You're Gonna Laugh

Over 750 of the Funniest Internet Jokes Ever!

A Compilation by Sandy Rozelman

8/8
You

Printed in the United States of America by Comfort Publishing, 9450 Moss Plantation Avenue N.W., Suite 204, Concord, NC 28027.
The views expressed in this book are not necessarily those of the publisher.

Library of Congress Control Number: 2009926148

ISBN 978-1-935361-44-2

To order copies of this book, go to:

www.youregonnalaugh.com or www.comfortpublishing. com

*Comfort*PUBLISHING

2/11
BOT

When asked to write a bio for my book, my first reaction was that I haven't done anything worth telling the world about except all the usual things that everyone does. But after some thought realized that I have done some very special things in my life.

I have a very eclectic work history ranging from retail sales to executive secretarial and from dental assistant to bookkeeping and manager of a print shop...and most recently, a Nanny. Years ago I was a volunteer teacher's assistant and tutor and edited the Year Book at my children's Jr. High School for two years.

Currently my most rewarding experience is volunteering at a nursing home as part of singing group where we entertain the residents once a week.

I have an interesting collection of frog figurines from all over the world. In my spare time I do puzzles and play games. Over the years I wrote a number of personal poems that I bound into a book. I also created a book of family recipes for my children.

I've always found that I am attracted to happy people and things that make me laugh; Hence, this Joke Book. To me a sense of humor is a person's most attractive quality. I have also found that laughter has helped me to cope with the challenges of Fibromyalgia. Compiling this book has been both therapeutic and fun. 'Laughter is the best medicine' is not just a trite cliché.

Watch for more books in the series to be coming out soon.

O ver ten years ago I began saving all the email jokes I received. I didn't know at the time why I was saving them except that they were funny, they made me laugh, and I didn't want to forget them. Also, I didn't know where the delete key was. They accumulated in files until I had several thousand jokes.

Figuring my children would find them when I died and wonder what their crazy mother was thinking saving all this stuff, they would toss them all in the trash.

Then I met Joe. And we got married. And he discovered the jokes and encouraged me to compile them into a book. This book is dedicated to him for his loving support and encouragement.

This is a compilation of the best of the best and the funniest of the funny from my personal email files.

This book is dedicated to my children:

My daughter Jamie, who could always make me laugh, even when, especially when, I wanted or needed to be serious.

My daughter Shelley, who has the best, most contagious laugh ever and always finds the fun and humor in everything.

My son Danny, who, in every picture in all of my photo albums, is smiling, except when he got his first haircut.

This book is also dedicated to all of my Computer Buddies for all the wonderful emails they have sent to me over the years. You know who you are. Thank you.

In Memory of my Mom & Dad, Rose & Philip Kasdan who would be so proud of me right now. I know they are smiling down on me because I can hear them laughing.

Take time to laugh, for it is the music of the soul

At one point during a game the coach said to one of his young players, "Do you understand what cooperation is? What a team is?"

The little boy nodded yes.

"So, when a strike is called or you're out at first, you don't argue or curse or attack the umpire. Do you understand all that?"

Again the little boy nodded.

"Good. Now go over there and explain it to your mother."

Max told his doctor, "I don't think my wife's hearing is as good as it used to be. What should I do?"

The doctor replied, "Try this test first. When your wife is at the sink doing dishes, stand fifteen feet behind her and ask her a question. If she doesn't respond keep moving closer, asking the question until she hears you."

He went home and saw his wife preparing dinner. Standing fifteen feet behind her he said, "Sadie, what's for dinner?"

Hearing no reply, he moved up to ten feet behind her and repeated the question. Still no reply, so he moved to five feet.

Finally, he stood directly behind her and said, "Honey, what's for dinner tonight?"

She turned around and yelled in his face, "For the fourth time, I SAID CHICKEN!"

A grandmother took her little grandson to the beach one summer day. They were having a good time until a huge wave came in and swept the boy out to sea.

She fell down on her knees and pleaded to the heavens, "Please return my grandson – that's all I ask – PLEASE!"

A moment later, lo and behold, a wave swelled from the ocean and deposited the wet, yet unhurt child at her feet. She checked him over to make sure that he was okay.

He was fine. She looked up to the heavens angrily and said, "When we came he had a hat!"

A man and a woman were sitting beside each other in the first class section of an airplane. The woman sneezed, took out a tissue, gently wiped her nose, and then visibly shuddered for ten to fifteen seconds.

The man went back to his reading. A few minutes later, the woman sneezed again, took a tissue, wiped her nose, and then shuddered violently once more. Assuming that the woman might have a cold, the man was still curious about the shuddering. A few more minutes passed when the woman sneezed yet again. As before she took a tissue, wiped her nose, her body shaking even more than before.

Unable to restrain his curiosity, the man turned to the woman and said, "I couldn't help but notice that you've sneezed three times, wiped your nose and then shuddered violently. Are you OK?"

"I am sorry if I disturbed you. I have a very rare medical condition; whenever I sneeze I have an orgasm."

The man, more than a bit embarrassed, was still curious. "I have never heard of that condition before," he said. "Are you taking anything for it?"

The woman nodded, "Pepper."

A wife went to the police station with her next-door neighbor to report her husband was missing. The policeman asked for a description.

She said, "He's 35 years old, 6 foot 4, has dark eyes, dark wavy hair, an athletic build, weighs 185 pounds, is soft-spoken and is good to the children.

The next-door neighbor protested, "Your husband is 5 foot 4, chubby, bald, has a big mouth and is mean to your children."

The wife replied, "Yeah, but who the hell wants HIM back?"

A rnold and his wife were cleaning out the attic one day when he came across a ticket from the local shoe repair shop. The date stamped on the ticket showed it was over eleven years old. They both laughed and tried to remember which of them might have forgotten to pick up a pair of shoes over a decade ago.

"Do you think the shoes will still be in the shop?" Arnold asked.

"Not very likely," his wife said.

"It's worth a try," said Arnold, pocketing the ticket.

He went downstairs, hopped into the car and drove to the store. With a straight face he handed the ticket to the man behind the counter. With a face just as straight, the man said, "Just a minute. I'll have to look for these." He disappeared into the back corner of the shop.

Two minutes later the man called out, "Here they are!"

"No kidding?" Arnold called back. "That's terrific! Who would have thought they'd still be here after all this time."

The man came back to the counter empty-handed. "They'll be ready Thursday," he said calmly.

A Canadian lumberjack camp advertises for a lumberjack. A skinny guy shows up at the camp the next day carrying an axe. The head lumberjack takes one look at the puny little guy and tells him to get lost.

"Give me a chance to show you what I can do," says the skinny guy.

"Okay, see that giant redwood over there? Take your axe and cut it down."

The guy heads for the tree and in five minutes he's knocking on the lumberjack's door. "I cut the tree down," he says.

The lumberjack can't believe his eyes. "Where did you learn to chop down trees like that?"

"In the Sahara Forest," says the puny man.

"You mean the Sahara Desert," says the lumberjack.

"Sure! That's what they call it now!"

How many women with MENOPAUSE (or PMS) does it take to change a light bulb?
 One! ONLY ONE!!!! And do you know WHY? Because no one else in this house knows HOW to change a light bulb! They don't even know that the bulb is BURNED OUT!! They would sit in the dark for THREE DAYS before they figured it out. And, once they figured it out, they wouldn't be able to find the #*&%@ light bulbs despite the fact that they've been in the SAME CABINET for the past 17 YEARS! But if they did, by some miracle of God, actually find them, TWO DAYS LATER, the chair they dragged to stand on to change the STUPID light bulb would STILL BE IN THE SAME SPOT!!!!! AND UNDERNEATH IT WOULD BE THE WRAPPER THE FREAKING LIGHT BULBS CAME IN!!! BECAUSE NO ONE EVER CARRIES OUT THE GARBAGE!!!! IT'S A WONDER WE HAVEN'T ALL SUFFOCATED FROM THE PILES OF GARBAGE THAT ARE A FOOT DEEP THROUGHOUT THE ENTIRE HOUSE!! IT WOULD TAKE AN ARMY TO CLEAN THIS PLACE! AND DON'T EVEN GET ME STARTED ON WHO CHANGES THE TOILET PAPER ROLL!!!

I'm sorry. What was the question?

Driving with his son in the car, the father tuned the radio to a country western station.

"How can you stand that stuff?" complained his teenage son. "It's all about lonesome cowboys, gunfights and broken hearts."

Knowing he preferred hard rock, the dad asked, "Well, what's your music about?"

"That's the beauty of it," the son said. "You just don't know."

A couple of guys in a pick up truck drove into the lumberyard. One of the men walked into the office and said, "We need some four-by-twos."

The clerk said, "You mean two-by-fours, don't you?"

The man said, "I'll go check," and went back to the truck. He returned a minute later and said, "Yeah, I meant two-by-fours."

"All right. How long do you need them?"

The customer paused for a moment and said, "I'd better go check."

He returned to the office and said, "A long time. We're gonna build a house."

My wife came home yesterday and said, "Honey, the car won't start, but I know what the problem is."

I asked her what it was and she said there was water in the carburetor. I thought for a moment, and then said, "You know, I don't mean this offensively, but you don't know the carburetor from the accelerator."

"No, there's definitely water in the carburetor," she insisted.

"Okay, honey, that's fine," I said. "I'll go take a look. Where is it?"

She replied, "In the lake."

An old country doctor went deep into the woods to deliver a baby. The cabin was so remote that it had no electricity. Upon arriving, the doctor realized that the laboring mother and her five-year-old child were the only people there. With no one else to help him, the doctor finally instructed the child to hold a lantern so he could see to deliver the baby.

The child was happy to help and held the lantern high while the mother pushed. After a while the baby was born and the doctor held the newborn by the feet and spanked him on the bottom to get him to take his first breath. With the excitement over, the doctor asked the five-year-old for his opinion about the baby.

"Hit him again," the little boy said. "He shouldn't have crawled up there in the first place."

Johnny goes to visit his 85-year-old grandfather in the hospital. "How are you grandpa?"
"Feeling fine," says the old man.
"What's the food like?" he questioned.
"Terrific, wonderful menus," answered his grandfather.
"And the nursing?" queried Johnny.
"Couldn't be better. These young nurses really take care of me.
"What about sleeping? Do you sleep okay?"

"No problem at all – nine hours solid every night. At 10:00 they bring me a cup of hot chocolate and a Viagra tablet, and that's it. I go out like a light."

Johnny was puzzled and a little alarmed by this so he rushed off to question the nurse in charge. "What are you people doing? I'm told you're giving an 85 year old Viagra on a daily basis. Surely that can't be true!"

"Oh yes," replies the nurse. "Every night at 10:00 we give him a cup of hot chocolate and a Viagra tablet. It works wonderfully well. The hot chocolate makes him sleepy and the Viagra keeps him from rolling out of bed."

For his birthday, little Patrick asked for a 10-speed bicycle. His father said, "Son, we'd give you one, but the mortgage on this house is $280,000 and your mother just lost her job. There's no way we can afford it."

The next day the father saw little Patrick heading out the front door with a suitcase. "Son, where are you going?"

Little Patrick told him, "I was walking past your room last night and heard you telling Mom you were 'pulling out.' Then I heard her tell you to 'wait because she was coming too.' And I'll be damned if I'm staying here by myself with a $280,000 mortgage and no bike!"

A dignified old lady was among a group looking at an art exhibition in a newly opened gallery. One rather risqué contemporary painting caught her eye.

"What on earth is that?" she inquired of the artist standing nearby.

He smiled condescendingly, "That my dear lady, is supposed to be a mother and her child."

The little old lady snapped back, "Well, then, why isn't it?"

Business conditions forced an executive to get rid of one of his staff. He narrowed it down to one of two people, Debra or Jack. They were both equally qualified and both did excellent work so he decided that in the morning whichever one used the water cooler first would have to go.

Debra came in the next morning, hung-over after partying the night before. She went to the cooler to get some water to take an aspirin and the executive approached her and said: "Debra, I've never done this before, but I have to lay you or Jack off."

Debra replied, "Could you jack off? I've got a headache."

A boy is assigned a paper on childbirth and asked his parents, "How was I born?"

"Well honey," said the slightly prudish parent, "the stork brought you to us."

"Oh. Well, how did you and daddy get born?"

"Oh, the stork brought us too."

"Well, how were grandma and grandpa born?" he persisted.

"Well darling, the stork brought them too." By now the parent is starting to squirm a little.

Several days later, the boy handed in his paper to the teacher who read with confusion, the opening sentence:

"This report has been very difficult to write because there hasn't been a natural childbirth in my family for three generations."

A little old lady, well into her eighties, slowly enters the front door of a sex shop. Obviously very unstable on her feet, she wobbles the few feet across the store to the counter. Finally arriving at the counter and grabbing it for support, she stutteringly asks the sales clerk: "Dddooo youuuu hhhave ddddddiillllldosss?"

The clerk, politely trying not to burst out laughing, replies: "Yes we do have dildos. Actually we carry many different models."

The old woman then asks: "Ddddddoooo yyyouuuu ccaarrryy aaa pppinkk onnee, tttenn inchessss lllong aaandd aabboutt ttwoo inchesss ththiickk . . . aaand rrunns by bbaatteries?

The clerk responds, "Yes we do."

"Ddddooo yyoooouuuu kknnnoooww hhhowww tttooo tttturrrnnn ttthe ssunoooffabbitch offfff?"

Two little old ladies had been very long-time close friends. But being old-fashioned, each went to a retirement home of her own respective religion. It was not long before Mrs. Murphy felt very lonesome for Mrs. Cohen, so one day she asked to be driven to the Jewish Home to visit her old friend. When she arrived she was greeted with open arms, hugs, and kisses.

Mrs. Murphy said "Don't be holdin' back, Mrs. Cohen, how do you like it here?"

Mrs. Cohen went on and on about the wonderful food, the facility and the caretakers. Then, with a twinkle in her eye, she said, "But the best thing is that I now have a boyfriend."

Mrs. Murphy said, "Now isn't that wonderful! Tell me all about it."

Mrs. Cohen said, "After lunch we go up to my room and sit on the edge of the bed. I let him touch me on the top, and then on the bottom, and then we sing Jewish songs."

Mrs. Murphy said, "For sure it's a blessing. I'm so glad for you Mrs. Cohen."

Mrs. Cohen said, "And how is it with you, Mrs. Murphy?"

Mrs. Murphy said it was also wonderful at her new facility, and that she also had a boyfriend.

Mrs. Cohen said, "Good for you! So what do you do?"

"We also go up to my room after lunch and sit on the edge of the bed. I let him touch me on top, and then I let him touch me down below."

Mrs. Cohen said, "Yes? And then?"

Mrs. Murphy said, "Well, since we don't know any Jewish songs, we fuck."

Mrs. Ward goes to the doctor's office to collect her husband's test results. The lab tech says to her, "I'm sorry, ma'am, but there has been a bit of a mix-up and we have a problem. When we sent the samples from your husband to the lab, the samples from another Mr. Ward were sent as well and we are now uncertain which one is your husband's. And frankly, your husband's results are either bad or terrible."

What do you mean?" Mrs. Ward asked.

"Well, one Mr. Ward has tested positive for Alzheimer's and the other has tested positive for AIDS. We can't tell which is your husband."

"That's terrible! Can't we do the test over?" questioned Mrs. Ward.

"Normally, yes. But you have an HMO, and they won't pay for these expensive tests more than once."

Mrs. Ward asked, "Well, what am I supposed to do now?"

"The HMO recommends that you drop your husband off in the middle of town. If he finds his way home, don't sleep with him."

God may have created man before woman, but there is always a rough draft before the masterpiece.

A wife came home just in time to find her husband in bed with another woman. With super-human strength borne of fury, she dragged him down the stairs, out the back door, and into the tool shed in the back yard and put his penis in a vice. She then secured it tightly and removed the handle. Next she picked up a hacksaw.

The husband was terrified, and screamed, "Stop! Stop! You're not going to cut it off, are you?"

The wife, with a gleam of revenge in her eye put the saw in her husband's hand and said, "Nope. I'm going to set the shed on fire. You do whatever you have to."

An extraordinarily handsome man decided he had to marry the perfect woman so they could produce beautiful children beyond compare. With that as his mission, he began searching for the perfect woman. Shortly there after he met a farmer who had three gorgeous daughters that positively took his breath away. So he explained his mission to the farmer, asking for permission to marry one of them.

The farmer simply replied, "You came to the right place. Look 'em over and pick the one you want."

The man dated the first daughter. The next day the farmer asked for the man's opinion.

"Well," said the man, "she's just a weeeeee bit, not that you can hardly notice . . . pigeon-toed."

The farmer nodded and suggested the man date one of the other girls; so the man went out with the second daughter.

The next day, the farmer again asked how things went.

"Well," the man replied, "she's just a weeeee bit, not that you can hardly tell . . . cross-eyed."

The farmer nodded and suggested he date the third girl to see if things might be better. So he did.

The next morning the man rushed in exclaiming, "She's perfect, just perfect. She's the one I want to marry."

So they were wed right away. Months later the baby was born. When the man visited the nursery he was horrified: the baby was the ugliest, most pathetic human you can imagine. He rushed to his father-in-law asking how such a thing could happen, considering the beauty of the parents.

"Well," explained the farmer, "She was just a weeeee bit, not that you could hardly tell . . . pregnant when you met her."

The nice thing about being senile is you can hide your own Easter eggs.

A very ugly woman walks into a shop with her two kids.
The shopkeeper asks, "Are they twins?"
The woman says, "No, he's 9 and she's 7. Why? Do you think they look alike?"
"No," he replies, "I just can't believe you got laid twice!"

She was in the kitchen doing the boiled eggs for breakfast.
He walks in and asks, "What's for breakfast?"
She turns to him and says, "You've got to make love to me this very moment."
He, thinking it's his lucky day, stands her over the kitchen table and they have sex.
Afterwards he says, "What was that all about?"
She says, "The egg timer's broken!"

There is more money being spent on breast implants and Viagra than Alzheimer's research.
This means that by the year 2020, there should be a large elderly population with perky boobs and huge erections and absolutely no recollection of what to do with them.

A Woman's View

Men are like a fine wine. They start out as grapes, and it's up to the woman to stomp the shit out of them and keep them in the dark until they mature into something respectable to have dinner with.

A Man's View

Women are like fine wine. They all start out fresh, fruity and intoxicating to the mind and then turn full-bodied with age until they go all sour and vinegary and give you a headache.

A lady walks into the drug store and asks the druggist for some arsenic.

The druggist asks, "Ma'am, what do you want with arsenic?"

The lady says, "To kill my husband."

"I can't sell you any for that reason," says the druggist.

The lady then reaches into her purse and pulls out a photo of a man and a woman in a compromising position. The man is her husband and the lady is the druggist's wife. She shows it to the druggist.

He looks at the photo and says, "Oh, I didn't know you had a prescription!"

Five Secrets to a Perfect Relationship with the Perfect Man:

1. It is important that a man helps you around the house and has a job.
2. It is important that a man makes you laugh.
3. It is important to find a man you can count on and doesn't lie to you.
4. It is important that a man is good in bed and loves making love to you.
5. It is really important that these four men don't know each other.

They finally released the ingredients in Viagra:

3%   Vitamin E
2%   Aspirin
2%   Ibuprofen
1%   Vitamin C
5%   Spray starch
87% Fix-A-Flat

What lies at the bottom of the ocean and twitches?
A nervous wreck

A drunken cowboy lay sprawled across three entire seats in the posh Amarillo Theater. When the usher came by and noticed this, he whispered to the cowboy, "Sorry, sir, but you're only allowed one seat."

The cowboy groaned but didn't budge.

The usher became more impatient: "Sir, if you don't get up from there I'm going to have to call the manager."

Once again, the cowboy just groaned.

The usher marched briskly back up the aisle, and in a moment he returned with the manager. Together the two of them tried repeatedly to move the cowboy, but with no success. Finally, they summoned the police. The Texas Ranger surveyed the situation briefly then asked, "All right buddy, what's your name?"

"Sam," the cowboy moaned.

"Where ya from, Sam?" asked the Ranger.

With pain in his voice, Sam replied, "The balcony."

A n old lady was standing at the rail of the cruise ship holding her hat so that it wouldn't blow away in the wind. A gentleman approached her and said, "Pardon me, madam. I do not intend to be forward, but did you know that your dress is blowing up in this wind?"

"Yes, I know," said the lady. "But I need my hands to hold onto my hat."

"But, madam," he said, "you must know that your derriere is exposed!"

The woman looked down, then back up at the man and said, "Sir, anything you see down there is 85 years old, but I just bought this hat yesterday!"

A Kindergarten teacher was observing her classroom of children while they were drawing. She would occasionally walk around to see each child's work.

As she got to one little girl who was working diligently, she asked what the drawing was.

The girl replied, "I'm drawing God."

The teacher paused and said, "But no one knows what God looks like."

Without missing a beat, the girl replied, "They will in a minute."

The children were lined up in the cafeteria of an elementary school for lunch. At the head of the table was a large pile of apples. The teacher made a note, and posted it on the apple tray:

"Take only ONE. God is watching."

Moving further along the lunch line, at the other end of the table was a large pile of chocolate chip cookies.

A child had written a note, "Take all you want. God is watching the apples."

Mary Clancy goes up to Father O'Grady after his Sunday morning service, and she's in tears.
He says, "So what's bothering you, Mary my dear?"
She says, "Oh, Father, I've got terrible news. My husband passed away last night."
The priest says, "Oh, Mary, that's terrible. Tell me, Mary, did he have any last requests?"
She says, "That he did, Father."
The priest says, "What did he ask, Mary?"
"He said, 'Please Mary, put down that damn gun.'"

A lonely spinster, aged 70, decided that it was time to get married. She put an ad in the local paper that read: "HUSBAND WANTED, must be in my age group, must not beat me, must not run around on me, and must still be good in bed! All applicants apply in person."

On the second day she heard the doorbell. Much to her dismay she opened the door to see a gray-haired gentleman sitting in a wheelchair.

He had no arms or legs. The woman said: "You're not really asking me to consider you, are you? Just look at you . . . you have no legs!"

The old man smiled: "Therefore I cannot run around on you!"

She snorted: "You don't have any hands either!"

Again the old man smiled: "Nor can I beat you!"

She raised an eyebrow and gazed intently: "Are you still good in bed?"

The old gentleman beamed a sly smile, "I rang the doorbell, didn't I?"

After she woke up, a woman told her husband, "I just dreamed you gave me a pearl necklace for my birthday. What do you think it means?"

"You'll know tonight," he said.

That evening the man came home with a small package and gave it to his wife. Delighted, she opened it – to find a book entitled "The Meaning of Dreams".

A young man wanted to get his beautiful blonde wife something nice for their first wedding anniversary. So he decides to buy her a cell phone. She is all excited, she loves her phone. He shows her and explains to her all the features on the phone.

The next day the blonde goes shopping. Her phone rings and it's her husband. "Hi hun," he says "How do you like your new phone?"

She replies, "I just love it, it's so small and your voice is clear as a bell. There's one thing I don't understand, though."

"What's that, baby?" asks the husband.

"How did you know I was at Wal-Mart?"

An old lady dies and goes to heaven. She's chatting it up with St. Peter at the Pearly Gates when all of a sudden she hears the most awful, blood-curdling screams.

"Don't worry about that," says St. Peter. "It's only someone having the holes put into her shoulder blades for wings."

The old lady looks a little uncomfortable but carries on with the conversation. Ten minutes later, there are more blood-curdling screams.

"Oh my God," says the old lady. "Now what is happening?"
"Not to worry," says St. Peter, "she's just having her head drilled to fit the halo."
"I can't do this," says the old lady, "I'm going to hell."
"You can't go there," says St. Peter. "You'll be raped and sodomized."
"Maybe so," says the old lady, "but I've already got the holes for that."

My memory's not as sharp as it used to be. Also, my memory's not as sharp as it used to be.

After the woman gave birth to a baby, her doctor stood solemnly at her bedside.
"I have something I must tell you about your baby."
"What's wrong?" the alarmed mother asked.
"Your baby is a hermaphrodite."
"What's that?"
"It means your baby has both male and female parts."
"Oh my God!" the woman exclaimed. "You mean he has a penis AND a brain?"

Woman's Life Cycle:

At age 8 -- You take her to bed and tell her a story.
At age 18 -- You tell her a story and take her to bed.
At age 28 -- You don't need to tell her a story to take her to bed.
At age 38 -- She tells you a story and takes you to bed.
At age 48 -- She tells you a story to avoid going to bed.
At age 58 -- You stay in bed to avoid her story.
At age 68 -- If you take her to bed, that'll be a story!
At age 78 -- What story??? What bed??? Who the hell are you???

A story is told about a vendor who sold bagels for 50 cents each at a street corner food stand. A jogger ran past and threw a couple of quarters into the bucket but didn't take a bagel. He did the same thing every day for months.

One day, as the jogger was passing by, the vendor stopped him. The jogger asked, "You probably want to know why I always put money in but never take a bagel, don't you?"

"No," said the vendor. "I just wanted to tell you that the bagels have gone up to 60 cents."

It's scary when your body starts making the same noises as your coffee maker.

Jim and Edna were both patients in a mental hospital. One day, while they were walking past the hospital swimming pool, Jim suddenly jumped into the deep end. He sank to the bottom of the pool and stayed there. Edna promptly jumped in to save him. She swam to the bottom and pulled Jim out.

When the director of nursing became aware of Edna's heroic act, she considered her to be mentally stable. When she went to tell Edna the news she said, "Edna, I have good news and bad news. The good news is you're being discharged; since you were able to rationally respond to a crisis by jumping in and saving the life of another patient, I have concluded that your act displays sound-mindedness.

The bad news is that Jim, the patient you saved, hung himself in his bathroom with the belt to his robe right after you saved him. I am sorry, but he's dead."

Edna replied, "He didn't hang himself. I put him there to dry. How soon can I go home?"

A married man goes to confessional and tells the priest, "I had an affair with a woman - almost."
The priest says, "What do you mean, 'almost'?"

The man says, "Well, we got undressed and rubbed together, but then I stopped."

The priest replies, "Rubbing together is the same as putting it in. You're not to go near that woman again. Now, say five Hail Marys and put $50 in the poor box."

The man leaves confessional, goes over and says his prayers, then walks over to the poor box. He pauses for a moment and then starts to leave.

The priest, who was watching him, quickly runs over to him and says, "I saw that. You didn't put any money in the poor box!"

The man replied, "Well, Father, I rubbed up against it. You said it was the same as putting it in!"

Bubba is showering in a locker room with his buddy when he notices his friend is very well endowed. "Damn, Bob, you're really well-hung!"

Bob exclaims. "I wasn't always this impressive; I had to work for it."

"What do you mean?" Bubba asked.

"Well, everyday for the past two years, I've spent an hour each night rubbing it with butter. I know it sounds crazy, but it actually made it grow four inches! You should try it."

Bubba agrees, and the two say good-bye.

A few months later, the two are in the same locker room, and Bob asks Bubba how his situation was developing.

Bubba replied, "I did what you said, Bob, but I've actually gotten smaller! I lost two inches already!"

"Did you do everything I told you? An hour each day with butter?"

"Well, we don't usually have real butter, so I've been using Crisco."

"Crisco!" Bob exclaimed. "Dammit, Bubba, Crisco is shortening!"

A mother and father took their 6-year-old son to a nude beach. As the boy walked along the beach, he noticed that some of the ladies had boobs bigger than his mother's and asked her why.

She told her son, "The bigger they are, the dumber the person is."

The boy, pleased with the answer, goes to play in the ocean, but returns to tell his mother that many of the men have larger members than his dad's.

His mother replied, "The bigger they are, the dumber the person is."

Again satisfied with his answer, the boy returned to the ocean to play. Shortly after, the boy returned again. He promptly told his mother, "Daddy is talking to the dumbest girl on the beach and the longer he talks the dumber he gets!"

The doctor, who had been seeing an 80-year-old woman for most of her life, finally retired. At her next checkup, the new doctor told her to bring a list of all the medicines that had been prescribed for her.

As the young doctor was looking through these, his eyes grew wide as he realized she has a prescription for birth control pills. "Mrs. Smith, do you realize these are BIRTH CONTROL pills?!"

"Yes, they help me sleep at night."

"Mrs. Smith, I assure you there is absolutely NOTHING in these that could possibly help you sleep!"

She reached out and patted the young doctor's knee. "Yes, dear, I know that. But every morning, I grind one up and mix it in the glass of orange juice that my 16-year-old granddaughter drinks. And believe me, it helps me sleep at night!"

Two old ladies were sitting on a park bench outside the local town hall where a flower show was in progress. One leaned over and said, "Life is so damned boring. We never have any fun anymore. For $5 I'd take my clothes off and streak through that stupid flower show!"
"You're on!" said the other old lady, holding up a $5 bill.

As fast as she could, the first little old lady fumbled her way out of her clothes and, completely naked, streaked through the front door of the flower show. Waiting outside, her friend soon heard a huge commotion inside the hall, followed by loud applause.

The naked lady burst out through the door surrounded by a cheering crowd. "What happened?" asked her waiting friend.

"I won first prize as Best Dried Arrangement."

A redhead walked into a bar and sat down next to a blonde and stared up at the TV. The 10 o'clock news was on. The news crew was covering a story of a man on a ledge of a large building preparing to jump. The redhead turned to the blonde and says, "You know, I bet he'll jump."

The blonde replied, "Well, I bet he won't."

The redhead placed $20 on the bar and said, "You're on!"

Just as the blonde placed her money on the bar, the guy did a swan dive off of the building, falling to his death. The blonde was very upset and handed her $20 dollars to the redhead and said, "All is fair. Here is your money."

The redhead replied, "Honey, I can't take your money, I saw this earlier on the 5 o'clock news and knew he would jump."

The blonde replied, "I did too, but I didn't think he'd do it again."

One day a duck went to the supermarket. He went up and down the aisles. Then he walked up to the store manager and said, "Got any duck food?"

The manager replied, "No, we only have people food here." The duck left.

The next day the duck went back to the supermarket. He went up and down the aisles. He walked up to the manager and said, "Got any duck food?"

He replied, "No! We only sell people food here and if you ask me again I will nail your feet to the ground!" The duck left.

The duck returned to the supermarket the next day. He walked up and down the aisles. He walked up to the manager and asked, "Got any nails?"

The manager replied, "No."

Then the duck asked, "Got any duck food?"

She left him on the sofa when the phone rang and was back in a few seconds.
"Who was it?" he asked.
"My husband," she replied.
"I better get going," he said. "Where was he?"
"Relax. He's downtown playing poker with you."

An elderly couple are having problems remembering things. During a checkup, the doctor tells them that they're physically okay, but they might want to start writing things down.

Later that night, while watching TV, the old man gets up from his chair. "Want anything while I'm in the kitchen?" he asks.

"Will you get me a bowl of ice cream?"

"Sure."

"Don't you think you should write it down so you can remember it?" she asks.

"No, I can remember it."

"Well, I'd like some strawberries on top, too. Maybe you should write it down, so's not to forget it?"

He says, "I can remember that. You want a bowl of ice cream with strawberries."

"I'd also like whipped cream. I'm certain you'll forget that; write it down."

Irritated, he says, "I don't need to write it down, I can remember it! Ice cream with strawberries and whipped cream – I got it, for goodness sake!"

After about 20 minutes, the old man returns from the kitchen and hands his wife a plate of bacon and eggs.

She stares at the plate for a moment. "Where's my toast?"

Intaxication: Euphoria at getting a tax refund, which lasts until you realize that it was your money to start with.

Arachnoleptic Fit: The frantic dance performed just after you've accidentally walked through a spider web.

How are a Texas tornado And a Tennessee divorce the same? Somebody's gonna lose a trailer.

An older, white-haired man walked into a jewelry store one Friday evening with a beautiful young gal at his side. He told the jeweler he was looking for a special ring for his girlfriend. The jeweler looked through his stock and brought out a $5,000 ring and showed it to him.

The old man said, "I don't think you understand, I want something very special." At that statement, the jeweler went to his special stock and brought another ring over. "Here's a stunning ring at only $40,000," the jeweler said. The young lady's eyes sparkled and her whole body trembled with excitement. The old man seeing this said, "We'll take it."

The jeweler asked how payment would be made and the old man stated, by check. "I know you need to make sure my check is good, so I'll write it now and you can call the bank Monday to verify the funds and I'll pick the ring up Monday afternoon," he said.

Monday morning, a very teed-off jeweler phoned the old man. "There's no money in that account."

"I know," said the old man, "but can you imagine the weekend I had?"

Patient: It's been one month since my last visit and I still feel miserable.

Doctor: Did you follow the instructions on the medicine I prescribed for you?

Patient: I sure did. The bottle said, "Keep Tightly Closed."

Definition of a truly wonderful gadget: Any mechanical device that performs a kitchen task in one-twentieth the time it takes to find it.

A woman went to the doctors' office where she was seen by one of the younger doctors. After about four minutes in the examination room, she burst out screaming as she ran down the hall.

An older doctor stopped her and asked what the problem was and she told him her story.

After listening, he had her sit down and relax in another room.

The older doctor marched down the hallway to the back where the young doctor was writing on his board.

"What's the matter with you?" the older doctor demanded. "Mrs. Reid is 62 years old, has four grown children and seven grandchildren, and you just told her she was pregnant?"

The younger doctor continued writing and without looking up said, "Does she still have the hiccups?"

A man left for work one Friday afternoon. But it was payday, so instead of going home, he stayed out the entire weekend partying with the boys and spending his entire paycheck.

When he finally appeared at home on Sunday night, he was confronted by his angry wife and was barraged for nearly two hours with a tirade befitting his actions. Finally his wife stopped the nagging and said to him, "How would you like it if you didn't see me for two or three days?"

He replied, "That would be fine with me."

Monday went by and he didn't see his wife. Tuesday and Wednesday came and went with the same results. But on Thursday, the swelling went down just enough where he could see her a little out of the corner of his right eye.

The Lone Ranger was ambushed and captured by an enemy Indian war party. The Indian Chief proclaims, "So, you are the great Lone Ranger. In honor of the Harvest Festival, you will be executed in three days. But, before I kill you, I will grant you three requests. What is your first request?"

The Lone Ranger responds, "I'd like to speak to my horse."

The Chief nods and Silver is brought before the Lone Ranger, who whispers in Silver's ear and the horse gallops away. Later that evening, Silver returns with a beautiful blonde woman on his back.

As the Indian Chief watches, the blonde enters the Lone Ranger's tent and spends the night. The next morning the Indian Chief admits he's impressed. "You have a very fine and loyal horse but I will still kill you in two days. What is your second request?"

The Lone Ranger again asks to speak to his horse. Silver is brought to him, and he again whispers in the horse's ear. As before, Silver takes off across the plains and disappears over the horizon.

Later that evening, to the Chief's surprise, Silver again returns, this time with a brunette, even more attractive than the blonde. She enters the Lone Ranger's tent and spends the night.

The following morning the Indian Chief is again impressed. "You are indeed a man of many talents but I will still kill you tomorrow. What is your last request?"

The Lone Ranger responds, "I'd like to speak to my horse . . . alone."

The Chief is curious but he agrees and Silver is brought to the Lone Ranger's tent.

Once they're alone, the Lone Ranger grabs Silver by both ears, looks him square in the eye and says, "Listen very carefully you dumb-ass horse. For the last time . . . BRING POSSE!"

I live life in the fast lane, but I'm married to a speed bump.

F ifty-one years ago, the Army drafted Herman James, a North Carolina mountain man. On his first day in basic training, the Army issued him a comb. That afternoon the Army barber sheared off all his hair.

On his second day, the Army issued Herman a toothbrush. That afternoon the Army dentist yanked seven of his teeth.

On the third day, the Army issued him a jock strap. The Army has been looking for Herman for 51 years!

A Polish immigrant went to the DMV to apply for a driver's license. First, of course, he had to take an eyesight test.

The optician showed him a card with the letters: C Z W I X N O S TA C Z

"Can you read this?" the optician asked.

"Read it?" the Polish guy replied, "I know the guy."

W hy don't blind people like to sky dive?
Because it scares the dog.

A cop stopped a woman for going 15 mph over the speed limit. After he handed her a ticket, she asked him, "Don't you give out warnings?"

"Yes, ma'am," he replied. "They're all up and down the road. They say, 'Speed Limit 55.'"

A man is having terrible headaches. He can't sleep, eat, think, or do much of anything because of the pain. Several doctors examined him and couldn't determine the cause of his problem. He finally went to one of the top neurological specialists in the country who examines him and says, "I've found the cause of the pain. Your testicles are pushing up into your spine. The constant pressure on the spine causes the headaches. The only thing I can do is perform surgery and remove your testicles." The man is shocked to hear this but the decision is not difficult, as he knows he cannot stand the pain of the headaches. He has the surgery and immediately feels like a new man. The pain is completely gone and he feels like he has a new life. He is so happy he decides to buy himself a new suit. He goes to a small men's shop and tells the old tailor that he wants to buy a suit.

"Sure," says the tailor. "You're a 42 long, right?"

"Wow, how did you know?"

"Hey, I've been in this business a long time. You learn a few things."

The tailor brought the man a suit that fit perfectly. It looked so good that the man decided to buy a new shirt to go with it.

"16, 34, right?" said the tailor.

"Right again!" said the man. "You're amazing."

"Hey, I've been in this business a long time. You learn a few things."

The tailor brought a shirt and tie and they looked great. The man said, "Hey, let's go for broke. Give me a pair of the silk boxers too."

The tailor said, "36 right?"

"I'm disappointed," said the man. "But 2 out of 3 is still good. I wear size 34 boxers."

The tailor said, "Hey, I've been in this business for a long time and I think you need 36."

The man replied, "It's obvious you know your business, but I've worn size 34 for as long as I can remember. I'm going to have to disagree with you on this one".

"Hey look," said the tailor, "I'll sell you whatever you want. But I've been in this business a long time. If you wear a size 34, it's gonna push your nuts up into your spine and give you terrible headaches."

Marriage is a relationship in which one person is always right, and the other is a husband.

Just wondering: Why do tourists go to the tops of tall buildings and then put money into telescopes so they can see things on the ground close up?

Sally was driving home from one of her business trips in Northern Arizona when she saw an elderly Navajo woman walking on the side of the road. As the trip was a long and quiet one, she stopped the car and asked the Navajo woman if she would like a ride. With a silent nod of thanks, the woman got into the car.

Resuming the journey, Sally tried in vain to make a bit of small talk with the Navajo woman. The old woman just sat silently, looking intently at everything she saw, studying every little detail, until she noticed a brown bag on the seat next to Sally.

"What in bag?" asked the old woman.

Sally looked down at the brown bag and said, "It's a bottle of wine. I got it for my husband."

The Navajo woman was silent for another moment or two. Then speaking with the quiet wisdom of an elder, she said, "Good trade."

Mother Superior called all the nuns together and said to them, "I must tell you all something. We have a case of gonorrhea in the convent."

"Thank God," said an elderly nun at the back. "I'm so tired of chardonnay."

Everyone has a photographic memory. Some people just don't have any film.

There was this couple that had been married for 20 years. Every time they made love the husband always insisted on shutting off the light.

Well, after 20 years the wife felt this was ridiculous. She figured she would break him out of this crazy habit. So one night, while they were in the middle of a wild, screaming, romantic session, she turned on the lights. She looked down and saw her husband was holding a battery-operated leisure device . . . a vibrator . . . soft, wonderful and larger than a real one.

She went completely ballistic. "You impotent bastard," she screamed at him. "How could you be lying to me all of these years? You better explain yourself!"

The husband looks her straight in the eyes and says calmly: "I'll explain the toy . . . you explain the kids."

There was a preacher whose wife was expecting a baby so he went before the congregation and asked for a raise. After much discussion, they passed a rule that whenever the preacher's family expanded, so would his paycheck.

After six children, this started to get expensive and the congregation decided to hold another meeting to discuss the preacher's salary. There was much yelling and bickering about how much the clergyman's additional children were costing the church.
Finally, the preacher got up and spoke to the crowd, "Having children is an act of God," he said.

Silence fell on the congregation. In the back pew, a little old lady stood up and in her frail voice said, "Rain and snow are also acts of God, but when we get too much, we wear rubbers."

These days half the stuff in my shopping cart says, "For fast relief."

Last night, my wife and I were sitting in the living room and I said to her, "I never want to live in a vegetative state, dependent on some machine and fluids from a bottle. If that ever happens, just pull the plug."

She got up, unplugged the TV and then threw out my beer.

She's such a bitch.

A cabbie picks up a nun. She gets into the cab, and notices that the VERY handsome cab driver won't stop staring at her. She asks him why he is staring.

He replies: "I have a question to ask you but I don't want to offend you."

She answers, " My son, you cannot offend me. When you're as old as I am and have been a nun as long as I have, you get a chance to see and hear just about everything. I'm sure that there's nothing you could say or ask that I would find offensive."

"Well, I've always had a fantasy to have a nun kiss me."

She responds, "Well, let's see what we can do about that. First, you have to be single and second, you must be Catholic."

The cab driver is very excited and says, "Yes, I'm single and Catholic!

"Okay," the nun says. "Pull into the next alley." The nun fulfills his fantasy with a kiss that would make a hooker blush.

But when they get back on the road, the cab driver starts crying.

"My dear child," says the nun, "why are you crying?"

"Forgive me, but I've sinned. I lied and I must confess. I'm married and I'm Jewish."

The nun says, "That's okay. My name is Kevin and I'm going to a Halloween party."

Good health is merely the slowest possible rate at which one can die.

Health nuts are going to feel stupid someday, lying in hospitals dying of nothing.

One winter morning a husband and wife in northern Ohio were listening to the radio during breakfast. They heard the announcer say, "We are going to have eight to 10 inches of snow today. You must park your car on the even-numbered side of the street so the snowplows can get through."

So the good wife went out and moved her car. A week later while they are eating breakfast again, the radio announcer said, "We are expecting 10 to 12 inches of snow today. You must park your car on the odd-numbered side of the street, so the snowplows can get through."

The good wife went out and moved her car again. The next week they are again having breakfast, when the radio announcer says, "We are expecting 12 to 14 inches of snow today. You must park..." Then the electricity went out.

The good wife was very upset, and with a worried look on her face she said, "Honey, I don't know what to do. Which side of the street do I need to park on so the snowplows can get through?"

With the love and understanding in his voice that all men who are married to blondes exhibit, the husband replied, "Why don't you just leave it in the garage this time?"

How do crazy people go through the forest?
They take the psychopath.

The Proper Work Ethic: Always give 100%

10% on Mondays
25% on Tuesdays
45% on Wednesdays
15% on Thursdays
5% on Fridays

What is the difference between a Harley and a Hoover?
The location of the dirt bag.

A woman was shopping at her local supermarket where she selected:

a half-gallon of 2% milk, a carton of eggs, a quart of orange juice, a head of romaine lettuce, a 2 lb. can of coffee, and a 1 lb. package of bacon.

As she was unloading her items on the conveyor belt to check out, a drunk standing behind her watched as she placed the items in front of the cashier. While the cashier was ringing up her purchases, the drunk calmly stated, "You must be single."

The woman was a bit startled by this proclamation, but she was intrigued by the derelict's intuition, since she was indeed single. She looked at her six items on the belt and saw nothing particularly unusual about her selections that could have tipped off the drunk to her marital status.

Curiosity getting the better of her, she said "Well, you know what, you're absolutely correct. But how on earth did you know that?"

The drunk replied, "'Cause you're ugly."

A dyslexic man walks into a bra.

I want to live my next life backwards:
You start out dead and get that out of the way.
Then you wake up in an old age home feeling better every day.
Then you get kicked out for being too healthy.
Enjoy your retirement and collect your pension.
Then when you start work, you get a gold watch on your first day.
You work 40 years until you're too young to work.
You get ready for High School: drink alcohol, party, and you're generally promiscuous.
Then you go to primary school, you become a kid, you play, and you have no responsibilities.
Then you become a baby, and then...
You spend your last 9 months floating peacefully in luxury, in spa-like conditions - central heating, room service on tap, and then...
You finish off as an orgasm.

A big earthquake with the strength of 8.1 on the Richter scale has hit Mexico. Two million Mexicans have died and over a million are injured. The country is totally ruined and the government doesn't know where to start with asking for help to rebuild.

The rest of the world is in shock. Canada is sending troopers to help the Mexican army control the riots. Saudi Arabia is sending oil. Other Latin American countries are sending supplies. The European community (except France) is sending food and money. The United States, not to be outdone, is sending four million replacement Mexicans.

On their way to get married, a young Catholic couple are involved in a fatal car accident. The couple find themselves sitting outside the Pearly Gates waiting for St. Peter to process them into Heaven. While waiting, they begin to wonder: Could they possibly get married in Heaven?

When St. Peter showed up, they asked him. St. Peter says, "I don't know. This is the first time anyone has asked. Let me go find out," and he leaves.

The couple sat and waited, and waited. Two months passed. As they waited, they discussed that IF they were allowed to get married in Heaven, what was the eternal aspect of it all. "What if it doesn't work?" they wondered, "Are we stuck together FOREVER?"

St. Peter finally returns and informs the couple, "You CAN get married in Heaven."

"Great!" said the couple, "But we were just wondering, what if things don't work out? Could we also get a divorce in Heaven?"

St. Peter, red-faced with anger, slams his clipboard onto the ground. "OH, COME ON! It took me three months to find a priest up here! Do you have ANY idea how long it'll take me to find a LAWYER?!?

Smith climbs to the top of Mt. Sinai to get close enough to talk to God. Looking up, he asks the Lord, "God, what does a million years mean to you?"

The Lord replies, "A minute."

Smith asks, "And what does a million dollars mean to you?"

The Lord replies, "A penny."

Smith asks, "Can I have a penny?"

The Lord replies, "In a minute."

An elderly couple was attending church services when about halfway through she leans over and says to him, "I just had a silent passing of gas. What do you think I should do?"

He leans over to her and replies, "Put a new battery in your hearing aid."

She told me we couldn't afford beer anymore and I'd have to quit. Then I caught her spending: $65 on make-up, $150 for a cut and color, $30 for a manicure, $40 for a pedicure, $50 on vitamins, $300 on clothes and $600 for a gym membership.

I asked her why I had to give up stuff and not her. She said she needed it to look pretty for me. I told her that was what the beer was for. I don't think she's coming back.

One afternoon a lawyer was riding in his limousine when he saw two men along the roadside eating grass. Disturbed, he ordered his driver to stop and he got out to investigate. He asked one man, "Why are you eating grass?"

"We don't have any money for food," the poor man replied. "We have to eat grass."

"Well, then, you can come with me to my house and I'll feed you," the lawyer said.

"But sir, I have a wife and two children with me. They are over there, under that tree."

"Bring them along" the lawyer replied. Turning to the other poor man he stated, "You come too."

The second man said, "But sir, I also have a wife and SIX children with me!"

"Bring them all, as well," the lawyer answered.

They all entered the car, which was no easy task, even for a car as large as the limousine was. Once underway, one of the poor fellows turned to the lawyer and said, "Sir, you are too kind. Thank you for taking all of us with you."

The lawyer replied, "Glad to do it. You'll really love my place. The grass is almost a foot high."

Three friends from the local congregation were asked, "When you're in your casket, and friends and congregation members are mourning over you, what would you like them to say?"

Artie said: "I would like them to say I was a wonderful husband, a fine spiritual leader, and a great family man."

Eugene commented: "I would like them to say I was a wonderful teacher and servant of God who made a huge difference in people's lives."

Al said: "I'd like them to say, 'Look, he's moving!'"

The woman applying for a job in a Florida lemon grove seemed way too qualified for the job.
"Look, miss," said the foreman. "Have you any actual experience in picking lemons?"
"Well, as a matter of fact, yes!" she replied? "I've been divorced three times."

Why are hurricanes usually named after women?
Because when they arrive, they're wet and wild, but when they go, they take your house and car.

An old man goes to the wizard to ask him if he can remove a curse he has been living with for the last 40 years.

The wizard says, "Maybe, but you will have to tell me the exact words that were used to put the curse on you."

The old man says without hesitation, "I now pronounce you man and wife."

Miss Beatrice, the church organist, was in her 80s and had never been married. She was admired for her sweetness and kindness to all. One afternoon the Pastor came to call on her. She showed him into her quaint sitting room. She invited him to have a seat while she prepared tea.

As he sat facing her old Hammond organ, the young minister noticed a cut-glass bowl sitting on top of it filled with water, and in the water floated, of all things, a condom!

The pastor tried to stifle his curiosity about the bowl of water and its strange floater, but soon it got the better of him. "Miss Beatrice," he said, "I wonder if you would tell me about this." as he pointed toward the bowl.

"Oh yes," she replied. "Isn't it wonderful? I was walking through the park a few months ago and I found this little package on the ground. The directions said to place it on the organ, keep it wet and that it would prevent the spread of disease. Do you know I haven't had the flu all winter?"

Because they had no reservations at a busy restaurant, an elderly man and his wife were told there would be a 45-minute wait for a table.

"Young man, we're both 90 years old," the husband said. "We may not have 45 minutes."

They were seated immediately.

A newlywed couple wanted to join a church. The pastor told them, "We have special requirements for new parishioners. You must abstain from sex for one whole month." The couple agreed and, after two-and-a-half weeks, returned to the Church. When the Pastor ushers them into his office, the wife is crying, and the husband is obviously very depressed.

"You are back so soon. Is there a problem?" the pastor inquired.

"We are terribly ashamed to admit that we did not manage to abstain from sex for the required month," the young man replied sadly.

The pastor asked him what happened.

"Well, the first week was difficult. However, we managed to abstain through sheer willpower. The second week was terrible, but with the use of prayer, we managed to abstain. However, the third week was unbearable. We tried cold showers, prayer, reading from the Bible, anything to keep our minds off carnal thoughts. One afternoon, my wife reached for a can of paint and dropped it. When she bent over to pick it up, I was overcome with lust and had my way with her right then and there," admitted the man, shamefacedly.

"You understand this means you will not be welcome in our church," stated the pastor.

"We know," said the young man, hanging his head. "We're not welcome at Home Depot, either."

A man goes to a shrink and says, "Doctor, my wife is unfaithful to me. Every evening, she goes to Larry's bar and picks up men. In fact, she sleeps with anybody who asks her! I'm going crazy. What do you think I should do?"

"Relax," says the doctor, "take a deep breath and calm down. Now, tell me, exactly where is Larry's bar?"

A Texan is drinking in a New York bar when, he gets a call on his cell phone. He hangs up, grinning from ear to ear, and orders a round of drinks for everybody in the bar announcing his wife has produced a typical Texas baby boy weighing 25 pounds.

Nobody can believe that any new baby can weigh in at 25 pounds, but the Texan just shrugs, "That's about average down home, folks. Like I said, my boy's a typical Texas baby boy."

Congratulations showered him from all around, and exclamations of "WOW!" One woman actually fainted due to sympathy pains. Two weeks later he returns to the bar. The bartender says, "Say you're the father of that typical Texas baby that weighed 25 pounds at birth. Everybody's been making bets about how big he'd be in two weeks. So how much does he weigh now?"

The proud father answers, "Seventeen pounds."

The bartender is puzzled, concerned, and a little suspicious.

"What happened? He already weighed 25 pounds the day he was born!" The Texas father takes a slow swig from his Lone Star beer, wipes his lips on his shirt sleeve, leans into the bartender and proudly says, "Had'm circumcised".

John was on his deathbed and gasped pitifully. "Give me one last request, dear," he said.
"Of course, John," his wife said softly.
"Six months after I die," he said, "I want you to marry Bob."
"But I thought you hated Bob," she said.
With his last breath John said, "I do!"

My husband and I divorced over religious differences. He thought he was God, and I didn't.

Marriage is a three-ring circus: Engagement ring, wedding ring, and suffering.

A woman, standing nude looks in her bedroom mirror and says to her husband, "I look horrible. I feel fat and ugly. Pay me a compliment."

The husband replies, "Well, your eyesight is still perfect."

He never heard the shot . . . . .

A man has six children and is very proud of his achievement. He is so proud of himself, that he starts calling his wife, "Mother of Six," in spite of her objections.

One night, they go to a party. The man decides that it's time to go home and wants to find out if his wife is ready to leave as well. He shouts at the top of his voice, "Shall we go home, Mother of Six?"

His wife, irritated by her husband's lack of discretion, shouts right back, "Anytime you're ready, Father of Four."

A man and his wife were having some problems at home and were giving each other the silent treatment. Suddenly, the man realized that the next day, he would need his wife to wake him at 5:00 am for an early morning business flight. Not wanting to be the first to break the silence (and LOSE), he wrote on a piece of paper, "Please wake me at 5:00 a.m." He left it where he knew she would find it.

The next morning the man woke up, only to discover it was 9:00 a.m. and he had missed his flight. Furious, he was about to go and see why his wife hadn't woken him, when he noticed a piece of paper by the bed. The paper said, "It is 5:00 a.m. Wake up."

Men are not equipped for these kinds of contests.

When the husband finally died his wife put the usual death notice in the paper, but added that he died of gonorrhea. No sooner were the papers delivered than a friend of the family phoned and complained bitterly, "You know very well that he died of diarrhea, not gonorrhea."

Replied the widow, "I nursed him night and day so of course I know he died of diarrhea, but I thought it would be better for posterity to remember him as a great lover rather than the big shit he always was."

A funeral service is being held for a woman who has just passed away. At the end of the service, the pallbearers are carrying the casket out when they accidentally bump into a wall, jarring the casket. They hear a faint moan. They open the casket and find that the woman is actually alive! She lives for ten more years, and then dies. Once again, a ceremony is held, and at the end of it, the pallbearers are again carrying out the casket.

As they carry the casket towards the door, the husband cries out, "Watch that wall!"

Two elderly women were eating breakfast in a restaurant one morning. Ethel noticed something funny about Mabel's ear and said, "Do you know you've got a suppository in your left ear?"

Mabel answered, "I have a suppository in my ear?" She pulled it out and stared at it.

"Ethel, I'm glad you saw this thing. Now I think I know where to find my hearing aid."

Before the funeral services, the undertaker came up to the very elderly widow and asked, "How old was your husband?"
"98," she replied. "Two years older than me."
"So you're 96," the undertaker commented.
She said, "Hardly worth going home, is it?"

An elderly couple was on a cruise and it was really stormy. They were standing on the back of the boat watching the moon, when a wave came up and washed the old woman overboard. They searched for days and couldn't find her, so the captain sent the old man back to shore with the promise that he would notify him as soon as they found something. Three weeks went by and finally the old man got a fax from the boat. It read: "Sir, sorry to inform you, we found your wife dead at the bottom of the ocean. We hauled her up to the deck and attached to her butt was an oyster and in it was a pearl worth $50,000. Please advise."

The old man faxed back: "Send me the pearl and re-bait the trap."

What makes men chase women they have no intention of marrying? The same urge that makes dogs chase cars they have no intention of driving.

I've sure gotten old! I've had two bypass surgeries, a hip replacement, new knees, fought prostate cancer and diabetes. I'm half blind, can't hear anything quieter than a jet engine, take 40 different medications that make me dizzy, winded and subject to blackouts. Have bouts with dementia. Have poor circulation; hardly feel my hands and feet anymore. Can't remember if I'm 85 or 92. Have lost all my friends. But, thank God, I still have my driver's license.

I feel like my body has gotten totally out of shape, so I got my doctor's permission to join a fitness club and start exercising. I decided to take an aerobics class for seniors. I bent, twisted, gyrated, jumped up and down and perspired for an hour. But, by the time I got my leotard on, the class was over.

Why is air a lot like sex? Because it's no big deal unless you're not getting any.

For sale: Wedding dress, size 8. Worn once by mistake.

Last year I replaced all the windows in my house with that expensive double-pane energy efficient kind, but this week, I got a call from the contractor who installed them. He was complaining that the work had been completed a whole year ago and I hadn't paid for them.

Just because I'm blonde doesn't mean that I am automatically stupid. So, I told him just what his fast-talking sales guy had told me last year . . . namely, that in ONE YEAR these windows would pay for themselves! Helllooooo? It's been a year!

There was only silence at the other end of the line; so I finally just hung up . . . He didn't call back. Guess I won that stupid argument.

Sixty is the worst age to be," said the 60-year-old man. "You always feel like you have to pee and most of the time you stand there and nothing comes out."

"Ah, that's nothin," said the 70-year-old. "When you're 70, you don't have a bowel movement any more. You take laxatives, eat bran, sit on the toilet all day and nothin' comes out!"

"Actually," said the 80-year-old, "Eighty is the worst age of all."

"Do you have trouble peeing, too?" asked the 60-year old.

"No, I pee every morning at 6 o'clock. I pee like a racehorse on a flat rock; no problem at all."

"So, do you have a problem with your bowel movement?"

"No, I have one every morning at 6:30."

Exasperated, the 60-year-old said, "You pee every morning at 6 and crap every morning at 6:30. So what's so bad about being 80?"

"I don't wake up until 7."

There are two times when a man doesn't understand a woman: Before marriage and after marriage.

A little boy goes to his father and asks, "Daddy, how was I born?"

The father answers: "Well son, I guess one day you will need to find out anyway!

Your mom and I first got together in a chat room on Yahoo. Then I set up a date via e-mail with your mom and we met at a cyber-cafe. We sneaked into a secluded room, where your mother agreed to a download from my hard drive. As soon as I was ready to upload, we discovered that neither one of us had used a firewall, and since it was too late to hit the delete button, nine months later a little pop-up appeared that said: You've Got Male!

A n Amish boy and his father were in a mall. They were amazed by almost everything they saw, but especially by two shiny, silver walls that could move apart and then slide back together again.

The boy asked, "What is this, Father?"

The father (never having seen an elevator) responded, "Son, I have never seen anything like this in my life, I don't know what it is."

While the boy and his father were watching with amazement, a fat old lady in a wheel chair moved up to the moving walls and pressed a button. The walls opened and the lady rolled between them into a small room. The walls closed and the boy and his father watched the small circular numbers above the walls light up sequentially.

They continued to watch until it reached the last number and then the numbers began to light in the reverse order. Finally the walls opened up again and a gorgeous 24-year-old blonde stepped out.

The father said quietly to his son . . . "Go and get your mother."

A very elderly gentleman (mid-nineties), very well-dressed, hair well-groomed, great-looking suit, flower in his lapel, smelling slightly of a good aftershave, presenting a well looked-after image, walks into an upscale cocktail lounge. Seated at the bar is an elderly looking lady (mid-eighties).

The gentleman walks over, sits alongside of her, orders a drink, takes a sip, turns to her and says, "So tell me, do I come here often?"

A priest and a rabbi were sitting next to each other on an airplane. After a while, the priest turned to the rabbi and asked, "Is it still a requirement of your faith that you not eat pork?"

The rabbi responded, "Yes, that is still one of our beliefs."

The priest then asked, "Have you ever eaten pork?"

To which the rabbi replied, "Yes, on one occasion I did succumb to temptation and tasted a ham sandwich."

The priest nodded in understanding and went on with his reading.

A while later, the rabbi spoke up and asked the priest, "Father, is it still a requirement of your church that you remain celibate?"

The priest replied, "Yes, that is still very much a part of our faith."

The rabbi then asked him, "Father, have you ever fallen to the temptations of the flesh?"

The priest replied, "Yes, rabbi, on one occasion I was weak and broke with my faith."

The rabbi nodded understandingly and remained silent, thinking, for about five minutes.

Finally, the rabbi said, "Beats the shit out of a ham sandwich, doesn't it?"

An elderly gentleman had serious hearing problems for a number of years. He went to the doctor and the doctor was able to have him fitted for a set of hearing aids that allowed the gentleman to hear 100%. The elderly gentleman went back in a month to the doctor and the doctor said, "Your hearing is perfect. Your family must be really pleased that you can hear again."

The gentleman replied, "Oh, I haven't told my family yet. I just sit around and listen to the conversations. I've changed my will three times!"

Joe's will specified that $30,000 was to be spent for an elaborate funeral.

As the last guests departed the affair, his wife, Helen, turned to her oldest friend.

"Well, I'm sure Joe would be pleased," the friend said. "How much did this really cost?"

"All of it," said Helen. "Thirty thousand."

"No!" Jody exclaimed. "I mean, it was very nice, but $30,000?"

Helen answered. "The funeral was $6,500. I donated $500 to the church. The wake, food and drinks were another $500. The rest went for the memorial stone."

Jody computed quickly. "$22,500 for a memorial stone? My God, how big is it?"

"Three carats."

Two elderly gentlemen from a retirement center were sitting on a bench under a tree when one turns to the other and says: "Slim, I'm 83 years old now and I'm just full of aches and pains. I know you're about my age. How do you feel?"

Slim says, "I feel just like a newborn baby."

"Really? Like a newborn baby?"

"Yep. No hair, no teeth, and I think I just wet my pants.

A woman walked up to the manager of a department store. "Are you hiring any help?"

"No," he said. "We already have all the staff we need."

"Then would you mind getting someone to wait on me?"

I went to the doctor for my yearly physical. The nurse starts with certain basics.

"How much do you weigh?" she asks.

"115," I say. The nurse puts me on the scale. It turns out my weight is 140.

The nurse asks, "Your height?"

"5 foot 8," I say. The nurse checks and sees that I only measure 5' 5".

She then takes my blood pressure and tells me it is very high.

"Of course it's high!" I scream. "When I came in here I was tall and slender! Now I'm short and fat!"

She put me on Prozac!

An elderly couple had dinner at another couple's house, and after eating the wives left the table and went into the kitchen. The two gentlemen were talking, and one said, "Last night we went out to a new restaurant and it was really great. I would recommend it very highly."

The other man said, "What is the name of the restaurant?"

The first man thought and thought and finally said, "What is the name of that flower you give to someone you love? You know . . . the one that's red and has thorns."

"Do you mean a rose?"

"Yes, that's the one," replied the man. He then turned towards the kitchen and yelled, "Hey Rose, what's the name of that restaurant we went to last night?"

What's the difference between a northern fairytale and a southern fairytale?
A northern fairytale begins "Once upon a time..."
A southern fairytale begins "Y'all ain't gonna believe this shit..."

An elderly Italian man went to the local church for confession. He said: "Father, during World War II, a beautiful Jewish woman knocked on my door and asked me to hide her from the enemy. So I hid her in my attic."

"That was a wonderful thing you did, my son, and you have no need to confess that."

"It's worse than that, Father. She started to repay me with sexual favors."

The priest said: "By doing that, you were both in great danger. However, two people together under those circumstances are greatly tempted to act that way. But if you are truly sorry for your actions, you are forgiven."

"Thank you Father. That's a great load off my mind. But I have one more question."

"Should I tell her the war is over?"

Ma was in the kitchen fiddling around when she hollers out, "Pa, You need to go out and fix the outhouse!"
Pa replies, "There ain't nuthin wrong with the outhouse."
Ma yells back, "Yes there is, now git out there and fix it."
So Pa mosies out to the outhouse, looks around and yells back,
"Ma, there ain't nuthin wrong with the outhouse! "
Ma replies, "Stick yur head in the hole!"
Pa yells back, "I ain't stickin my head in that hole!"
Ma says, "Ya have to stick yur head in the hole to see what to fix."
So with that, Pa sticks his head in the hole, looks around and yells back,
"Ma, there ain't nuthin wrong with this outhouse!"
Ma hollers back, "Now take your head out of the hole!"
Pa proceeds to pull his head out of the hole, then starts yelling,
"Ma Help! My beard is stuck in the cracks in the toilet seat!"
To which Ma replies, "Hurts, don't it?"

Know how to prevent sagging? Just eat till the wrinkles fill out.

Why is a Laundromat a really bad place to pick up a woman? Because a woman who can't even afford a washing machine will probably never be able to support you.

When I had been married for 30 years, I took a look at my wife one day and said, "Honey, 30 years ago we had a cheap apartment, a cheap car, slept on a sofa bed and watched a 10-inch black and white TV, but I got to sleep every night with a hot 25-year-old blonde."

Now, we have a nice house, nice car, big bed and plasma screen TV, but I'm sleeping with a 60-year-old woman. It seems to me that you are not holding up your side of things."

My wife is a very reasonable woman. She told me to go out and find a hot 25-year-old blonde, and she would make sure that I would once again be living in a cheap apartment, driving a cheap car, sleeping on a sofa bed, and watching a 10-inch black and white TV.

Aren't older women great? They really know how to solve your mid-life crisis.

A woman stopped by unannounced at her recently married son's house. She rang the doorbell and walked in. She was shocked to see her daughter-in-law lying on the couch, totally naked. Soft music was playing and the aroma of perfume filled the room.

"What are you doing?" she asked.
"Waiting for my husband when he gets home from work," the daughter-in-law answered.

"But you're naked!" the mother-in-law exclaimed.

"This is my love dress," the daughter-in-law explained.

"Love dress? But you're naked!"

"My husband loves me to wear this dress," she explained. "It excites him to no end. Every time he sees me in this dress, he instantly becomes romantic and ravages me for hours on end. He can't get enough of me."

When the mother-in-law got home, she undressed, showered, put on her best perfume, dimmed the lights, put on a romantic CD, and lay on the couch waiting for her husband to arrive. Finally her husband came home. He walked in and saw her lying there so provocatively.

"What are you doing?" he asked.

"This is my love dress," she whispered, sensually.

"Needs ironing," he said. "What's for dinner?"

His funeral is Thursday."

Mildred and Chester knew each other from childhood, but were in their seventies when they got married. They had to wait for Mildred's mother to pass away first. Back in those days there was no hanky panky before marriage, so Chester and Mildred were both virgins. Needless to say Chester was pretty excited on their wedding night, having waited so patiently all these years. However, Mildred was very apprehensive as she had developed a heart condition and would have to tell Chester that they could not do it.

Chester is now sitting on the bed wanting Mildred to hurry up. He detects a little reluctance on her part. Thinking that she is shy, he sends her off to the bathroom to get undressed. When she reappears in her satin nightie, he gets her to sit next to him on the bed. Not knowing how to get things started he pulls the first strap on her nightie. She blushes just as red as her satin nightie. She is really concerned about telling Chester about her heart condition.

In the meantime Chester is looking at the first breast he has seen since his own mother's. It is hanging there down to her belly button, gravity having taken its course over some sixty years. He realizes her anxiety but figures she is going to have to be helped a little more. Now he pulls the second strap and sees the second breast unroll downward before him.

Poor Mildred is now beside herself. She is going to have to tell Chester about her heart. With a quivering voice, and mustering up all her courage, she says, "Chester, I have acute angina."

Chester says, "I sure hope so. 'Cause your boobs are really ugly."

While attending a marriage seminar dealing with communication, Larry and his wife Nancy listened to the instructor, "It is essential that husbands and wives know each other's likes and dislikes."

He addressed the man, "Can you name your wife's favorite flower?"

Larry leaned over, touched his wife's arm gently and whispered, "It's Pillsbury, isn't it?"

A woman goes into a tattoo parlor and tells the tattoo artist that she wants a tattoo of a turkey on her right thigh just below her bikini line. She also wants him to put "Happy Thanksgiving" under the turkey. So the guy does it and it comes out looking really good.

The woman then instructs him to put a ham tattoo with "Merry Christmas" on her left thigh. So the guy does it and it comes out looking good, too.

As the woman is getting dressed to leave, the tattoo artist asks "If you don't mind, could you tell me why you had me put such unusual tattoos on your thighs?"

She says, "I'm sick and tired of my husband complaining all the time that there's nothing good to eat between Thanksgiving and Christmas!"

A man is like a deck of playing cards. You need:

• A Heart to love him,
• A Diamond to marry him,
• A Club to smash his f _ _ king head in, and
• A Spade to bury the bastard.

A couple drove down a country road for several miles, not saying a word. An earlier discussion had led to an argument and neither of them wanted to concede their position. As they passed a barnyard of mules, goats, and pigs, the husband asked sarcastically, "Relatives of yours?"

"Yep," the wife replied, "in-laws."

On their wedding night, the young bride approached her new husband and asked for $20 for their first lovemaking encounter. In his highly aroused state, her husband readily agreed.

This scenario was repeated each time they made love, for more than 30 years, with him thinking that it was a cute way for her to afford new clothes and other incidentals that she needed.

Arriving home around noon one day, she was surprised to find her husband in a very drunken state. During the next few minutes, he explained that his employer was going through a process of corporate downsizing, and he had been let go. It was unlikely that, at the age of 59, he'd be able to find another position that paid anywhere near what he'd been earning, and therefore, they were financially ruined.

Calmly, his wife handed him a bankbook, which showed more than thirty years of steady deposits and interest totaling nearly $1 million. Then she showed him certificates of deposits issued by the bank, which were worth over $2 million, and informed him that they were one of the largest depositors in the bank.

She explained that for the more than three decades she had "charged" him for sex, these holdings had multiplied and these were the results of her savings and investments.

Faced with evidence of cash and investments worth over $3 million, her husband was so astounded he could barely speak, but finally he found his voice and blurted out, "If I'd had any idea what you were doing, I would have given you all my business!"

That's when she shot him. Sometimes men just don't know when to keep their mouths shut.

A little girl, when asked her name would reply, "I'm Mrs. Smith's daughter."
Her mother told her this was wrong, she must say, "I'm Jane Smith."
A woman approached her at church and said, "Aren't you Mrs. Smith's daughter?"
"I thought I was, but my mother says I'm not," she replied.

A man walking along a California beach was deep in prayer. Suddenly the sky clouded above his head and in a booming voice the Lord said, "Because you have tried to be faithful to me in all ways, I will grant you one wish."

The man said, "Build a bridge to Hawaii so I can drive over anytime I want."

The Lord said, "Your request is very materialistic. Think of the enormous challenges for that kind of undertaking. The supports required to reach the bottom of the Pacific! The concrete and steel it would take! It will nearly exhaust several natural resources. I can do it, but it is hard for me to justify your desire for worldly things. Take a little more time and think of something that would honor and glorify me."

The man thought about it for a long time. Finally he said, "Lord, I wish that I could understand my wife! I want to know how she feels inside, what she's thinking when she gives me the silent treatment, why she cries, what she means when she says 'nothing's wrong,' and how I can make a woman truly happy."

The Lord replied, "You want two lanes or four on that bridge?"

For centuries, Hindu women have worn a spot on their foreheads. We have always naively thought that it had something to do with their religion.

The Indian Embassy in Washington, D.C. has recently revealed the true story.

When one of these women gets married, she brings with her a dowry. On her wedding night, the husband scratches off the spot to see if he has won either a convenience store, a gas station, a donut shop or a motel in the United States.

A young family moved into a house next door to a vacant lot. One day a construction crew turned up to start building a house on the empty lot. The young family's five-year-old daughter naturally took an interest in all the activity going on next door and spent much of each day observing the workers.

Eventually the construction crew, all of them gems-in-the-rough, more or less adopted her as a kind of project mascot. They chatted with her, let her sit with them while they had coffee and lunch breaks, and gave her little jobs to do here and there to make her feel important.

At the end of the first week they even presented her with a pay envelope containing a couple of dollars. The little girl took this home to her mother who said all the appropriate words of admiration and suggested that they take the two-dollar "pay" she had received to the bank the next day to start a savings account. When they got to the bank, the teller was equally impressed and asked the little girl how she had come by her very own pay check at such a young age.

The little girl proudly replied, "I worked last week with the crew building the house next door to us."

"My goodness gracious," said the teller, "and will you be working on the house this week, too?"

The little girl replied, "I will if those assholes at Home Depot ever deliver the fucking sheet rock."

If you yelled for 8 years, 7 months and 6 days you would have produced enough sound energy to heat one cup of coffee. (Hardly seems worth it.)

If you farted consistently for 6 years and 9 months, enough gas is produced to create the energy of an atomic bomb. (Now that's more like it!)

The human heart creates enough pressure when it pumps out to the body to squirt blood 30 feet. (OMG!)

A pig's orgasm lasts 30 minutes. (In my next life, I want to be a pig.)

A cockroach will live nine days without its head before it starves to death! (Creepy) (I'm still not over the pig.)

Banging your head against a wall uses 150 calories an hour. (Don't try this at home.)

The male praying mantis cannot copulate while its head is attached to its body. The female initiates sex by ripping the male's head off. ("Honey, I'm home. What the....?!")

The flea can jump 350 times its body length. It's like a human jumping the length of a football field. (30 minutes - lucky pig! Can you imagine?)

The catfish has over 27,000 taste buds. (What could be so tasty on the bottom of a pond?)

Some lions mate over 50 times a day. (I still want to be a pig in my next life . . . quality over quantity.)

Butterflies taste with their feet. (Something I always wanted to know.)

The strongest muscle in the body is the tongue. (Hmmm...)

Right-handed people live, on average, nine years longer than left-handed people. (If you're ambidextrous, do you split the difference?)

Elephants are the only animals that cannot jump. (So that's a good thing.)

A cat's urine glows under a black light. (Who was paid to figure that out?)

An ostrich's eye is bigger than its brain. (I know some people like that.)

Starfish have no brains. (I know some people like that, too.)

Polar bears are left-handed. (If they switch, they'll live a lot longer.)

Humans and dolphins are the only species that have sex for pleasure. (What about that pig??)

Two antennas met on a roof, fell in love and got married. The ceremony wasn't much, but the reception was excellent.

A counselor was helping his kids put their stuff away on their first morning of summer camp. He was surprised to see that one of the youngsters was unpacking an umbrella. The counselor asked, "Why did you bring an umbrella to camp?"

The kid answered, "Did you ever have a mother?"

What then, would a fly without wings be called . . . a walk?

Mid-life is a time when you become more reflective. You start pondering the "big" questions: What is life? Why am I here? How much Healthy Choice ice cream can I eat before it's no longer a healthy choice?

What do you see when the Pillsbury Dough Boy bends over? Doughnuts.

An irate woman burst into the baker's shop and said, "I sent my son in here for 2 pounds of cookies this morning, but when I weighed them there was only 1 pound. I suggest that you check your scales."

The baker looked at her calmly and replied, "Ma'am, I suggest you weigh your son."

Why is divorce so expensive? Because it's worth it

Why are married women heavier than single women? Single women come home, see what's in the fridge and go to bed. Married women come home, see what's in bed and go to the fridge.

Mahatma Gandhi, as you know, walked barefoot most of the time, which produced an impressive set of calluses on his feet. He also ate very little, which made him rather frail. And with his odd diet, he suffered from bad breath. All of this made him . . . what?

A super callused fragile mystic hexed by halitosis.

Thoughts to Ponder

Life is sexually transmitted.

Men have two emotions: Hungry and Horny. If you see him without an erection, make him a sandwich.

Give a person a fish and you feed them for a day; teach a person to use the Internet and they won't bother you for weeks.

Some people are like a Slinky . . . . not really good for anything, but you still can't help but smile when you shove them down the stairs.

All of us could take a lesson from the weather. It pays no attention to criticism.

Why does a slight tax increase cost you $200 and a substantial tax cut save you 30 cents?

In the '60s, people took acid to make the world weird. Now the world is weird and people take Prozac to make it normal.

We know exactly where one cow with mad cow disease is located among the millions and millions of cows in America, but we haven't got a clue as to where thousands of illegal immigrants and terrorists are located. Maybe we should put the Department of Agriculture in charge of immigration.

A guy was typing away at his home computer, when his six-year-old daughter sneaked up behind him. Suddenly, she turned and ran into the kitchen, squealing to the rest of the family, "I know Daddy's password! I know Daddy's password!"

"What is it?" her sisters asked eagerly.

Proudly she replied, "Asterisk, asterisk, asterisk, asterisk, asterisk!"

What is the difference between men and government bonds?
The bonds mature.

Little Johnny watched, fascinated, as his mother gently rubbed cold cream on her face.

"Why are you rubbing that cold cream on your face, mommy?" he asked.

"To make myself beautiful," said his mother.

A few minutes later, she began removing the cream with a tissue.

"What's the matter?" asked little Johnny. "Giving up?"

The only difference between a rut and a grave is its depth.

What do you call a boomerang that doesn't work?
A stick.

Marriage changes passion . . . suddenly you're in bed with a relative.

Why is it that if someone tells you that there are a billion stars in the universe you will believe them, but if they tell you a wall has wet paint, you will have to touch it to be sure?

Liz goes to her first art show and is looking at the paintings. One is a huge canvas that has black with yellow blobs of paint splattered all over it. The next painting is a murky gray color that has drips of purple paint streaked across it.

Liz walks over to the artist and says, "I don't understand your paintings."

"I paint what I feel inside me," explained the artist.

"Have you ever tried Alka-Seltzer?"

THE SHIT LIST

THE GHOST SHIT - The kind where you feel shit come out, see shit on the toilet paper, but there's no shit in the bowl.

THE CLEAN SHIT - The kind where you feel shit come out, see shit in the bowl, but there's no shit on the toilet paper.

THE WET SHIT - You wipe your ass fifty times and it still feels unwiped. So you end up putting toilet paper between your ass and your underwear so you don't ruin them with those dreadful skid marks.

THE WET CHEEKS SHIT - That's the kind that comes out of your ass so fast that your butt cheeks get splashed with the toilet water, or splash-back.

THE LIQUID SHIT - That's the sort where yellowish brown liquid shoots out of your ass and splatters all over the inside of the toilet bowl.

THE MEXICAN FOOD SHIT - In a class all its own.

THE SECOND WAVE SHIT - This shit happens when you think you've finished, your pants are up to your knees and you suddenly realize you have to shit some more.

THE BRAIN HEMORRHAGE THROUGH YOUR NOSE SHIT - You have to strain so much to get it out that you turn purple and practically have a stroke.

THE CORN SHIT - No explanation necessary.

THE LINCOLN LOG SHIT - The kind of shit that's so enormous you're afraid to flush it down without first breaking it up into little pieces with the toilet brush.

THE NOTORIOUS DRINKER'S SHIT - The kind of shit you have the morning after a long night of drinking. Its most noticeable trait is the tread mark left on the bottom of the toilet bowl after you flush.

THE 'GEE I REALLY WISH I COULD SHIT' SHIT - The kind where you want to shit, but even after straining your guts out, all you can do is sit on the toilet, cramped and farting.

THE POWER DUMP SHIT - The kind that comes out so fast you've barely got your pants down and you're done.

THE LIQUID PLUMBER SHIT - This kind of shit is so big it plugs up the toilet and it overflows all over the floor. You should have followed the advice from the Lincoln Log Shit.

THE SPINAL TAP SHIT - The kind of shit that hurts so much coming out that you'd swear it got to be coming out sideways.

THE 'I THINK I'M GIVING BIRTH THROUGH MY ASSHOLE' SHIT - Similar to the Lincoln Log and the Spinal Tap Shits. The shape and size of the turd resembles a tallboy beer can. Vacuous air space remains in the rectum for some time afterwards.

THE PORRIDGE SHIT - The type that comes out like toothpaste, and just keeps on coming. You have 2 choices: a) flush and keep going; or b) risk it piling up to your butt while you sit there, helpless.

THE 'I'M GOING TO CHEW MY FOOD BETTER' SHIT - When the bag of Dorritos you ate last night lacerates the insides of your rectum on the way out in the morning.

THE 'I THINK I'M TURNING INTO A BUNNY' SHIT - When you drop lots of cute, little round ones that look like marbles and make tiny splishy sounds when they hit the water.

THE 'WHAT THE HELL DIED IN HERE' SHIT - Also sometimes referred to as The Toxic Dump. Of course, you don't warn anyone of the poisonous bathroom odor. Instead, you stand innocently near the door and enjoy the show as they run out gagging and gasping for air.

THE 'I JUST KNOW THERE'S A TURD STILL DANGLING THERE' SHIT - Where you just sit there patiently and wait for the last cling-on to drop.

A mother was working in the kitchen listening to her son playing with his new electric train set in the living room. She heard the train stop and her son saying, "All of you sons of bitches who want off, get the hell off now, cause this is the last stop! And all of you sons of bitches who are getting on, get your asses on the train, cause we're going down the tracks."

The horrified mother went in and told her son, "We don't use that kind of language in this house. Now I want you to go to your room and you are to stay there for two hours. When you come out, you may play with your train, but I want you to use nice language."

Two hours later, the son came out of the bedroom and resumed playing with his train. Soon the train stopped and the Mother heard her son say, "All passengers who are disembarking the train, please remember to take all your belongings with you. We thank you for riding with us today and hope your trip was a pleasant one. We hope you will ride with us again soon."

She hears the little boy continue, "For those of you just boarding, we ask you to stow all of your hand luggage under your seat. Remember, there is no smoking on the train. We hope you will have a pleasant and relaxing journey with us today."

As the Mother began to smile, the child added, "For those of you who are pissed off about the two hour delay, please see the bitch in the kitchen."

When a wealthy businessman choked on a fish bone at a restaurant, he was fortunate that a doctor was seated at a nearby table.

Springing up, the doctor skillfully removed the bone and saved his life.

As soon as the fellow had calmed himself and could talk again, he thanked the surgeon enthusiastically and offered to pay him for his services.

"Just name the fee," he said gratefully.

"Okay," replied the doctor. "How about half of what you would have offered when the bone was still stuck in your throat?"

A mild-mannered man was tired of being bossed around by his wife so he went to a psychiatrist. The psychiatrist said he needed to build his self-esteem so he gave him a book on assertiveness, which he read on the way home. He had finished the book by the time he reached his house.

The man stormed into the house and walked up to his wife. Pointing a finger in her face, he said, "From now on, I want you to know that I am the man of this house, and my word is law! I want you to prepare me a gourmet meal tonight, and when I'm finished eating my meal, I expect a sumptuous dessert afterward. Then, after dinner, you're going to draw me my bath so I can relax. And when I'm finished with my bath, guess who's going to dress me and comb my hair?"

"The funeral director," said his wife.

What would you call it when an Italian has one arm shorter than the other?
A speech impediment.

A couple, age 67, went to the doctor's office.
The doctor asked, "What can I do for you?"

The man said, "Will you watch us have sexual intercourse?"

The doctor looked puzzled, but agreed. When the couple had finished, the doctor said, "There is nothing wrong with the way you have intercourse," and he charged them $32. This happened several weeks in a row. The couple would make an appointment, have intercourse, pay the doctor and leave. Finally, the doctor asked, "Just exactly what are you trying to find out?

The old man said, "We are not trying to find out anything. She is married and we can't go to her house. I am married so we can't go to my house. The Holiday Inn charges $60. The Hilton charges $78. We do it here for $32 and I get back $28 from Medicare for a visit to the doctor's office.

A man walks into a psychiatrist's office wearing only underwear made of Saran Wrap.
The psychiatrist says, "Well, I can clearly see your're nuts."

A recent survey was conducted to discover why men get out of bed in the middle of the night:
    5% said it was to get a glass of water.
    12% said it was to go the toilet.
    83% said it was to go home.

PRISON VS. WORK

*I*N PRISON...You spend the majority of your time in an 8x10 cell.
AT WORK...You spend most of your time in a 6x8 cubicle.

IN PRISON...You get three meals a day.
AT WORK...You only get a break for 1 meal and you have to pay for it.

IN PRISON...You get time off for good behavior.
AT WORK...You get rewarded for good behavior with more work.

IN PRISON...A guard locks and unlocks all the doors for you.
AT WORK...You must carry around a security card and unlock and open all the doors yourself.

IN PRISON...You can watch TV and play games.
AT WORK...You get fired for watching TV and playing games.

IN PRISON...You get your own toilet.
AT WORK...You have to share.

IN PRISON...They allow your family and friends to visit.
AT WORK...You cannot even speak to your family and friends.

IN PRISON...All expenses are paid by taxpayers with no work required.
AT WORK...You get to pay all the expenses to go to work and then they deduct taxes from your salary to pay for prisoners.

IN PRISON...You spend most of your life looking through bars from the inside wanting to get out.
AT WORK...You spend most of your time wanting to get out and go inside bars.

IN PRISON...There are wardens who are often sadistic.
AT WORK...They are called supervisors.

A couple is golfing one day on a very, very exclusive golf course lined with million-dollar houses. On the third tee the husband says, "Honey, be very careful when you drive the ball. Don't knock out any windows; it'll cost us a fortune to fix."

The wife tees up and promptly shanks it right through the window of the biggest house on the course. The husband cringes and says, "I told you to watch out for the houses! Okay, let's go up there, apologize, and see how much this is going to cost us."

They walk up and knock on the door and a voice says, "Come in." When they open the door, they see glass all over the floor and a broken bottle lying on its side in the foyer. A man on the couch says, "Are you the people that broke my window?"

"Uh, yeah," the husband says. "Sorry about that."

"No, actually, I want to thank you, I'm a genie that was trapped for a thousand years in that bottle. You've released me. I'm allowed to grant three wishes - I'll give you each one wish, and I'll keep the last one for myself."

"OK, great!" the husband says. "I want a million dollars a year for the rest of my life."

"No problem, it's the least I could do. And you, what do you want?" the genie says, looking at the wife.

"I want a house in every country of the world," she says.

"Consider it done."

"And what's your wish, Genie?" the husband asks.

"Well, since I've been trapped in that bottle, I haven't had sex with a woman in a thousand years. My wish is to sleep with your wife."

The husband looks at his wife and says, "Well, we did get a lot of money and all those houses. I guess it's okay with me if it's okay with you." So the genie takes the wife upstairs and ravishes her for two hours. Afterward, he rolls over, looks at the wife, and says, "How old is your husband, anyway?'

"35. Why?"

"And he still believes in genies?"

A cop was patrolling at night in a well-known spot. He sees a couple in a car, with the interior light brightly glowing. The cop carefully approaches the car to get a closer look. Then he sees a young man behind the wheel, reading a computer magazine. He immediately notices a young woman in the rear seat, knitting. Puzzled by this surprising situation, the cop walks to the car and gently raps on the driver's window.

The young man lowers his window . . . . . "Uh, yes, officer?"

"What are you doing?"

"Well, isn't it obvious? I'm reading a magazine, sir."

Pointing towards the young woman in the back seat the cop says, "And her, what is she doing?"

The young man shrugs: "Sir, I believe she's knitting a pullover sweater."

Now, the cop is totally confused; a young couple alone in a car at night in a lovers' lane. And nothing obscene is happening!

"What's your age, young man?"

"I'm 25, sir."

"And her ... what's her age?"
The young man looks at his watch and replies: "She'll be 18 in 11 minutes."

An old cowboy sat down at the bar and ordered a drink. As he sat sipping his drink, a young woman sat down next to him. She turned to the cowboy and asked, "Are you a real cowboy?"

He replied, "Well, I've spent my whole life breaking colts, working cows, going to rodeos, fixing fences, pulling calves, baling hay, doctoring calves, cleaning my barn, fixing flats, working on tractors and feeding my dogs, so I guess I am a cowboy."

She said, "I'm a lesbian. I spend my whole day thinking about women. As soon as I get up in the morning, I think about women. When I shower, I think about women. When I watch TV, I think about women. I even think about women when I eat. It seems that everything makes me think of women."

The two sat sipping in silence.

A little while later, a man sat down on the other side of the old cowboy and asked, "Are you a real cowboy?"

He replied, "I always thought I was, but I just found out I'm a lesbian."

There were two brooms in a closet, a girl broom and a boy broom. The girl and boy brooms decided to get married. The girl broom was all in white and the boy broom looked great in his tuxedo. After they were married, all was great but then the girl broom said to the boy broom, "I think we are going to have a little whisk broom." And the boy broom replied . . . . .

"That's impossible!   WE'VE NEVER EVEN SWEPT TOGETHER!"
Sounds to me like she's been sweeping around!

Why are you IN a movie, but you're ON TV?

THE PERFECT BREAKFAST . . . as a man sees it . . .
You're sitting at the table and your son is on the cover of the box of Wheaties.
Your mistress is on the cover of Playboy.
And your wife is on the back of the milk carton.

Birthdays are good for you: The more you have, the longer you live.

A chicken and an egg are lying in bed. The chicken is leaning against the headboard smoking a cigarette, with a satisfied smile on its face. The egg, looking a bit pissed off, grabs the sheet, rolls over, and says, "Well, I guess we finally answered THAT question!"

A mafia godfather finds out that his bookkeeper has screwed him for ten million bucks. This bookkeeper is deaf. It was considered an occupational benefit, and why he got the job in the first place, since it was assumed that a deaf bookkeeper would not be able to hear anything he'd never have to testify about in court. When the Godfather goes to shakedown the bookkeeper about his missing $10 million bucks, he brings along his attorney, who knows sign language.

The godfather asks the bookkeeper: "Where is the 10 million bucks you embezzled from me?"

The attorney, using sign language, asks the bookkeeper where the 10 million dollars is hidden.

The bookkeeper signs back: "I don't know what you are talking about."

The attorney tells the godfather: "He says he doesn't know what you're talking about." That's when the godfather pulls out a pistol, puts it to the bookkeeper's temple, cocks it, and says: "Ask him again!"

The attorney signs to the underling: "He'll kill you for sure if you don't tell him!"

The bookkeeper signs back: "OK! You win! The money is in a brown briefcase, buried behind the shed in my backyard in Queens!"

The godfather asks the attorney: "Well, what'd he say?"

The attorney replies: "He says you don't have the guts to pull the trigger."

A couple of rednecks are out in the woods hunting when one of them suddenly grabs his chest and falls to the ground.

He doesn't seem to be breathing; his eyes are rolled back in his head. The other guy whips out his cell phone and calls 911. He gasps to the operator, "I think Bubba is dead! What should I do?"

The operator, in a calm soothing voice says, "Just take it easy and follow my instructions. First, let's make sure he's dead."

There is a silence . . . and then a shot is heard.
The guy's voice comes back on the line, "Okay, now what?"

A woman was in bed with her lover when she heard her husband opening the front door.

"Hurry," she said, "stand in the corner." She quickly rubbed baby oil all over him and then dusted him with talcum powder. "Don't move until I tell you to," she whispered. "Just pretend you're a statue."

"What's this, honey?" the husband inquired as he entered the room.

"Oh, it's a statue," she replied nonchalantly. "The Smiths bought one for their bedroom. I liked it so much, I got one for us too."

No more was said about the statue, not even later when they went to sleep. Around two in the morning, the husband got out of bed, went to the kitchen and returned a while later with a sandwich and a glass of milk.

"Here," he said to the statue, "eat something. I stood like an idiot at the Smiths' for three days, and nobody offered me as much as a glass of water."

Three mothers, a blonde, a brunette, and a redhead were all talking about their daughters.

The brunette said, "I was looking through my daughter's things and I found cigarettes. I can't believe my daughter smokes."

The redhead said, "Ladies, I was looking through my daughter's things and I found a bottle of liquor. I can't believe my daughter drinks."

The blonde said, "I was looking through my daughter's things and I found a pack of condoms. I can't believe my daughter has a penis."

An attorney arrived home late, after a very tough day trying to get a stay of execution for a client who was due to be hanged for murder at midnight. His last minute plea for clemency to the governor had failed and he was feeling worn out and depressed.

As soon as he walked through the door at home, his wife started on him about, 'What time of night to be getting home is this? Where have you been?' 'Dinner is cold and I'm not reheating it'. And on and on and on.

Too shattered to play his usual role in this familiar ritual, he poured himself a shot of whiskey and headed off for a long hot soak in the bathtub, pursued by the predictable sarcastic remarks as he dragged himself up the stairs. While he was in the bath, the phone rang. The wife answered and was told that her husband's client, John Wright, had been granted a stay of execution after all. Wright would not be hanged tonight.

Finally realizing what a terrible day he must have had, she decided to go upstairs and give him the good news. As she opened the bathroom door, she was greeted by the sight of her husband, bent over naked, drying his legs and feet.

'They're not hanging Wright tonight,' she said to which he whirled Around and screamed,
'FOR THE LOVE OF GOD WOMAN, DON'T YOU EVER STOP?'

Toward the end of the golf course, Dave somehow managed to hit his ball into the woods finding it in a patch of pretty yellow buttercups. Trying to get his ball back in play, he ended up thrashing just about every buttercup in the patch.

All of a sudden . . . POOF! In a flash and puff of smoke, a little old woman appeared.

She said, "I'm Mother Nature! Do you know how long it took me to make those buttercups? Just for that, you won't have any butter for your popcorn the rest of your life; better still, you won't have any butter for your toast for the rest of your life . . . as a matter of fact you won't have any butter for anything the rest of your life!"

THEN POOF! . . . she was gone.

After Dave got hold of himself, he hollered for his friend, Fred. "Fred, where are you?"

Fred yells back, "I'm over here, in the pussy willows."

Dave yells back: "DON'T SWING, FRED! For the love of God, DON'T SWING!

A kindergarten class had a homework assignment to find out about something exciting and relate it to the class the next day. The first little boy called upon, walked up to the front of the class, and with a piece of chalk, made a small white dot on the blackboard, then sat back down.

Puzzled, the teacher asked him just what it was. "It's a period," said the little boy.

"Well, I can see that." she said, "but what is so exciting about a period?"

"Darned if I know," said the little boy, "but this morning my sister was missing one. Dad had a heart attack, Mom fainted, and the man next door shot himself."

A Chinese couple gets married - and she's a virgin. Truth be told, he is none too experienced either. On the wedding night, she cowers naked under the bed sheets as her husband undresses. He climbs in next to her and tries to be reassuring: "My darring" he says, "I know dis yo firs time and you berry frighten. I pomise you, I give you anyting you want, I do anyting - jus anyting you want, you say. Whatchou want?" he says, trying to sound experienced, which he hopes will impress his virgin bride. A thoughtful silence follows and he waits patiently (and eagerly) for her request.

She eventually replies shyly and unsure, "I want . . . numba 69."

More thoughtful silence, this time from him. Eventually, in a puzzled tone, he queries, "You want Beef wif Broccori?"

A t a convention of biological scientists, one prominent researcher remarked to another, "Did you know that in our lab we have switched from rats to lawyers for our experiments?"

"Really?" the other researcher replied. "Why did you switch?"

"Well, for three reasons. First, we found that lawyers are far more plentiful. Second, the lab assistants don't get so attached to them, and thirdly, there are some things even a rat won't do."

A guy went to a travel agent and tried to book a two-week cruise for himself and his girlfriend. The travel agent said that all the ships were booked up and things were very tight, but that he would see what he could do. A couple of days later, the travel agent phoned and said he could now get them onto a three-day cruise.

The guy agreed and went to the drugstore to buy three Dramamines and three condoms.

Next day, the agent called back and said that he now could book a five-day cruise.

The guy said, "I'll take it," and returned to the pharmacy to buy two more Dramamines and two more condoms.

The following day, the travel agent called yet again and said he could now book an eight-day cruise.

The guy agreed, and went back to the drugstore. He asked for three more Dramamine and three more condoms.

The pharmacist looked sympathetically at him and said, "Look, if it makes you sick, why do you keep doing it?"

She was sooo blonde:
she sent me a fax with a stamp on it.
she thought a quarterback was a refund.
she tried to put M&M's in alphabetical order.
she thought Boyz II Men was a day care center.
she tripped over a cordless phone.
she spent 20 minutes looking at the orange juice can because it said "concentrate."
at the bottom of the application where it says, "sign here," she put "Sagittarius."
she studied for a blood test.
she sold the car for gas money!
she thinks Taco Bell is the Mexican phone company.
if she spoke her mind, she'd be speechless.
she thought that she could not use her AM radio in the evening.
she had a shirt that said "TGIF" which she thought stood for: "This Goes In Front."
when she went to the airport and saw a sign that said "Airport Left," she turned around and went home.

After three weeks in the Garden of Eden, God came to visit Eve. "So, how is everything going?" inquired God.

"It is all so beautiful, God," she replied, "the sunrises & sunsets are breathtaking, the smells, the sights, everything is wonderful, but I have just this one problem. It is these breasts that you have given me. The middle one pushes the other two out and I am constantly knocking them with my arms, catching them on branches and snagging them on bushes. They are a real pain," reported Eve.

And Eve went on to tell God that since many other parts of her body came in pairs, such as her limbs, eyes, ears, etc., she felt that having only two breasts might leave her body more "symmetrically balanced," as she put it.

"That is a fair point," replied God, "but it was my first shot at this, you know. I gave the animals six breasts, so I figured that you needed only half of those, but I see that you are right. I will fix it up right away." And God reached down, removed the middle breast and tossed it into the bushes. Three weeks passed & God once again visited Eve in the Garden of Eden.

"Well, Eve, how is my favorite creation?"

"Just fantastic," she replied, "but for one oversight. All of the animals have a mate except me. I feel so alone."

God thought for a moment and said, "You know, Eve, you are right. How could I have overlooked this? You do need a mate and I will immediately create a man from a part of you. Now, let's see. . . where did I put that useless boob?"

You know you are getting old when everything either dries up or leaks.

Why do you have to "put your two cents in," but it's only a "penny for your thoughts"? Where's that extra penny going?

While sitting in a chair, lift your right foot off the floor and make clockwise circles. Now, while doing this, draw the number "6" in the air with your right hand. Your foot will change direction and there's nothing you can do about it!

Deep in the back woods of Kentucky, a redneck's wife went into labor in the middle of the night, and the doctor was called out to assist in the delivery.

Since there was no electricity, the doctor handed the father-to-be a lantern and said, "Here, you hold this high so I can see what I am doing."

Soon, a baby boy was brought into the world. "Whoa there," said the doctor. "Don't be in such a rush to put that lantern down. I think there's another one coming."

Sure enough, within minutes he had delivered a baby girl.

"Hold that lantern up, don't set it down, there's another one!" said the doctor.

Within a few minutes he had delivered a third baby.

"Don't put down that lantern, it seems there's yet another one coming!" cried the doctor.

The redneck scratched his head in bewilderment and asked the doctor, "You reckon it might be the light that's attractin' 'em?"

A priest was called to a local nursing home to perform a wedding. An anxious old man met him at the door. The priest sat down to counsel the old man and asked several questions.

"Do you love her?"
The old man replied, "I guess."
"Is she a good Christian?"
"I don't know for sure," the old man answered.
"Does she have lots of money?" asked the priest.
"I doubt it."
"Then why are you marrying her?" he asked.
"She can drive at night," the old man said.

A man walks into a shoe store and tries on a pair of shoes.

"How do they feel?" asks the sales clerk.

"Well, they feel a bit tight," replied the man.

The clerk bends down and has a look at the shoes and says, "Try pulling the tongue out."

"Well, theyth sthill feelth a bith thighth."

R emember all the years you spent watching carefully what you ate and how you exercised so you could get an extra twenty years of life? Well, THESE ARE THOSE TWENTY YEARS. Why did you bother?

B ob calls his buddy Sam, the horse rancher, and says he's sending a friend over to look at a horse. Sam asks, "How will I recognize him?"

"That's easy - he's a midget with a speech impediment."

So, the midget shows up, and Sam asks him if he's looking for a male or female horse. "A female horth." So he shows him a prized filly. "Nith lookin horth. Can I thee her eyeth"?

Sam picks up the midget and he gives the horse's eyes the once over. "Nith eyeth, can I thee her earzth"? So he picks the little fella up again, and shows him the horse's ears.

"Nith earzth, can I see her mouf"? The rancher is gettin' pretty ticked off by this point, but he picks him up again and shows him the horse's mouth. "Nith mouf, can I see her twat"?

Totally mad at this point, the rancher grabs him under his arms and rams the midget's head as far as he can up the horse's crotch, pulls him out, and slams him on the ground.

The midget gets up, sputtering and coughing. "Perhapth I should rephrase that: Can I thee her wun awound a widdle bit?"

In the beginning God covered the earth with broccoli and cauliflower and spinach, green and yellow and red vegetables of all kinds, so Man and Woman would live long and healthy lives.

Then using God's bountiful gifts, Satan created ice cream and doughnuts. And Satan said, "You want hot fudge with that?" And Man said, "Yes!" and Woman said, "I'll have another with sprinkles." And lo they gained 10 pounds.

So God said, "Try my fresh green salad."

And Satan presented crumbled Bleu Cheese dressing and garlic toast on the side. And Man and Woman unfastened their belts following the repast.

God then said, "I have sent you heart healthy vegetables and olive oil in which to lightly sauté the wholesome vegetables."

And Satan brought forth deep fried coconut shrimp, chicken-fried steak so big it needed its own platter and chocolate cheesecake for dessert. And Man's glucose levels spiked through the roof.

God then brought forth running shoes so that his children might lose those extra pounds.

And Satan came forth with a cable TV with remote control so Man would not have to toil changing the channels. And man and woman laughed and cried before the flickering light and started wearing stretch jogging suits.

Then God brought forth lean meat so that Man might consume fewer calories and still satisfy his appetite.

And Satan created the 99-cent double cheeseburger, and said, "You want fries with that?" And Man replied, "Yes! And super size 'em!" And Man went into cardiac arrest.

God sighed and created quadruple bypass surgery.

And Satan created HMOs.

Who was the first person to look at a cow and say, "I think I'll squeeze these dangly things here, and drink whatever comes out?"

Mid-life is when the growth of hair on our legs slows down. This gives us plenty of time to care for our newly-acquired mustache.

Mid-life is when women no longer have upper arms, we have wing spans. We are no longer women in sleeveless shirts, we are flying squirrels in drag.

Mid-life is when you can stand naked in front of a mirror and you can see your rear without turning around.

Mid-life is when you go for a mammogram and you realize that this is the only time someone will ask you to appear topless.

Mid-life is when you want to grab every firm young lovely in a tube top and scream, "Listen honey, even the Roman Empire fell and those will too."

Mid-life brings wisdom to know that life throws us curves and we're sitting on our biggest ones.

Mid-life is when you look at your-know-it-all, (cell phone) beeper-wearing teenager and think: "For this I have stretch marks?"

In mid-life your memory starts to go. In fact the only thing we can retain is water.

Mid-life means that your Body By Jake now includes Legs By Rand McNally -- more red and blue lines than an accurately scaled map of Wisconsin.

Once you're in heaven, do you get stuck wearing the clothes you were buried in for eternity?

A woman and a man are involved in a car accident on a snowy, cold Monday morning; it's a bad one. Both of their cars are totally demolished but amazingly neither of them is hurt. God works in mysterious ways.

After they crawl out of their cars, the woman says, "So . . . you're a man. That's interesting. I'm a woman. Wow, just look at our cars! There's nothing left, but we're unhurt. This must be a sign from God that we should meet and be friends and live together in peace for the rest of our days."

Flattered, the man replies, "Oh yes, I agree with you completely, this must be a sign from God!"

The woman continues, "And look at this, here's another miracle. My car is completely demolished but this bottle of wine didn't break. Surely God wants us to drink this wine and celebrate our good fortune."

Then she hands the bottle to the man. The man nods his head in agreement, opens it and drinks half the bottle and then hands it back to the woman.

The woman takes the bottle and immediately puts the cap back on, and hands it back to the man. The man asks, "Aren't you having any?"

The woman replies, "No. I think I'll just wait for the police."

Diary entries of a young woman on a cruise ship:

MONDAY: What a wonderful cruise this is going to be! I felt singularly honored this evening. The Captain asked me to dine at his table.

TUESDAY: I spent the entire afternoon on the bridge with the Captain.

WEDNESDAY: The Captain made proposals to me unbecoming an officer and a gentleman.

THURSDAY: Tonight the Captain threatened to sink the ship if I do not give in to his indecent proposals.

FRIDAY: This afternoon I saved 1600 lives. Twice.

A new young monk arrives at the monastery. He is assigned to help the other monks in copying the old canons and laws of the church by hand. He notices, however, that all of the monks are copying from copies, not from the original manuscript. So, the new monk goes to the head abbot to question this, pointing out that if someone made even a small error in the first copy, it would never be picked up. In fact, that error would be continued in all of the subsequent copies.

The head monk, says, "We have been copying from the copies for centuries, but you make a good point, my son." So, he goes down into the dark caves underneath the monastery where the original manuscript is held as archives in a locked vault that hasn't been opened for hundreds of years. Hours go by and nobody sees the old abbot. So, the young monk gets worried and goes downstairs to look for him. He hears sobbing coming from the back of the cellar and finds the abbot leaning over one of the original books and crying,

"We forgot the "R," we forgot the "R."

The young monk asks the old abbot, "What's wrong, father?"

With a choking voice, the old abbot replies, "The word is celebrate. The word is celebRate."

Mildred, the church gossip, and self-appointed monitor of the church's morals, kept sticking her nose in to other people's business. Several members did not approve of her extra curricular activities, but feared her enough to maintain their silence.

She made a mistake, however, when she accused Frank, a new member, of being an alcoholic after she saw his old pickup parked in front of the town's only bar one afternoon. She emphatically told Frank (and several others) that everyone seeing it there would know what he was doing.

Frank, a man of few words, stared at her for a moment and just turned and walked away. He didn't explain, defend, or deny. He said nothing.

Later that evening, Frank quietly parked his pickup in front of Mildred's house, walked home and left it there all night!

An old woman's car breaks down on the interstate one day. So she eases it over onto the shoulder of the road. She carefully steps out of the car and opens the trunk. Out of the trunk jump two men in trench coats, who walk away from the rear of the vehicle where they stand facing oncoming traffic and opening their coats to expose their nude bodies to approaching drivers. Not surprisingly, one of the worst pile-ups in the history of this highway occurs.

It's not very long before a police car shows up. The cop, clearly enraged, runs towards the old woman's disabled vehicle yelling, "What the heck is going on here?"

My car broke down," says the old lady, calmly.

"Well, what are these perverts doing here by the road?" asks the cop.

And she said, "Those are my emergency flashers."

What disease did cured ham actually have?

One day a physics professor was discussing a particularly complicated concept. A pre-med student rudely interrupted to ask, "Why do we have to learn this stuff?"

"To save lives," the professor responded before continuing the lecture.

"So how does physics save lives?" the student persisted.

"It keeps the ignoramuses out of medical school."

Can a hearse carrying a corpse drive in the carpool lane?

It was entertainment night at the senior center and the Amazing Claude was topping the bill. People came from miles around to see the famed hypnotist do his stuff. As Claude went to the front of the meeting room, he announced, "Unlike most hypnotists who invite two or three people up here to be put into a trance, I intend to hypnotize each and every member of the audience."

The excitement was almost electric as Claude withdrew a beautiful antique pocket watch from his coat. "I want you each to keep your eye on this antique watch. It's a very special watch. It's been in my family for 6 generations."

He began to swing the watch gently back and forth while quietly chanting, "Watch the watch, watch the watch, watch the watch . . ."

The crowd became mesmerized as the watch swayed back and forth, light gleaming off its polished surface. Hundreds of pairs of eyes followed the swaying watch, until, suddenly, it slipped from the hypnotist's fingers and fell to the floor, breaking into a hundred pieces.

"Shit!" said the hypnotist.

It took three weeks to clean up the senior center.

A young man saw an elderly couple sitting down to lunch at McDonald's. He noticed that they had ordered only one meal and an extra drink cup. As he watched, the older gentleman carefully divided the hamburger in half, then counted out the fries, one for him, one for her, until each had exactly half of them. Then the old man poured half of the soft drink into the extra cup and set that in front of his wife. The old mad then began to eat while his wife sat watching with her hands folded in her lap.

The young man decided to ask if they would allow him to purchase another meal for them so that they didn't have to split theirs.

The old gentleman said, "Oh, no. We've been married 50 years and everything has always been and always will be shared 50/50."

The young man then asked the wife if she was going to eat, and she replied, "Not yet. It's his turn with the teeth."

Why do they call it PMS? Mad Cow was already taken!!!

A man is dining in a fancy restaurant and there is a gorgeous redhead sitting at the next table. He has been checking her out since he sat down, but lacks the nerve to talk with her. Suddenly she sneezes, and her glass eye comes flying out of its socket towards the man. He reflexively reaches out, grabs it out of the air, and hands it back.

"Oh my, I am so sorry," the woman says as she pops her eye back in place. "Let me buy your dinner to make it up to you, " she says.

They enjoy a wonderful dinner together, and afterwards they go to the theater followed by drinks. They talk, they laugh, she shares her deepest dreams and he shares his. She listens. After paying for everything, she asks him if he would like to come to her place for a nightcap and stay for breakfast.

They had a wonderful, wonderful time.

The next morning, she cooks a gourmet meal with all the trimmings. The guy is amazed! Everything had been SO incredible!

"You know, " he said, "you are the perfect woman. Are you this nice to every guy you meet? "

"No, " she replies, "you just happened to catch my eye."

How is it that we put man on the moon before we figured out it would be a good idea to put wheels on luggage?

A psychiatrist's secretary walked into his study and said, "There's a gentleman in the waiting room asking to see you. Claims he's invisible."

The psychiatrist responded, "Tell him I can't see him."

Why is it that people say they "slept like a baby" when babies wake up like every two hours?

Why do toasters always have a setting that burns the toast to a horrible crisp, which no decent human being would eat?

Three girls all worked in the same office with the same female boss. Each day, they noticed the boss left work early. One day the girls decided that, when the boss left, they would leave right behind her. After all, she never called or came back to work, so how would she know they went home early?

The brunette was thrilled to be home early. She did a little gardening, spent play time with her son and went to bed early.

The redhead was elated to be able to get in a quick workout at the spa before meeting a dinner date.

The blonde was happy to get home early and surprise her husband, but when she got to her bedroom, she heard a muffled noise from inside. Slowly and quietly, she cracked open the door and was mortified to see her husband in bed with her lady boss! Gently, she closed the door and crept out of her house.

The next day, at their coffee break, the brunette and redhead planned to leave early again and they asked the blonde if she was going to go with them. The blonde responded, "No way, I almost got caught yesterday!"

They call it DIET because all the other four-letter words were taken.

Four Catholic ladies are having coffee together, discussing how important their children are. The first Catholic woman tells her friends, "My son is a priest. When he walks into a room, everyone calls him 'Father.'"

The second Catholic woman chirps, "Well, my son is a bishop. When he walks into a room, everyone says 'Your Grace.'"

The third Catholic woman says smugly, "Well, not to put you down, but my son is a cardinal. When he walks into a room, people say 'Your Eminence.'"

The fourth Catholic woman sips her coffee in silence. The first three women give her this subtle, "Well . . . . . ?"

She replies: "My son is a gorgeous, 6'2," hard-bodied, well-hung male stripper. When he walks into a room, women say 'My God.'"

A door-to-door vacuum cleaner salesman knocks on the door of a house and a lady opens the door. Before she has a chance to say anything, he runs inside and dumps a bag of dirt all over her carpet.

He says, "Lady, if this vacuum cleaner doesn't clean up all that dirt, I'll eat every last bit of it."

She turns to him with a smirk and says, "Do you want ketchup on that?"

The salesman says, "Why do you ask?"

"We just moved in to this place and we haven't got the electricity turned on yet."

B ambi, a blonde in her fourth year as a UCLA freshman, sat in her US government class. The professor asked Bambi if she knew what Roe vs. Wade was about.

Bambi pondered the question then finally said, "That was the decision George Washington had to make before he crossed the Delaware."

I f a deaf person has to go to court, is it still called a hearing?

W hy do they call it an asteroid when it's outside the hemisphere, but call it a hemorrhoid when it's in your butt?

I f the professor on Gilligan's Island can make a radio out of a coconut, why can't he fix a hole in a boat?

T he doctor comes in and informs the dad that his son was born without a torso, arms or legs. The son is just a head! But the dad loves his son and raises him as well as he can, with love and compassion.

After 21 years, the son is now old enough for his first drink. Dad takes him to the bar, tearfully tells the son he is proud of him and orders up the biggest, strongest drink for his boy. With all the bar patrons looking on curiously and the bartender shaking his head in disbelief, the boy takes his first sip of alcohol.

Swoooop! A torso pops out! The bar is dead silent; then bursts into a whoop of joy. The father, shocked, begs his son to drink again.

The patrons chant, "Take another drink"! The bartender still shakes his head in dismay.

Swoooop! Two arms pops out! The bar goes wild. The father, crying and wailing, begs his son to drink again.

The patrons chant, "Take another drink!" The bartender ignores the whole affair. By now the boy is getting tipsy, and with his new hands he reaches down, grabs his drink and guzzles the last of it. Swoooop! Two legs pop out. The bar is in chaos. The father falls to his knees, tearfully giving thanks!!

The boy stands up on his new legs and stumbles to the left . . . then to the right - right through the front door, into the street, where a truck runs over him and kills him instantly.

The bar falls silent. The father moans in grief.

The bartender sighs and says, "He should have quit while he was a head!"

A woman awoke during the night to find that her husband was not in their bed. She put on her robe and went downstairs to look for him. She found him sitting at the dining room table with a cup of coffee in front of him. He appeared deep in thought, just staring at the wall. She watched as he wiped a tear from his eye and took a sip of coffee.

"What's the matter, dear?" she whispered as she stepped into the room. "Why are you down here at this time of night?"

The husband looked up. "Do you remember 40 years ago when we were dating, and you were only 18?" he asked solemnly. The wife was touched to tears thinking that her husband was so caring and sensitive.

"Yes, I do," she replied.

The husband paused. The words were not coming easily. Do you remember when your mother caught us behind the couch making love?"

"Yes, I remember," said the wife, lowering herself into a chair beside him.

The husband continued. "Do you remember when she shoved a shotgun in my face and said, 'Either you marry my daughter, or I will send you to jail for 40 years!'"

"I remember that, too," she replied softly.

He wiped another tear from his cheek and said, "I would have gotten out today."

ROMANCE MATHEMATICS
Smart man + smart woman = romance
Smart man + dumb woman = affair
Dumb man + smart woman = marriage
Dumb man + dumb woman = pregnancy

These four friends were so confident, that the weekend before finals, they decided to visit some friends and have a big party. They had a great time, but after all the hearty partying, they slept all day Sunday and didn't make it back to Duke until early Monday morning.

Rather than taking the final then, they decided that after the final they would explain to their professor why they missed it. They said they visited friends but on the way back they had a flat tire. As a result, they missed the final. The professor agreed they could make up the final the next day.

The guys were excited and relieved. They studied that night for the exam. The Professor placed them in separate rooms and gave them a test booklet. They quickly answered the first problem worth 5 points. Cool, they thought! Each one in separate rooms, thinking this was going to be easy . . . then they turned the page.

On the second page was written: For 95 points: Which tire?

If you take an Asian person and spin him around several times, does he become disoriented?

Jennifer's wedding day was fast approaching. Nothing could dampen her excitement - not even her parents' nasty divorce. Her mother had found the PERFECT dress to wear and would be the best-dressed mother-of-the-bride ever! A week later, Jennifer was horrified to learn that her father's new young wife had bought the exact same dress! Jennifer asked her to exchange it, but she refused.

"Absolutely not. I look like a million bucks in this dress, and I'm wearing it," she replied.

Jennifer told her mother who graciously said, "Never mind sweetheart. I'll get another dress. After all, it's your special day."

A few days later, they went shopping and did find another gorgeous dress. When they stopped for lunch, Jennifer asked her mother, "Aren't you going to return the other dress? You really don't have another occasion where you could wear it."

Her mother just smiled and replied, "Of course I do, dear. I'm wearing it to the rehearsal dinner the night before the wedding!"

A married couple was asleep when the phone rang at 2 in the morning. The wife (undoubtedly blonde), picked up the phone, listened a moment and said, "How should I know, that's 200 miles from here!" and hung up.

The husband said, "Who was that?"

The wife said, "I don't know, some woman wanting to know if the coast is clear."

George, age 90, went for his annual physical. All of his tests came back with normal results. Dr. Smith said, "George, everything looks great physically. How are you doing mentally and emotionally? Are you at peace with yourself, and do you have a good relationship with God?"

George replied, "God and me are tight. He knows I have poor eyesight, so he's fixed it so that when I get up in the middle of the night to go to the bathroom, poof, the light goes on, when I'm done, poof, the light goes off."

"Wow!" commented Dr. Smith, "That's incredible!"

A little later in the day, Dr. Smith called George's wife. "Ethel," he said, "George is doing fine. Physically he's great. But, I had to call because I'm worried about his so-called relationship with God. He says he gets up during the night and, poof, the light goes on in the bathroom, and then when he is through, poof, the light goes off?"

Ethel exclaimed, "Oh, my God! He's peeing in the refrigerator again!"

M ost people don't know that back in 1912, Hellmann's mayonnaise was manufactured in England. In fact, the Titanic was carrying 12,000 jars of the condiment scheduled for delivery in Vera Cruz, Mexico, which was to be the next port of call for the great ship after its stop in New York.

This would have been the largest single shipment of mayonnaise ever delivered to Mexico. But as we know, the great ship did not make it to New York. The ship hit an iceberg and sank, and the cargo was forever lost.

The people of Mexico, who were crazy about mayonnaise, and were eagerly awaiting its delivery, were disconsolate at the loss. Their anguish was so great, that they declared a National Day of Mourning, which they still observe to this day.

The National Day of Mourning occurs each year on May 5th and is known, of course, as Sinko de Mayo.

I f you choke a Smurf, what color does it turn?

A man boarded an airplane and took his seat. As he settled in, he glanced up and saw a most beautiful woman boarding the plane and heading straight towards his row. As fate would have it, she took the seat right beside his. Eager to strike up a conversation he blurted out,

"Business trip or pleasure?"

She turned, smiled and said, "Business. I'm going to the Annual Nymphomaniacs of America Convention in Chicago."

Struggling to maintain his composure, he calmly asked, "What's your business role at this convention?"

"Lecturer," she responded. "I use information that I have learned from my personal experiences to debunk some of the popular myths about sexuality."

"Really?" he said. "And what kind of myths are there?"

"Well," she explained, "one popular myth is that African-American men are the most well-endowed of all men, when in fact it is the Native American Indian who is most likely to possess that trait. Another popular myth is that Frenchmen are the best lovers when actually it is men of Jewish descent who are the best. I have also discovered that the lover with absolutely the best stamina is the Southern redneck."

Suddenly the woman became a little uncomfortable and blushed. "I'm sorry," she said, "I shouldn't really be discussing all of this with you. I don't even know your name."

"Tonto," the man said, "Tonto Goldstein, but my friends call me Bubba."

Is it okay to use an AM radio after noon?

A woman marries a man expecting he will change, but he doesn't.
A man marries a woman expecting that she won't change, and she does.

To be happy with a man, you must understand him a lot and love him a little.
To be happy with a woman, you must love her a lot and not try to understand her at all.

A woman worries about the future until she gets a husband.
A man never worries about the future until he gets a wife.

A successful man is one who makes more money than his wife can spend.
A successful woman is one who can find such a man.

M arried men live longer than single men do, but married men are a lot more willing to die.

A blonde suspects her boyfriend of cheating on her, so she goes out and buys a gun.

She goes to his apartment unexpectedly and when she opens the door she finds him in the arms of a redhead. Well, the blonde is really angry. She opens her purse to take out the gun, and as she does so, she is overcome with grief. She takes the gun and puts it to her head.

The boyfriend yells, "No, honey, don't do it!"

The blonde replies, "Shut up, you're next!"

W hat did the blonde ask her doctor when he told her she was pregnant? "Is it mine?"

T wo blondes are walking down the street. One notices a compact on the sidewalk and leans down to pick it up. She opens it, looks in the mirror and says, "Hmm, this person looks familiar."

The second blonde says, "Here, let me see!"

So the first blonde hands her the compact.

The second one looks in the mirror and says, "You dummy, it's me!"

She spent the first day packing her belongings into boxes, crates and suitcases. On the second day, she had the movers come and collect her things. On the third day, she sat down for the last time at their beautiful dining room table by candlelight, put on some soft background music, and feasted on a pound of shrimp, a jar of caviar, and a bottle of Chardonnay.

When she had finished, she went into each and every room and deposited a few half-eaten shrimp shells, dipped in caviar, into the hollow of the curtain rods. She then cleaned up the kitchen and left.

When the husband returned with his new girlfriend, all was bliss for the first few days. Then slowly, the house began to smell. They tried everything: cleaning and mopping and airing the place out. Vents were checked for dead rodents, and carpets were steam cleaned. Air fresheners were hung everywhere. Exterminators were brought in to set off gas canisters, during which they had to move out for a few days, and in the end they even paid to replace the expensive wool carpeting.

Nothing worked. People stopped coming over to visit. Repairmen refused to work in the house. The maid quit. Finally they could not take the stench any longer and decided to move.

A month later, even though they had cut the price in half, they could not find a buyer for their stinky house. Word got out, and eventually, even the local Realtors refused to return their calls. Finally, they had to borrow a huge sum of money from the bank to purchase a new place.

The ex-wife called the man, and asked how things were going. He told her a little about the saga of the house. She listened politely, and said that she missed her old home terribly, and would be willing to reduce her divorce settlement in exchange for getting the house back.

Knowing his ex-wife had no idea how bad the smell was, he agreed on price that was about 1/10th of what the house had been worth . . . But only if she were to sign the papers that very day. She agreed, and within the hour, his lawyers delivered the paperwork.

A week later, the man and his new girlfriend stood smirking as they watched the moving company pack everything to take to their new home.

Including the curtain rods!!

Toward the end of the service, the Minister asked, "How many of you have forgiven your enemies?" 80% held up their hands.

The Minister then repeated his question. All responded this time, except one small elderly lady.

"Mrs. Jones? Are you not willing to forgive your enemies?"

"I don't have any," she replied, smiling sweetly.

"Mrs. Jones, that is very unusual. How old are you?"

"Ninety-eight," she replied.

"Oh, Mrs. Jones, would you please come down in front and tell us all how a person can live ninety-eight years & not have an enemy in the world?"

The little sweetheart of a lady tottered down the aisle, faced the congregation, and said:

"I outlived the bitches."

A woman has the last word in any argument.
Anything a man says after that is the beginning of a new argument.

What do people in China call their good plates?

I recently picked a new primary care doctor.
After two visits and exhaustive lab tests, he said I was doing "fairly well" for my age.
A little concerned, I couldn't resist asking him, "Do you think I'll live to be 90?"
He asked, "Do you smoke tobacco or drink beer or wine?"
"Oh no," I replied. "I'm not doing drugs, either."
Then he asked, "Do you eat rib-eye steaks and barbecued ribs?"
I said, "No, my former doctor said that all red meat is very unhealthy!"
"Do you spend a lot of time in the sun, like playing golf, sailing, hiking, or bicycling?"

"No, I don't," I said.
He asked, "Do you gamble, drive fast cars, or have a lot of sex?"
"No," I said. "I don't do any of those things."
He looked at me and said, "Then, why do you give a shit?"

Returning home from work, a blonde was shocked to find her house ransacked and burglarized. She telephoned the police at once and reported the crime.

The police dispatcher broadcast the call on the radio, and a K-9 unit, patrolling nearby was the first to respond. As the K-9 officer approached the house with his dog on a leash, the blonde ran out on the porch, shuddered at the sight of the cop and his dog, and then sat down on the steps.

Putting her face in her hands, she moaned, "I come home to find all my possessions stolen. I call the police for help, and what do they do? They send me a BLIND policeman."

What hair color do they put on the driver's license of a bald man?

A woman went to her doctor for a follow-up visit after the doctor had given her a prescription for the male hormone testosterone. The woman was a little worried about some of the side effects she was experiencing.

"Doctor, the hormones you've been giving me have really helped, but I'm afraid you're giving me too much. I've started growing hair in places where I've never grown hair before."

The doctor reassured her, "A little hair growth is a perfectly normal side effect of testosterone. Just where has this hair appeared?"

"On my balls."

A second grader came home from school and said to her mother, "Mom, guess what? We learned how to make babies today."

The mother, more than a little surprised, tried to keep her cool. "That's interesting," she said. "How do you make babies?"

"It's simple," replied the girl. "You just change "y" to "i" and add "es."

Now that we have automatic teller machines, we no longer have to tell our children that money does not grow on trees.

They think it comes out of a wall.

A grandmother was surprised by her seven-year-old grandson one morning. He had made her coffee. She drank what was the worst cup of coffee in her life. When she got to the bottom, there were three of those little green Army men in the cup. She said, "Honey, what are these army men doing in my coffee?"

Her grandson said, "Grandma, it says on TV, 'The best part of waking up is soldiers in your cup!'"

The spin cycle on the washing machine will make cats dizzy. Cats throw up twice their body weight when dizzy.

Two Irishmen were sitting at a pub having beer and watching the brothel across the street.

They saw a Baptist minister walk into the brothel, and one of them said, "Aye, 'tis a shame to see a man of the cloth goin' bad."

Then they saw a rabbi enter the brothel, and the other Irishman said, "Aye, 'tis a shame to see that the Jews are fallin' victim to temptation as well."

Then they see a Catholic priest enter the brothel, and one of the Irishmen said, "What a terrible pity. One of the girls must be dying."

Irving was just coming out of anesthesia after a series of tests in the hospital, and his wife, Sarah, was sitting at his bedside. His eyes fluttered open, and he murmured, "You're beautiful."

Flattered, Sarah continued her vigil while he drifted back to sleep.

Later he woke up and said, "You're cute."

What happened to 'beautiful?'" Sarah asked.

"The drugs are wearing off," he replied.

What would Geronimo say if he jumped out of an airplane?

A senior citizen bought himself a brand new convertible. He took off down I-75, speeding at 85 mph, enjoying the wind blowing through what little hair he had left on his head. "This is great," he thought, as he roared down the highway. He pushed the pedal to the metal even more. Then he looked in his rear view mirror, and discovered a Florida State Patrol officer right behind him, blue lights flashing, and siren blaring.

"I can get away from him with no problem," thought the man. He pushed the gas pedal all the way to the floor, and flew down the highway at 100 mph. Then 110, and 120. Then he thought, "What am doing? I'm too old for this kind of thing."

So he pulled over to the side of the road, and waited for the officer to catch up with him. The officer pulled in behind the Corvette, and calmly walked up to the driver's door. "Sir," he said, looking at his watch. "My shift ends in 20 minutes. If you can explain why you were speeding away from me, with an excuse that I've never heard before, I'll let you go."

The man looked at the officer and said, "Ten years ago, my wife ran off with a Florida State Patrol Officer, and I thought you were bringing her back."

"Have a good day, sir," said the officer.

Why are they called apartments when they are all stuck together?

What Doctors say . . . . . What they mean

This should be taken care of right away...
I planned a trip to Hawaii next month, but this is so easy and profitable,
I want to fix it before it cures itself.

Well, what have we here???
He has no idea and is hoping you will give him a clue.

Let me check your medical history...
I want to see if you've paid your last bill before spending any more time
with you.

I have some good news and some bad news...
The good news is I'm buying a new BMW; the bad news is you're paying
for it.

Do you suppose all this stress could be affecting your nerves?
You're crazier than an outhouse rat. Now if I can only find a shrink who'll
split the fees with me.

If it doesn't clear up in a week, give me a call...
I don't know what it is; maybe it will go away by itself.

That's quite a nasty looking wound...
I think I'm going to throw up.

This may smart a little...
Last week two patients bit off their tongues.

Well, we're not feeling so well today are we?
I'm stalling for time, who are you and why are you here?

There's a lot of that going around...
Wow, that's the third one this week. Maybe I should learn something
about this.

A mortician was working late one night. It was his job to examine the dead bodies before they were sent off to be buried or cremated. As he examined the body of Mr. Schwartz who was about to be cremated, he made an amazing discovery: Schwartz had the longest private part he had ever seen!

"I'm sorry, Mr. Schwartz," said the mortician, "but I can't send you off to be cremated with a tremendously huge private part like this. It has to be saved for posterity." With that, the coroner used his tools to remove the dead man's schlong. He stuffed his prize into a briefcase and took it home.

The first person he showed it to was his wife. "I have something to show you that you won't believe," he said, and opened up his briefcase.

"Oh my God!" she screamed. "Schwartz is dead!"

R odney wakes up at home with a huge hangover. He forces himself to open his eyes, and the first thing he sees is a couple of aspirins and a glass of water on the side table. He sits down and sees his clothing in front of him, all clean and pressed. Rodney looks around the room and sees that it is in a perfect order, spotless and clean. So's the rest of the house. He takes the aspirins and notices a note on the table: "Honey, breakfast is on the stove. I left early to go shopping. Love you."

So he goes to the kitchen and sure enough there is a hot breakfast and the morning newspaper. His son is also at the table, eating. Rodney asks, "Son, what happened last night?"

His son says, "Well, you came home after 3 a.m., drunk and delirious. Broke some furniture, puked in the hallway, and gave yourself a black eye when you stumbled into the door."

Confused, Rodney asks, "So, why is everything in order and so clean, and breakfast is on the table waiting for me?"

His son replies, "Oh, that! Mom dragged you to the bedroom, and when she tried to take your pants off you said, 'Lady leave me alone, I'm married!'"

A man always loved fast cars. Taking advantage of the empty roads one morning, he accelerated down a wide-open stretch. Unfortunately, a young police officer was waiting at the other end and the man was flagged down. He greeted the officer with a cheery, "Good Morning."

"And a good morning to you, Wing Commander," replied the officer. "Having trouble taking off?"

WOMEN'S ENGLISH:

Yes = No.
No = Yes.
Maybe = No.
We need = I want.
I'm sorry = You'll be sorry.
We need to talk = I need to complain.
Sure, go ahead = I don't want you to.
Do what you want = You'll pay for this later.
I'm not upset = Of course I'm upset, you moron!
Are you listening to me?? = Too late, you're dead.
You have to learn to communicate = Just agree with me.
Be romantic, turn out the lights = I have flabby thighs.
You're so ... manly = You need a shave and you sweat a lot.
Do you love me? = I'm going to ask for something expensive.
It's your decision = The correct decision should be obvious by now.
You're certainly attentive tonight = Is sex all you ever think about?
I'll be ready in a minute = Kick off your shoes and find a good game on TV.
How much do you love me? = I did something today that you're really not
   going to like.

MEN'S ENGLISH:

I'm hungry = I'm hungry.
I'm sleepy = I'm sleepy.
I'm tired = I'm tired.
Nice dress = Nice cleavage!
I love you = Let's have sex now.
I'm bored = Do you want to have sex?
What's wrong? = I guess sex is out of the question.
May I have this dance? = I'd like to have sex with you.
Can I call you sometime? = I'd like to have sex with you.

Do you want to go to a movie? = I'd like to have sex with you.
Can I take you out to dinner? = I'd like to have sex with you.
Will you marry me? = I want to make it illegal for you to have sex with
    other guys.
You look tense, let me give you a massage = I want to have sex with you
    within the next ten minutes.
Let's talk = I am trying to impress you by showing that I am a deep
    person . . . and then I'd like to have sex with you.
I don't think those shoes go with that outfit = I'm gay

Two women went out one weekend without their husbands. As they
came back, right before dawn, both of them drunk, they felt the
urge to pee. They noticed the only place to stop was a cemetery. Scared
and drunk, they stopped and decided to go there anyway.

The first one did not have anything to clean herself with, so she took off
her panties, used them to clean herself and discarded them.

The second not finding anything either, thought "I'm not getting rid of
my panties," so she used the ribbon of a flower wreath to clean herself.

The morning after, the two husbands were talking to each other on the
phone, and one says to the other: "We have to be on the look-out. It
seems that these two were up to no good last night, my wife came home
without her panties."

The other one responded: "You're lucky, mine came home with a card
stuck to her butt that read, "We will never forget you".

Gay Bob goes into the doctor's office and has some tests run. The doctor come
back and says, "Bob, I'm not going to beat around the bush. You have AIDS."

Bob is devastated. "Doc, what can I do?"

"Eat one sausage, one head of cabbage, 20 unpeeled carrots drenched in hot sauc
10 Jalapeno peppers, 40 walnuts and 40 peanuts, one-half box of Grape Nuts
cereal, and top it off with a gallon of prune juice."

Bob asks, "Will that cure me, Doc?"

Doc says, "No, but it should leave you with a better understanding of what your a
is for."

A Jewish lady is sitting at home when the phone rings. "Hello," she says.

"Hello," says the male voice at the other end, "I bet you'd really like it if I came 'round, ripped off your blouse and bra and pants, then threw you to the floor and made hot, sweaty love to you."

The Jewish lady replies, "From 'hello,' you can tell all this?"

What do you call a male ladybug?

Morris and his wife Esther went to the state fair every year and every year Morris would say, "Esther, I'd like to ride in that airplane."

Esther always replied, "I know Morris, but that airplane ride costs $50, and $50 is $50."

One year Morris and Esther went to the fair and Morris said, "Esther, I'm 85 years old. If I don't ride that airplane I might never get another chance."

Esther replied, "Morris, that airplane ride costs $50, and $50 is $50."

The pilot overheard them and said, "Folks, I'll make you a deal. I'll take you both up for a ride. If you can stay quiet for the entire ride and not say one word, I won't charge you, but if you say one word it's $50."

Morris and Esther agreed and up they went. The pilot did all kinds of twists and turns, rolls and dives, but not a word was heard. He did all his tricks over again, but still not a word.

When they landed, the pilot turned to Morris and said, "By golly, I did everything I could think of to get you to yell out, but you didn't."

Morris replied, "Well, I was gonna say something when Esther fell out, but $50 is $50."

Snowmen fall from Heaven unassembled.

Bernie had a fight with his wife, Rachel, and went to the movies to cool off. Later that evening, he decided to phone home to see what the situation was and maybe even apologize. "Hello, darling," he said, "What are you making for dinner?"

"What am I making for dinner? After all the horrible things you said to me earlier, you want to know what I am making for dinner? Poison, that's what I'm making, poison."

Bernie replies, "Okay then, just make one portion. I'm not coming home."

Miriam was on her deathbed, and she gave final instructions to her husband Sidney.

"Sidney, you've been so good to me all these years. I know you never even thought about another woman. But now that I'm going, I want you to marry again as soon as is possible and I want you to give your new wife all my expensive clothes."

"I can't do that, darling," Sidney said. "You're a size 16 and she's only a 10."

There were two blonde guys working for the city council. One would dig a hole; the other would follow behind him and fill the hole in. They worked furiously all day without rest, one guy digging a hole, the other guy filling it in again.

An onlooker was amazed at their hard work, but couldn't understand what they were doing. So he asked the hole digger, "I appreciate the effort you are putting into your work, but what's the story? You dig a hole and your partner follows behind and fills it up again."

The hole digger wiped his brow and sighed, "Well, normally we are a three-man team, but the guy who plants the trees is sick today."

If flying is so safe, why do they call the airport a terminal?

If the 7-11 is open 24 hours a day, 365 days a year, why does it have locks on the doors?

"Can I go outside and play with the boys?" a little girl asks her mother. "No, they're too rough," she says.

"If I can find a smooth one, can I play with him?"

A young man called his mother and announced excitedly that he had just met the woman of his dreams. Now what should he do?

His mother had an idea. "Why don't you send her flowers and on the card invite her over for a home-cooked meal?"

He thought this was a great strategy and arranged a date for that weekend. His mother called the morning after to see how things went.

"The evening was a disaster," he moaned.

"Why, didn't she show up?"

"Oh, she showed up, but she refused to cook."

Men are like . . . . .

Laxatives . . . They irritate the shit out of you.
Bananas . . . The older they get, the less firm they are.
Vacations . . . They never seem to be long enough.
Weather . . . Nothing can be done to change them.
Blenders . . . You need one, but you're not quite sure why.
Chocolate bars . . . Sweet, smooth, and they usually head right for your hips.
Coffee . . . The best ones are rich, warm, and can keep you up all night long.
Commercials . . . You can't believe a word they say.
Department stores . . . Their clothes are always 1/2 off.
Government bonds . . . They take sooooooooo long to mature.
Mascara . . . They usually run at the first sign of emotion.
Popcorn . . . They satisfy you, but only for a little while.
Lava lamps . . . Fun to look at, but not very bright.
Parking spots . . . All the good ones are taken, the rest are handicapped.
Snowstorms . . . You never know when they're coming, how many inches you'll get, or how long they will last.

A little boy got on the bus, sat next to a man reading a book, and noticed he had his collar on backwards. The little boy asked why he wore his collar that way. The man, who was a priest, said, "I am a father."

The little boy replied, "My daddy doesn't wear his collar like that."

The priest looked up from his book and answered, "I am the father of many."

The boy said, "My dad has four boys and four girls and he doesn't wear his collar that way."

The priest, getting impatient, said, "I am the father of hundreds," and went back to reading his book.

The little boy sat quietly thinking for a while, then leaned over and said, "Maybe you should wear your pants backwards instead of your collar."

Rachel and Esther meet at their 40th high school reunion after having not seen each other since their graduation.

Rachel begins to tell Esther about her children. "My son is a doctor and he's got four children. My daughter is married to lawyer and they have three great kids. So tell me, Esther, how about your family?"

Esther replies, "Unfortunately, Marty and I never had any children and so we don't have any grandchildren either."

Rachel says, "No children? And no grandkids? What do you do for aggravation?"

A man has spent many days crossing the desert without water. His camel dies of thirst. He's crawling through the sands, certain that he has breathed his last, when all of a sudden he sees an object before him.

He crawls to the object, pulls it out of the sand, and discovers what looks to be an old brief case. He opens it and out pops a genie. But this is no ordinary genie. He is wearing an IRS ID badge and dull gray suit. There's a calculator in his pocket. He has a pencil tucked behind his ear.

"Well, kid," says the genie, "you know how it works. You have three wishes."

"I'm not falling for this," says the man. "I'm not going to trust an IRS auditor."

"What do you have to lose? You've got no transportation, and it looks like you're a goner anyway!"

The man thinks about this for a minute and decides that the genie is right. "OK, I wish I were in a lush oasis with plentiful food and drink."

POOF! The man finds himself in the most beautiful oasis he has ever seen. And he is surrounded with jugs of wine and platters of delicacies.

"OK, kid, what's your second wish?"

"My second wish is that I were rich beyond my wildest dreams."

POOF! The man finds himself surrounded by treasure chests filled with rare gold coins and precious gems. "OK, kid, you have just one more wish. Better make it a good one!"

After thinking for a few minutes, the man says, "I wish that no matter where I go beautiful women will want and need me."

POOF! He is turned into a tampon.

The moral of the story: If the government offers you anything, there's going to be a string attached!

After you've heard two eyewitness accounts of an auto accident it makes you wonder about history.

A fine is a tax for doing wrong. A tax is a fine for doing well.

IT'S GOOD TO BE A WOMAN

We got off the Titanic first.
We can scare male bosses with mysterious gynecological disorder excuses.
Taxis stop for us.
We don't look like a frog in a blender when dancing.
No fashion faux pas we make could ever rival the Speedo.
We don't have to pass gas to amuse ourselves.
If we forget to shave, no one has to know.
We can congratulate our teammate without ever touching her rear.
We never have to reach down every so often to make sure our privates are still there.
We can talk to people of the opposite sex without having to picture them naked.
There are times when chocolate really can solve all your problems.
We'll never regret piercing our ears.
We can fully assess a person just by looking at their shoes.

IT'S GOOD TO BE A MAN

Your last name stays put.
The garage is all yours.
Wedding plans take care of themselves.
Chocolate is just another snack.
You can wear a white T-shirt to a water park.
Car mechanics tell you the truth.
You don't give a rat's behind if someone notices your new haircut.
The world is your urinal.
You never have to drive to another gas station because this one's just too icky.
Same work... more pay.
Wrinkles add character.
Wedding dress $5,000, tux rental $100.
People never stare at your chest when you're talking to them.
The occasional well-rendered belch is practically expected.
Your pals can be trusted never to trap you with: "So, notice anything different?"
One mood, ALL the dang time.
Phone conversations are over in 30 seconds flat.
Your belly usually hides your big hips.
One wallet and one pair of shoes, one color, all seasons.
You can "do" your nails with a pocketknife.

John was working at a fish plant when he accidentally cut off all ten of his fingers. He went to the emergency room. The doctor looked at John and said "Let's have the fingers, and I'll see what I can do."

John said, "I haven't got the fingers."

"What do you mean, you haven't got the fingers? It's 2003. We've got microsurgery and all kinds of incredible techniques. I could have put them back on and made you like new. Why didn't you bring the fingers?"

Furious, John says, "How the hell was I supposed to pick them up!"

A wife, one evening, drew her husband's attention to the couple next door and said, "Do you see that couple? How devoted they are? He kisses her every time they meet. Why don't you do that?"

"I would love to," replied the husband, "but I don't know her well enough."

A husband and wife were involved in a petty argument, both of them unwilling to admit they might be in error.

"I'll admit I'm wrong," the wife told her husband in a conciliatory attempt, "if you'll admit I'm right."

He agreed and, like a gentleman, insisted she go first. "I'm wrong," she said.

With a twinkle in his eye, he responded, "You're right!"

After listening to an old Simon & Garfunkel tune, my young daughter asked, "Well, did he?"
"Did he what?" I asked back.
"Did Parsley save Rosemary in time?"

When dog food is new and improved tasting, who tests it?

You know that indestructible black box that is used on airplanes? Why don't they make the whole plane out of that stuff?

Two boys from the Tennessee mountains, Leroy and Jasper, have been promoted from privates to sergeants. Not long after, they're out for a walk and Leroy says, "Hey, Jasper, there's the NCO Club. Let's you and me stop in."

"But we's privates," protests Jasper.

"We's sergeants now," says Leroy, pulling him inside. "Now, Jasper, I'm a-gonna sit down and have me a drink."

"But we's privates," says Jasper.

"Are you blind, boy?" asks Leroy, pointing at his stripes. "We's sergeants now." So they have their drink, and pretty soon a hooker comes up to Leroy. "You're cute," she says, "and I'd like to date you, but I've got a bad case of gonorrhea."

Leroy pulls his friend to the side and whispers, "Jasper, go look in the dictionary and see what gonorrhea means. If it's okay, give me the okay sign."

So Jasper goes to look it up, comes back, and gives Leroy the big okay sign. Three weeks later Leroy is laid up in the infirmary with a terrible case of gonorrhea.

"Jasper," he says, "why did you give me the okay?"

"Well, Leroy, in the dictionary, it says gonorrhea affects only the privates." He points to his stripes. "But we's sergeants now."

A group of American tourists were being guided through an ancient castle in Europe.

"This place," the guide told them, "is 600 years old. Not a stone in it has been touched, nothing altered, and nothing replaced in all those years."

"Wow," said one woman dryly, "they must have the same landlord that I have."

It seems a pastor from Maine skipped services one Sunday to go bear hunting in the mountains. As he turned the corner along the path, he and a bear collided. The pastor stumbled backwards, slipped off the trail and began tumbling down the mountain with the bear in hot pursuit.

Finally the pastor crashed into a boulder sending his rifle flying and breaking both his legs. As the bear closed in the pastor cried out in desperation, "Lord, I'm sorry for what I have done. Please forgive me and save me! Lord, please make that bear a Christian."

Suddenly, the bear skidded to a halt at the pastor's feet, fell to its knees, clasped its paws together and said, "God Bless this food which I am about to eat."

She was on vacation, playing the slot machines. It was her first time in a casino and she wasn't sure how to use the machines.

"Excuse me," she said to a casino employee, "How does this work?"

He showed her how to insert a bill, hit the spin button and operate the release handle.

"And where does the money come out?" she asked.

He smiled and motioned to a far wall, "Usually at the ATM."

An elderly woman walked into the Bank of Canada one morning with a purse full of money. She wanted to open a savings account and insisted on talking to the president of the Bank because, she said, she had a lot of money. After many lengthy discussions (after all, the client is always right), an employee took the elderly woman to the president's office.

The president of the bank asked her how much she wanted to deposit.

She placed her purse on his desk and replied, "$165,000."

The president was curious and asked her how she had been able to save so much money. The elderly woman replied that she made bets. The president was surprised and asked, "What kind of bets?"

The elderly woman replied, "Well, I bet you $25,000 that your testicles are square." The president started to laugh and told the woman that it was impossible to win a bet like that.

The woman never batted an eye. She just looked at the president and said, "Would you like to take my bet?"

"Certainly," replied the president. "I bet you $25,000 that my testicles are not square."

"Done," the elderly woman answered. "But given the amount of money involved, if you don't mind I would like to come back at 10 o'clock tomorrow morning with my lawyer as a witness."

"No problem," said the president of the bank confidently.

That night, the president became very nervous about the bet and spent a long time in front of the mirror examining his testicles, turning them this way and that, checking them over again and again until he was positive that no one could consider his testicles as square and reassuring himself that there was no way he could lose the bet.

The next morning at exactly 10 o'clock, the elderly woman arrived at the president's office with her lawyer and acknowledged the $25,000 bet made the day before that the president's testicles were square. The president confirmed that the bet was the same as the one made the day before. Then the elderly woman asked him to drop his pants so that she and her lawyer could see clearly. The president was happy to oblige.

The elderly woman came closer so she could see better and asked the president if she could touch them. "Of course," said the president. "Given the amount of money involved, you should be 100% sure." The elderly woman did so with a little smile. Suddenly the president noticed that the lawyer was banging his head against the wall.

He asked the elderly woman why he was doing that and she replied, "Oh, it's probably because I bet him $100,000 that around 10 o'clock in the morning, I would be holding the balls of the President of the Bank of Canada!"

If a firefighter fights fire and a crime fighter fights crime, what does a freedom fighter fight?

Three men were drinking at a bar – a doctor, an attorney and a biker. As the doctor was drinking his white wine, he said, "For her birthday, I'm going to buy my wife a fur coat and a diamond ring. This way if she doesn't like the fur coat, she will still love me because she got a diamond ring."

As the attorney was drinking his martini, he said, "For my wife's birthday, I'm going to buy her a designer dress and a gold bracelet. This way if she doesn't like the dress, she will still love me because she got the gold bracelet.

As the biker was drinking his shots of whiskey, he said, "I'm going to buy my wife a T-shirt and a vibrator. This way if she doesn't like the T-shirt, she can go f _ _ k herself!"

Why do they sterilize the needle for lethal injections?

One Liners:

I had amnesia once -- or twice.
Protons have mass? I didn't even know they were Catholic.
All I ask is a chance to prove that money can't make me happy.
If the world were a logical place, men would ride horses sidesaddle.
What is a "free" gift? Aren't all gifts free?
Is it my imagination, or do buffalo wings taste like chicken?

Two can live as cheaply as one, for half as long.
Experience is the thing you have left when everything else is gone.
What if there were no hypothetical questions?
They told me I was gullible . . . and I believed them.
Teach a child to be polite and courteous in the home and, when he grows up, he'll never be able to merge his car onto a freeway.

One nice thing about egotists: They don't talk about other people.
When the only tool you own is a hammer, every problem begins to look

like a nail.
What was the greatest thing before sliced bread?
I used to be indecisive. Now I'm not sure.
It's not an optical illusion. It just looks like one.

The cost of living hasn't affected its popularity.
How can there be self-help "groups"?
Is there another word for synonym?
Where do forest rangers go to "get away from it all"?
The speed of time is one second per second.

Is it possible to be totally partial?
What's another word for thesaurus?
Is Marx's tomb a communist plot?
If swimming is so good for your figure, how do you explain whales?
Show me a man with both feet firmly on the ground, and I'll show you a
    man who can't get his pants off.

If you are driving at the speed of light and you turn your headlights
on, what happens?

One particular Christmas a long time ago, Santa was getting ready
for his annual trip, but there were problems everywhere. Four of
his elves got sick, and the trainee elves did not produce the toys as
quickly as the regular ones, so Santa was beginning to feel the pressure
of being behind schedule.

Then, Mrs. Claus told him that her mom was coming to visit, which
stressed Santa out even more. When he went to harness the reindeer,
he found that three of them were about to give birth and two had
jumped the fence and were out, heaven knows where. More stress.

When he began to load the sleigh, one of the boards cracked and the toy
bag fell to the ground, scattering the toys. Frustrated, Santa went back
into the house for a cup of coffee and a shot of whisky. When he went
to the cupboard, he discovered that the elves had hidden the liquor and
there was nothing to drink. In his frustration, he accidentally dropped
the coffee pot and it broke into hundreds of little pieces.

So he went to get the broom and found that mice had eaten the straw it was made from. Just then, the doorbell rang and Santa cussed his way to the door.

He opened the door and there was a little angel with a great big Christmas tree. The angel said very cheerfully, "Merry Christmas Santa! Isn't it just a lovely day? I have this beautiful tree for you. Where would you like me to stick it?"

Thus began the tradition of the little angel atop the Christmas tree.

O ne night as a couple lay down for bed the husband gently taps his wife on the shoulder and starts rubbing her arm. The wife turns over and says, "I'm sorry, honey, I've got a gynecologist appointment and I want to stay fresh."

The husband, rejected, turns over and tries to sleep. A few minutes later he rolls back over and taps his wife again. This time he whispers, "Do you have a dentist appointment tomorrow too?"

A fireman is at the station house working outside on the fire truck when he notices a little boy next door. The little boy is in a little red wagon with little ladders hung off the side. He is wearing a fireman's hat and has the wagon tied to a dog.

The fireman says, "Hey, little boy. What are you doing?"

The little boy says, "I'm pretending to be a fireman and this is my fire truck."

The fireman walks over to take a closer look and says, "That sure looks like a nice fire truck!" The fireman looks a little closer and notices the little boy has tied the dog to the wagon by its testicles. "Little boy, I don't want to tell you how to run your fire truck, but if you were to tie that rope around the dog's neck, I think you could go faster."

The little boy says, "You're probably right, mister, but then I wouldn't have a siren."

I t has recently been discovered that research causes cancer in rats.

Sadie and Max live in the same nursing home in Florida. (Where else?)

Sadie says, "Max, will you take me to a movie?"

Max says, "Sure, but I have one request. When I take a lady to the movies I like her to hold my penis."

Sadie says, "No problem."

The next day Bessie goes up to Max and asks him if he'll take her to a movie.

Max says, "I can't. I'm taking Sadie to a movie tonight."

Bessie says, "But you took Sadie last night. What does Sadie have that I don't have?"

PARKINSON'S

A woman could never get her husband to do anything around the house. He would come home from work, sit in front of the TV, eat dinner and sit some more – would never do those little household repairs that most husbands take care of. This frustrated the woman quite a bit.

One day the toilet stopped up. When her husband got home she said sweetly, "Honey, the toilet is clogged. Would you please look at it?"

Her husband snarled, "What do I look like? The Tidy-Bowl Man?" and he sat down on the sofa.

The next day the garbage disposal wouldn't work. When her husband got home she said very nicely, "Honey, the disposal won't work. Would you try to fix it for me?"

Once again he growled, "What do I look like? Mr. Plumber?"

The next day the washing machine was on the blink. When her husband got home she steeled her courage and said, "Honey, the washer isn't running. Would you check on it?"

And again she was met with a snarl, "What do I look like? The Maytag repairman?"

Finally she had had enough. The next morning the woman called three repairmen to fix the toilet, the garbage disposal and the washer. When her husband got home she said, "Honey, I had the repairmen out today.

He frowned, "Well, how much is that going to cost?"

"Well honey, they all said I could pay them by baking them a cake or having sex with them."

"Well, what kind of cakes did you bake them?" he asked.

She smiled. "What do I look like? Betty Crocker?"

A man came home from work one day to find his wife sitting on the front porch with her bags packed. He asked her where she was going and she replied, "I'm going away from here."

He questioned her as to why she was going and she told him, "I just found out that I can make $400 bucks a night doing what I give you for free."

He pondered that and then went back into the house and packed his bags and returned to the porch and his wife.

She said, "And just where do you think you are going?"

He replied, "I'm going too."

"Why?" she asked.

He said, "I want to see how you are going to live on $800 a year."

An elderly couple were sitting at the breakfast table one morning when the old gentleman said to his wife, "Just think, honey, we've been married for 50 years."

"Yes," she replied, "Just think, 50 years ago we were sitting here at this very same table."

"I know," the old man said, "We were probably sitting here naked as jaybirds 50 years ago."

"Well," Granny snickered, "What do you say, should we get naked?" The two stripped to the buff and sat down at the table.

"You know honey," the little old lady breathlessly replied, "my nipples are as hot for you today as they were 50 years ago."

"I wouldn't be surprised," replied Gramps. "One's in your coffee and the other is in your oatmeal!"

A guy walks into a bar with a pet alligator by his side. He puts the alligator up on the bar and turns to the astonished patrons. "I'll make you a deal. I'll open this alligator's mouth and place my genitals inside. Then the alligator will close his mouth for one minute. He'll then open his mouth and I'll remove my unit unscathed. In return for witnessing this spectacle, each of you will buy me a drink."

The crowd murmured their approval. The man stood up on the bar, dropped his trousers and placed his privates in the alligator's open mouth. The gator closed his mouth as the crowd gasped. After a minute the man grabbed a beer bottle and rapped the alligator hard on the top of its head. The gator opened his mouth and the man removed his genitals unscathed as promised. The crowd cheered and the first of his free drinks was delivered.

The man stood up again and made another offer. "I'll pay anyone $100 who's willing to give it a try."

A hush fell over the crowd. After a while a hand went up in the back of the bar. A woman timidly spoke up. "I'll try, but you have to promise not to hit me on the head with the beer bottle."

This guy goes out on his front lawn to fly a kite and was really having a difficult time. The kite was swinging wildly, not exactly what you'd describe as stable, so his wife sticks her head out the door and says, "Gee, Ralph, it looks like you need more tail."

Ralph replies, "Would you make up your mind? Last night you told me to go fly a kite."

Why is it called tourist season if we can't shoot at them?

Bill had been employed in a pickle factory for a number of years when he came home and confessed to his wife that he had a terrible compulsion. He had an urge to stick his penis into the pickle slicer. His wife suggested that he should see a sex therapist to talk about it, but Bill indicated that he'd be too embarrassed. He vowed to overcome the compulsion on his own.

One day a few weeks later, Bill came home absolutely ashen. His wife could see at once that something was seriously wrong.

"What's wrong, Bill?

Do you remember that I told you how I had this tremendous urge to put my penis into the pickle slicer?"

"Oh Bill, you didn't."

"Yes I did."

"My God, Bill, what happened?"

"I got fired."

"No, Bill. I mean what happened with the pickle slicer?"

"Oh . . . she got fired too."

Why are there interstates in Hawaii?

A man was telling his neighbor, "I just bought a new hearing aid. It cost me four thousand dollars, but it's state of the art."

"Really," answered the neighbor. "What kind is it?"

"Twelve thirty."

A woman is in a coma. Nurses are in her room giving her a sponge bath. One of them is washing her 'private area' and notices that there is a response on the monitor when he touches her. He goes to her husband and explains what had happened, telling him, "Crazy as this sounds, maybe a little oral sex will do the trick and bring her out of the coma."

The husband is skeptical, but they assure him that they will close the curtains for privacy. It was worth a try.

The hubby finally agrees and goes into his wife's room. After a few minutes the woman's monitor flat lines, no pulse, no heartbeat. The nurses run into the room. The husband is standing there pulling up his pants and says, "I think she choked."

D efinition of a consultant: A guy who knows 50 ways to make love but doesn't know any women.

Y our sexual dysfunction can be corrected," the physician said, "but it would be very expensive. One procedure costs $14,000 and is about 70 percent effective. Another procedure costs $20,000 and is 100 percent effective." The doctor advised the dejected fellow to go home and talk it over with his wife before making a decision. "Come back in a few days," he suggested.

The next morning the man returned to the doctor's office. "Well, I'm surprised to see you back here so quickly," the medic said. "Which procedure have you decided on?"

"Neither," the fellow replied. "We've decided to remodel the kitchen."

W hat do you get when you cross a pit bull and a collie? A dog that rips your arm off and then goes for help.

W hy are there flotation devices in the seats of planes instead of parachutes?

Two elderly ladies had been friends for many decades. Over the years they had shared all kinds of activities and adventures. Lately, their activities had been limited to meeting a few times a week to play cards.

One day they were playing cards when one looked at the other and said, "Now don't get mad at me. I know we've been friends for a long time, but I just can't remember your name. I've thought and thought but I can't recall it. Please tell me what your name is."

Her friend glared at her. For at least three minutes she just looked at her. Finally she said, "How soon do you need to know?"

A woman accompanied her husband to the doctor's office. After his check-up, the doctor called his wife into his office alone.

He said, "Your husband is suffering from a very serious disease, combined with horrible stress. If you don't do the following, your husband could die. Each morning, fix him a healthy breakfast. Be pleasant and make sure he is in a good mood. For lunch, fix him a nutritious meal. For dinner, prepare an especially nice meal for him. Don't burden him with chores. Don't discuss your stress, as this will probably make him feel worse. And most importantly, you must be intimate with your husband every day of the week. If you can do this for at least 10 months to a year, I think your husband will regain his health completely."

On the way home, the husband asked his wife, "What did the doctor say to you?"

"You're going to die."

Have you ever imagined a world without hypothetical situations?

A little old lady goes to the doctor and says, "Doctor, I have this problem with gas, but it really doesn't bother me too much. They never smell and are always silent. As a matter of fact I have farted at least 20 times since I've been here in your office. You didn't know I was farting because they don't smell and they are silent."

The doctor says, "I see. Take these pills and come back to see me next week."

The next week the lady returns. "Doctor," she says, "I don't know what the heck you gave me, but now my farts, although still silent, stink terribly."

"Good," the doctor said. "Now that we've cleared up your sinuses, let's work on your hearing."

This man was in a long line at the grocery store. As he got to the register he realized he had forgotten to get condoms. So he asked the checkout girl if she could have some condoms brought up to the register. She asked what size condoms he needed. The customer replied that he didn't know. She asked him to drop his pants. He did, she reached over the counter, grabbed hold of him, then picked up the intercom and said, "One box of large condoms to register 5."

The next man in line thought this was interesting and, was up for a cheap thrill. When he got to the register he told the checker that he too had forgotten to get condoms. She asked what size and he stated that he didn't know. She asked him to drop his pants. She gave him a quick feel, picked up the intercom and said, "One box of medium-sized condoms to register 5."

A few customers back was a teenaged boy. He thought what he had witnessed was way too cool. He had never had any type of sexual contact with a live female, so he thought this was his chance. When he got up to the register, he told the checker he needed some condoms. She asked him what size and he said he didn't know. She asked him to drop his pants and he did. She reached over the counter, gave him a quick squeeze, then picked up the intercom and said,

"Clean up at register 5."

Sterilize: What you do to your first baby's pacifier by boiling it and to your last baby's pacifier by blowing on it.

A man told his doctor that he wasn't able to do all the things around the house that he used to do.

When the exam was complete, he said, "Now, Doc, I can take it. Tell me in plain English what is wrong with me."

"Well, in plain English," the doctor said, "you're just lazy."

"Okay," said the man. "Now give me the medical term so I can tell my wife."

There was this really old guy at an old-timers dance who hadn't had any sex for a long time. He'd been dancing with the grandmas all night, but he still hadn't scored. Frustrated, he approached an old grandma and said, "Listen, I'm having no luck scoring a woman. How about coming back to my place for a piece? I'll give you $20 if you oblige."

"I'm willing, let's go," she said.

They arrived back at his place and after a bit of foreplay they headed for the bedroom. The old guy loved sex and couldn't get over how tight the old grandma was for such an old woman. Surely she's got to be a virgin.

After the wonderful performance, he rolled over and said, "WOW! If I had known you were a virgin, I would have given you $50."

Surprised, she replied, "If I had known you were actually going to get an erection, I would have taken off my pantyhose!"

The school of agriculture's dean of admissions was interviewing a prospective student. "Why have you chosen this career?" he asked.

"I dream of making a million dollars in farming, like my father," the student replied.

"Your father made a million dollars in farming?" echoed the dean, much impressed.

"No," replied the applicant. "But he always dreamed of it."

Amnesia: A condition that enables a woman who has gone through labor and childbirth to have sex again.

A waitress walks up to one of her tables in a New York City restaurant and notices that the three Japanese businessmen seated there are furiously masturbating.

She says, "What the hell do you guys think you are doing?"

One of the Japanese men says, "Can't you see? We are all berry hungry."

The waitress says, "So how is whacking off in the middle of the restaurant going to help that situation?"

One of the other businessmen replies, "The menu say, FIRST COME, FIRST SERVE."

Mother was having a hard time getting her son to go to school in the morning.

"Nobody in school likes me," he complained. "The teachers don't like me, the kids don't like me, the superintendent wants to transfer me, the bus drivers hate me, the school board wants me to drop out, and the custodians have it in for me. I don't want to go to school."

"But you have to go to school," said his mother sternly. "You're healthy, you have a lot to learn, you have something to offer others, and you are a leader. And besides, you are 45 years old and you are the principal."

How does the guy who drives the snowplow get to work?

Why don't cannibals eat clowns?
Because they taste funny.

A nun is sitting with her Mother Superior chatting. "I used some horrible language this week and feel absolutely terrible about it."

"When did you use this awful language?" asks the elder.

"Well, I was golfing and hit an incredible drive that looked like it was going to go over 250 yards, but it struck a phone line that was hanging over the fairway and fell straight to the ground after going only about 75 yards."

"Is that when you swore?"

"No, Mother," says the nun. "After that, a squirrel ran out of the bushes and grabbed my ball in his mouth and began to run away."

"Is THAT when you swore?" asks the Mother Superior again.

"Well, no," says the nun. "You see, as the squirrel was running, an eagle came down out of the sky, grabbed the squirrel in his talons and began to fly away!"

"Is THAT when you swore?" asked the amazed elder nun.

"No, not yet. As the eagle carried the squirrel away in its claws, it flew near the green and the squirrel dropped my ball."

"Did you swear THEN?" asked Mother Superior, becoming impatient.

"No, because the ball fell on a big rock, bounced over the sand trap, rolled onto the green and stopped about six inches from the hole."

The two Nuns were silent for a moment. The Mother Superior sighed and said, "You missed the fucking putt, didn't you?!?!"

A guy says, "For our 20th anniversary, I'm taking my wife to Australia."

His friend says, "That's going to be tough to beat. What will you do for your 25th anniversary?"

The first guy says, "I'm going to go back and get her."

Two guys sat down for lunch in the office cafeteria.

"Hey, whatever happened to Pete in payroll?" one asked.

"He got this harebrained notion he was going to build a new kind of car," his coworker replied.

"How was he going to do it?"

"He took a an engine from a Pontiac, tires from a Chevy, seats from a Lincoln, hubcaps from a Caddy, and well, you get the idea."

"So, what did he end up with?"

"Ten years to life."

Why is a bra singular and panties plural?

A momma mole, papa mole and baby mole lived in a hole outside of a farmhouse in the country. One day the papa mole poked his head out of the mole hole and said, "Mmmmmmmm, I smell sausage!"

The momma mole poked her head outside of the hole and said, "Mmmmmmmm, I smell pancakes!"

The baby mole tried to poke his head out of the hole but couldn't get past the two bigger moles.

Finally giving up, he said, "The only thing I can smell is molasses."

Do you realize that in about 40 years, we'll have millions of old ladies running around with tattoos and pierced navels? (Now that's scary!)

As an elderly man was putting on his coat, his wife said, "Where are you going?"

The elderly man replied, "To the doctor."

Surprised, his wife asked, "Why, are you sick?"

"No," he said, "I'm going to get me some of those new Viagra pills."

With that his equally elderly wife got up out of her rocker and started putting on her sweater. Surprised, he asked, "Where are you going?"

"I'm going to the doctor too."

"Why?"

She said, matter-of-factly, "If you're going to start using that rusty old thing again, I'm going to get a tetanus shot."

Two little kids are in the hospital, lying on stretchers next to each other outside the operating room. The first kid leans over and asks, "What are you in here for?"

The second kid says, " I'm here to get my tonsils out and I'm a little nervous."

The first kid says, "You've got nothing to worry about. I had that done when I was 4. They put you to sleep and when you wake up they give you lots of Jell-O and ice cream. It's a breeze."

The second kid then asks, "What are you here for?"

The first kid says, "A circumcision."

And the second kid says, "Whoa, I had that done when I was born. Couldn't walk for a year."

Why do they put Braille dots on the keypad of a drive-up ATM?

In line at the company cafeteria, Joe says to Mike behind him, "My elbow hurts like hell. I guess I'd better see a doctor."

"Listen, you don't have to spend that kind of money," Mike replies. "There's a diagnostic computer down at Wal-Mart. Just give it a urine sample and the computer will tell you what's wrong and what to do about it. It takes 10 seconds and costs $10 – a lot cheaper than a doctor."

So, Joe deposits a urine sample in a small jar and takes it to Wal-Mart.

He deposits $10, and the computer lights up and asks for the urine sample. He pours the sample into the slot and waits.

Ten seconds later, the computer ejects a printout:

"You have tennis elbow. Soak your arm in warm water and avoid heavy activity. It will improve in two weeks. Thank you for shopping at Wal-Mart."

That evening, while thinking how amazing this new technology was, Joe began wondering if the computer could be fooled.

He mixed some tap water, a stool sample from his dog, urine samples from his wife and daughter and a sperm sample for good measure.

Joe hurries back to Wal-Mart, eager to check the results. He deposits $10, pours in his concoction, and awaits the results.

The computer prints the following:

1. Your tap water is too hard. Get a water softener. (Aisle 9)
2. Your dog has ring worm. Bathe him with anti-fungal shampoo. (Aisle 7)
3. Your daughter has a cocaine habit. Get her into rehab.
4 Your wife is pregnant. Twins. They aren't yours. Get a lawyer.
5. If you don't stop playing with yourself, your elbow will never get better!

Thank you for shopping at Wal-Mart!

A young girl was doing a project on '70s rock groups and she asked her mom to name two of them.

"Yes!" the mom said.

"Who?" the girl asked.

"There you go," the mom answered.

A kind-hearted fellow was walking through Central Park in New York and was astonished to see an old man, fishing rod in hand, fishing over a beautiful bed of red roses.

"What a sad sight," said the passerby to himself. "That poor old man is fishing over a bed of flowers. I'll see if I can help." So the kind fellow walked up to the old man and asked, " What are you doing, my friend?"

"Fishin', sir."

"Fishin', eh. Well how would you like to come and have a drink with me?"

The old man stood up, put his rod away and followed the kind stranger to the corner bar. He ordered a large glass of vodka and a fine cigar. His host felt good about helping the old man and he asked, "Tell me, old friend, how many did you catch today?"

The old fellow took a long drag on the cigar, blew a careful smoke ring and replied, "You're the sixth today, sir."

Her husband bought her a mood ring for her birthday. When she is in a good mood, it turns green. When she is in a bad mood, it leaves a red mark on his forehead!

Prosecutor: "Did you kill the victim?"
Defendant: "No, I did not."
Prosecutor: "Do you know what the penalties are for perjury?"
Defendant: "Yes, I do. And they're a lot better than the penalty for murder."

If 4 out of 5 people SUFFER from diarrhea . . . . does that mean that one enjoys it?

A crusty old man walks into a bank and says to the woman at the teller window, "I want to open a damn checking account."

The astonished woman replies, "I beg your pardon, sir. I must have misunderstood you. What did you say?"

"Listen up, damn it. I said I want to open up a damn checking account now!"

"I'm very sorry sir, but that kind of language is not tolerated in this bank."

The teller leaves the window and goes over to the bank manager to inform him of her situation. The manager agrees that the teller does not have to listen to that foul language. They both return to the window and the manager asks the old geezer, "Sir, what seems to be the problem here?"

"There is no damn problem," the man says. "I just won 50 million bucks in the damn lottery and I want to open a damn checking account in this damn bank."

"I see," says the manager. "And is this bitch giving you a hard time?"

Lord, grant me the serenity to accept the things I cannot change, courage to change the things I can, and the wisdom to hide the bodies of those people I had to kill because they pissed me off!

A customer sent an order to a distributor for a large amount of goods totaling a great deal of money. The distributor noticed that the previous bill hadn't been paid. The collections manager left a voice mail for them saying, "We can't ship your new order until you pay for the last one."

The next day the collections manager received a collect phone call, "Please cancel the order. We can't wait that long."

If American mothers feed their babies with tiny little spoons and forks, what do Chinese mothers use? Toothpicks?

Wendi Sue passed away and Bubba called 911. The 911 operator told Bubba that she would send someone out right away.

"Where do you live?" she asked.

Bubba replied, "At the end of Eucalyptus Drive."

The operator asked, "Can you spell that for me?"

There was a long pause and finally Bubba said, "How's 'bout if I drag her over to Oak Street and you can pick her up there?"

When Diane found out she was pregnant, she told the good news to anyone who would listen. But her 4-year-old son overheard some of her parents' private conversations. One day when Diane and her 4-year-old were shopping a woman asked the little boy if he was excited about the new baby.

"Yes!" the 4-year-old said, "and I know what we're going to name it, too. If it's a girl we're going to call her Christine and if it's another boy we're going to call it quits!"

A man was reading the newspaper when an ad caught his eye: $100 Porsche! New! The man thought that it was very unusual to sell a Porsche for $100 and he thought it might be a joke or a typo. He soon decided it was worth a shot. He went to the lady's house and sure enough, she had an almost brand new Porsche.

"Wow!" the man said. "Can I take it for a test drive?" Unlike what he expected, the man found that the car ran perfectly and took it back to the lady's house. "Why are you selling me this great Porsche for only $100?"

"My husband just ran off with his secretary and he told me I could have the house and all the furniture as long as I sold his Porsche and sent him the money."

Obsessive - compulsive disorder: Been there, done that and done that and done that and done that . . . . .

A farmer walked into an attorney's office wanting to file for a divorce. The attorney asked, "May I help you?"

The farmer said, "Yeah, I want to get one of those dayvorces."

The attorney said, "Well, do you have any grounds?"

The farmer said, "Yeah, I got about 140 acres."

The attorney said, "No, you don't understand, do you have a case?"

The farmer said, "No, I don't have a Case, but I have a John Deere."

The attorney said, "No, you don't understand, I mean do you have a grudge?"

The farmer said, "Yeah, I got a grudge, that's where I park my John Deere."

The attorney said, "No sir, I mean do you have a suit?"

The farmer said, "Yes sir, I got a suit. I wear it to church on Sundays."

The attorney said, "Well sir, does your wife beat you up or anything?"

The farmer said, "No sir, we both get up about 4:30."

The attorney then said, "Well, is she a nagger or anything?"

The farmer said, "No, she's a little white gal, but our last child was a nagger and that's why I want this dayvorce!"

Why is it that when you transport something by car it's called a shipment, but when you transport something by ship it's called cargo?

RELIGIONS OF THE WORLD:

TAOISM:	Shit happens.
HINDUISM:	This shit happened before.
CONFUCIANISM:	Confucius say, "Shit happens."
BUDDHISM:	If shit happens, it isn't really shit.
ZEN:	What is the sound of shit happening?
ISLAM:	If shit happens, it is the Will of Allah.
JEHOVAH'S WITNESS:	Knock, Knock. "Shit Happens."
ATHEISM:	There is no shit.
AGNOSTICISM:	I don't know whether shit happens.
PROTESTANTISM:	Shit won't happen if I work harder.
CATHOLICISM:	If shit happens, I deserved it.
JUDAISM:	Why does shit always happen to us?

A priest walked into a barbershop in Washington, D.C. After he got his haircut he asked how much it would be. The barber said, "No charge. I consider it a service to the Lord."

The next morning the barber came to work and there were 12 prayer books and a thank you note from the priest in the front door.

Later that day a police officer came in and got his haircut. When he asked how much he owed, the barber said, "No charge. I consider it a service to the community."

The next morning he came to work and there were a dozen donuts and a thank you note from the police officer.

Then a Senator came in and got a haircut. When he was done he asked how much it was. The barber said, "No charge. I consider it a service to the country."

The next morning when the barber got to work there were 12 Senators waiting at the door.

W hy don't sheep shrink when it rains?

A little boy goes to his dad and asks, "Daddy, what is politics?"

Dad says, "Well son, let me try to explain it this way: I'm the breadwinner of the family, so let's call me Capitalism. Your Mom, she's the administrator of the money, so we'll call her the Government. We're here to take care of your needs, so we'll call you People. The nanny, we'll consider her the Working Class. Your baby brother, we'll call him the Future. Now think about that and see if that makes sense."

So the little boy goes off to bed thinking about what his Dad had said. Later that night he hears his baby brother crying so he gets up to check on him. He finds that the baby has severely pooped in his diaper. So the little boy goes to his parents' room and finds his mother sound asleep. Not wanting to wake her, he goes to the nanny's room. Finding the door locked, he peeks in the keyhole and sees his father getting it on with the nanny. He gives up and goes back to bed.

The next morning the little boy says to his father, "Dad, I think I understand the concept of politics now."

The father says, "Good, son, tell me in your own words what you think politics is all about."

The little boy replies, "Well, while Capitalism is screwing the Working Class, the Government is asleep, the People are being ignored and the Future is in deep shit."

A man goes to his doctor for a complete checkup. He hasn't been feeling well and wants to find out what's wrong. After the checkup, the doctor comes in with the results of his examination.

"I'm afraid I have some bad news. You're dying and you don't have much time," he says.

"Oh no, that's terrible! How long have I got?
"10 . . ." says the doctor.
"10? 10 what? Months? Weeks? What?!"
"10 . . . 9 . . . 8 . . . 7 . . ."

Just think: if it weren't for marriage, men would go through life thinking they had no faults at all.

Take time to stop and smell the roses and sooner or later you'll inhale a bee.

After 4 years of separation, my wife and I finally divorced amicably. I wanted to date again, but I had no idea of how to start so I decided to look in the personals column of the local newspaper. After reading through all the listings I circled three ads that seemed possible in terms of age and interests, but I put off calling them.

Two days later, there was a message on my answering machine from my ex-wife. "I came over to your house to borrow some tools today and saw the ads you circled in the paper. Don't call the one in the second column. It's me."

When weeding your garden, the best way to make sure you are removing a weed and not a valuable plant is to pull on it. If it comes out of the ground easily, it was a valuable plant.

A cute young woman was giving a manicure to a man in the barbershop. The man said, "How about a date later?"

"I'm married," she answered.

With a wink he said, "So, just tell him you're going out with your girlfriends."

"Tell him yourself," she said, "he's shaving you."

Seen on the headstone of an atheist, "Here lies an atheist. All dressed up and no place to go."

A wife was making a breakfast of fried eggs for her husband. Suddenly, her husband burst into the kitchen.

"Careful," he said, "CAREFUL! Put in some more butter! Oh my GOD! You're cooking too many at once. TOO MANY! Turn them! TURN THEM NOW! We need more butter. Oh my GOD! WHERE are we going to get MORE BUTTER? They're going to STICK! Careful ... CAREFUL! I said be CAREFUL! You NEVER listen to me when you're cooking. Never! Turn them! Hurry up! Are you CRAZY? Have you LOST your mind? Don't forget to salt them. You know you always forget to salt them. Use the salt. USE THE SALT! THE SALT!"

The wife stared at him. "What in the world is wrong with you? You think I don't know how to fry a couple of eggs?"

The husband calmly replied, "I wanted to show you what it feels like when I'm driving."

A cop pulls a guy over for weaving across two lanes of traffic. He walks up to the driver's window and asks, "You drinkin'?"

The driver says, "Well, that depends . . . . . You buyin'?"

A golfer hit his drive on the first hole 300 yards right down the middle. When it came down, however, it hit a sprinkler and the ball went sideways into the woods. He was angry, but he went into the woods and hit a very hard 2 iron, which hit a tree and bounced back straight at him. It hit him in the head and killed him.

The next thing he knew he was at the Pearly Gates. St. Peter looked at the big book and said, "I see you were a golfer, is that correct?"

"Yes, I am," he replied.

St. Peter then said, "Do you hit the ball a long way?"

The golfer replied, "You bet. After all, I got here in 2, didn't I?"

Whose cruel idea was it to put an "S" in the word LISP?

An 85-year-old lady finished her annual physical examination, whereupon the doctor said, "You are in fine shape for your age, but tell me, do you still have intercourse?"

"Just a minute, I'll have to ask my husband," she said.

She went out to the reception room and said, "Morris, do we still have intercourse?"

Morris answered impatiently, "If I've told you once, I've told you a thousand times . . . . . We have Blue Cross!"

A man goes into the men's room and is barely sitting down when he hears a voice from the other stall saying, "Hi, how are you?"

This guy was not the type to start a conversation or fraternize in men's rooms at a rest stop, so he doesn't know what gets into him when he answered, somewhat embarrassedly, "Not bad."

And the other guy says, "So what's up with you?"

What a question! At that point he's thinking this is too bizarre, so he says, "I'm like you, just traveling east."

He then hears the guy say nervously, "Listen, I'll have to call you back. There's an idiot in the other stall who keeps answering all my questions."

I've learned . . . . .

that you cannot make someone love you. All you can do is stalk them and hope they panic and give in.

that no matter how much I care, some people are just assholes,

that it takes years to build up trust, and it only takes suspicion, not proof, to destroy it.

that you can get by on charm for about 15 minutes. After that, you'd better have a big weenie or huge boobs.

that you shouldn't compare yourself to others – they are more screwed up than you think.

that you can keep puking long after you think you're finished.

that we are responsible for what we do, unless we are celebrities.

that the people you care about the most in life are taken from you too soon and all the less important ones just never go away.

When Beethoven passed away, he was buried in a churchyard. A couple of days later, the town drunk was walking through the cemetery and heard some strange noise coming from the area where Beethoven was buried.

Terrified, the drunk ran and got the priest to come and listen to it. The priest bent close to the ground and heard some faint, unrecognizable music coming from the grave. Frightened, the priest ran and got the town magistrate.

When the magistrate arrived, he bent his ear to the grave, listened for a moment and said, "Ah, yes, that's Beethoven's Ninth Symphony, being played backwards."

He listened a while longer, and said, "There's the Eighth Symphony, and it's backwards too. Most puzzling."

So the magistrate kept listening, "There's the Seventh . . . the Sixth . . . the Fifth . . ."

Suddenly the realization of what was happening dawned on him. He stood up and announced to the crowd that had gathered in the cemetery.

"My fellow citizens, there is nothing to worry about. Beethoven is decomposing."

A veterinarian was feeling ill and went to see her doctor. The doctor asked her all the usual questions about symptoms, how long had they been occurring, etc., when she interrupted him.

"I'm a veterinarian and I don't need to ask my patients these kinds of questions. I can tell what's wrong just by looking." She added irritably, "Why can't you?"

The doctor nodded, stood back, and looked her up and down. He then quickly wrote out a prescription, handed it to her and said, "There you are. Of course you realize, if that doesn't work, we'll have to put you to sleep."

A meek little fellow in a restaurant timidly touched the arm of a man putting on an overcoat. "Excuse me," he said, "but do you happen to be Mr. Smith of Newport?"

"No I'm not," answered the man impatiently.
"Oh, well, you see," continued the first man, "I am, and that's his overcoat you're putting on."

I've been so busy . . . I don't know if I found a rope or lost my horse.

A lady, on her first trip to Texas, goes into a bar where she sees a tall cowboy wearing boots and a ten-gallon hat. His boot-clad feet were propped up on a table. He had the biggest feet she'd ever seen. The woman asked the cowboy if it's true what they say about men with big feet.

The cowboy says, "Sure is, why don't you come back to my place and let me prove it?"

The woman figures why not and spends the night with him. The next day she hands the cowboy a $100 bill.

Blushing, he says, "Nobody has ever paid me for my services before. I'm flattered."

The woman replies, "Well don't be. Take this money and buy yourself some boots that fit."

There were three little old ladies sitting on a park bench having a quiet conversation when a flasher approached from across the park.

The flasher came up to the ladies, stood right in front of them and opened his trench coat.

The first lady immediately had a stroke.

Then the second lady also had a stroke.

But the third lady, being older and feebler, couldn't reach that far.

A scout for one of the leading colleges went to the office of the athletic director and announced, "Have I got an athlete for you? This guy can play every sport and excels at every position. He is absolutely the finest athlete I have ever seen play."

The athletic director was very impressed but had to ask the question, "But how is he scholastically?"

The scout replied, "He makes straight A's in every subject. However, I must tell you his B's are a little crooked."

Sometimes I wish I was what I was when I wished I was what I am now.

A young boy went up to his father and asked him, "Dad, what is the difference between potentially and realistically?

The father thought for a moment, then answered, "Go ask your mother if she would sleep with Robert Redford for a million dollars. Then ask your sister if she would sleep with Brad Pitt for a million dollars and ask your brother if he'd sleep with Tom Cruise for a million dollars. Come back and tell me what you learn from that."

So the boy went to his mother and asked, "Would you sleep with Robert Redford for a million dollars?"

The mother replied, "Of course I would! I wouldn't pass up an opportunity like that!"

The boy then went to his sister and asked, "Would you sleep with Brad Pitt for a million dollars?"

The girl replied, "Oh my God! I would just love to do that. I would be nuts to pass up a chance like that."

The boy then went to his brother and asked, "Would you sleep with Tom Cruise for a million dollars?"

"Of course," the brother replied. "Do you know how much stuff a million dollars could buy?"

The boy pondered that for a few days, and then went back to his dad. His father asked him, "Did you find out the difference between potentially and realistically?"

The boy replied, "Yes sir. Potentially, we're sitting on three million dollars, but realistically, we're living with two sluts and a fag."

When my wife quit work to take care of our new baby daughter, countless hours of peek-a-boo and other games slowly took its toll. One evening my wife smacked her bare toes on the corner of the dresser, and grabbing her foot, sank to the floor.

I rushed to her side and asked what she hurt.

She looked at me through tear-filled eyes and managed to moan, "It's the piggy that ate the roast beef."

A day without sunshine is like, well, night.

There's a new really strong sun block that will be out soon, to use when going to the beach or if you are just going to be out in the midday sun. It has an SPF of 80. You squeeze the tube and a sweater comes out.

A minister decided that a visual demonstration would add emphasis to his Sunday sermon. He put four worms into four separate jars:

The first worm was put into a jar of alcohol.
The second worm was put into a jar of cigarette smoke.
The third worm was put into a jar of semen.
The fourth worm was put into a jar of good, clean soil.

At the conclusion of the sermon, the Minister reported the following results:

The worm in alcohol – dead
The worm in cigarette smoke – dead
The worm in semen – dead
The worm in good, clean soil – alive.

The minister asked his congregation, "What can we learn from this demonstration?"

A little old woman in the back quickly raised her hand and said, "

As long as you drink, smoke and have sex, you won't have worms."

Two little potatoes are standing on a street corner. How can you tell which one is the prostitute?

It's the one with the little sticker that says, "IDAHO".

Twin brothers were named Joe and John. Joe was the owner of an old dilapidated boat. It happened that John's wife died the same day that Joe's old boat sank. A few days later a kindly old lady met Joe on the street and mistaking him for John said, "I'm so sorry to hear about your great loss. You must feel terrible."

Joe said, "Oh Hell no!!! She was a rotten old thing from the very beginning. Her bottom was all shriveled up and she smelled like a dead fish. She had a bad crack in the back and a pretty big hole in front. The hole got bigger every time I used her and she leaked like crazy. But what really finished her off was the time these four guys rented her for a good time. I warned them she wasn't any good but they wanted to have a go at her anyhow. The damned fools all tried to get in her at the same time and it was just too much for the ol' girl and she split right down the middle." The old lady fainted dead away.

A man had 50-yard line tickets for the Super Bowl. As he sits down, a man comes down and asks if anyone is sitting in the seat next to him.

"No," he says. "The seat is empty."

"This is incredible," says the man. "Who in their right mind would have a seat like this for the Super Bowl, the biggest sporting event in the world and not use it?"

"Well, actually, the seat belongs to me. I was supposed to come with my wife, but she passed away. This is the first Super Bowl we haven't been to together since we got married in 1969."

"Oh, I'm so sorry to hear that. That's terrible. But couldn't you find someone else – a friend or relative or even a neighbor to take the seat?"

The man shakes his head. "No. They're all at the funeral."

Do not walk behind me, for I may not lead. Do not walk ahead of me, for I may not follow. Do not walk beside me, either. Just leave me alone.

One Sunday John was praying in church, "God, I really need to win the lottery, although I'm not being greedy. It's for my family. You see my wife and I have bills to pay, braces to put on my son and need money to send our daughter to college. Please help me."

A week goes by and John returns to church to pray again to win the lottery, adding this time that his dog is sick and they need money to pay for his treatments. He goes week after week and prays to God to win the lottery. "God I have prayed and prayed and still you do not help me with my many problems. What have I done?"

All of a sudden a white light shines down and John hears the voice of God. "John, meet me half way. Buy a ticket."

A defendant was on trial for murder. There was strong evidence indicating guilt, but there was no corpse. In the defense's closing statement the lawyer, knowing that his client would probably be convicted, resorted to a trick.

"Ladies and gentleman of the jury. I have a surprise for you all. Looking at his watch, the lawyer said, "Within one minute, the person presumed dead in this case will walk into this courtroom. He looked toward the courtroom door. The jurors, somewhat stunned, all looked on eagerly. A minute passed. Nothing happened.

Finally the lawyer said, "Actually, I made up the previous statement. But you all looked on with anticipation. I therefore put to you that you have a reasonable doubt in this case as to whether anyone was killed and insist that you return a verdict of not guilty."

The jury, clearly confused, retired to deliberate. A few minutes later, the jury returned and pronounced a verdict of guilty.

"But how?" inquired the lawyer. "You must have had some doubt. I saw all of you stare at the door."

The jury foreman replied, "Oh, we looked . . . but your client didn't."

An Amish lady is trotting down the road in her horse and buggy when she is pulled over by a cop. "Ma'am, I'm not going to ticket you, but I do have to issue you a warning. You have a broken reflector on your buggy."

"Oh, I'll let my husband, Jacob, know as soon as I get home."

"That's fine. Another thing, ma'am, I don't like the way that one rein loops across the horse's back and around one of his balls. I consider that animal abuse. Have your husband take care of that right away."

The lady got home and told her husband about her encounter with the cop.

"Well, dear, what exactly did he say?"
"He said the reflector is broken."
"I can fix that in two minutes. What else?"
"I'm not sure, Jacob . . . something about the emergency brake."

An old guy approaches the window of the movie theater with a chicken on his shoulder and asks for 2 tickets. The girl at the counter wants to know who is going in with him.

He replies, "Why, my pet chicken, of course!"

"I'm sorry," the girl tells him. "We can't allow animals in the theater."

The guy goes around the corner and stuffs the chicken into his pants and returns to the window, buys his ticket, goes inside and sits down. The chicken starts to get hot and begins to squirm. The man unzips his pants so the chicken can stick its head out and watch the movie.

Seated next to him is a woman. She looks over at his lap and is horrified. She elbows her friend and whispers, "Myrtle, this man over here has just unzipped his pants!"

Myrtle whispers back," Oh, don't worry about it, if you've seen one, you've seen them all."

Agnes says, "I know, but this one's . . . . . EATING MY POPCORN!"

Junk is something you've kept for years and throw away three weeks before you need it.

The mother of three unruly young boys was asked whether or not she'd have children if she could do it all over again.

"Sure," she replied, "just not the same ones."

The way to find inner peace, the article stated, is to finish things you have started.

Today I finished two bags of potato chips, a chocolate pie, a bottle of wine and a box of candy. I feel better already.

An 80-year-old man went into the confessional and told the priest the following:

"Father, I am an 80-year-old man, I'm married, I have four children and 11 grandchildren. Last night I strayed and had an affair with two 18-year-old girls. We partied and made love all night long."

The priest said, "My son, when was the last time you were at confession?"

The old man said, "I have never been to confession. I'm Jewish."

The priest said, "Then why are you here telling me this?"

The old man said, "Father, I'm telling everyone."

A kindergartener told his teacher he'd found a frog. She asked whether it was alive or dead.
"Dead," he informed her.
"How do you know?"
"Because I pissed in his ear," said the child, innocently.
"You did what?!?" squealed the teacher in surprise.
"You know," explained the boy, "I leaned over and went 'Psssst' and he didn't move."

If you don't like my driving, don't call anyone. Just take another road. That's why the highway department made so many of them.

A father was reading Bible stories to his young son. "The man named Lot was warned to take his wife and flee out of the city, but his wife looked back and was turned into a pillar of salt."

His son asked, "What happened to the flea?"

WHAT IS A CAT?

Cats do what they want.
They rarely listen to you.
They're totally unpredictable.
When you want to play, they want to be alone.
When you want to be alone, they want to play.
They expect you to cater to their every whim.
They're moody.
They leave hair everywhere.

CONCLUSION: They're tiny women in little fur coats.

WHAT IS A DOG?

Dogs spend all day sprawled on the most comfortable piece of furniture in the house.
They can hear a package of food opening half a block away, but don't hear you when you're in the same room.
They can look dumb and lovable all at the same time.
They growl when they are not happy.
When you want play, they want to play.
When you want to be alone, they want to play.
They leave their toys everywhere.
They do disgusting things with their mouths and then try to kiss you.
They go right for your crotch as soon as they meet you.

CONCLUSION: They're tiny men in little fur coats.

Love is like a roller coaster: When it's good you don't want to get off, and when it isn't, you can't wait to throw up.

A baby was born so advanced in development he could talk. He looked around the delivery room and saw the doctor. "Are you my doctor?" he asked.

"Why, yes, I am," said the doctor.

The baby said, "Thank you for taking such good care of me during the birth."

He looked at his mother and asked, "Are you my mother?"

"Yes, dear, I am," said the mother beaming.

"Thank you for taking such good care of me before I was born."

He then looked at his father and asked, "Are you my father?"

"Yes, I am," his father proudly answered.

The baby motioned him closer and poked him on the forehead with his index finger.

"Hurts, doesn't it!"

A father was at the beach with his children when his four-year-old son ran up to him, grabbed his hand and led him to the shore where a seagull lay dead in the sand.

"Daddy, what happened to him?"

"He died and went to heaven."

The boy thought a moment and then said, "Why did God throw him back down?"

It now costs more to amuse a child than it once did to educate her father.

At the Russian War College, the general is a guest lecturer and tells the class of officers that the session will focus on potential problems and the resulting strategies. One of the officers in the class asks the first question.

"Will we have to fight in a World War Three?"

"Yes, comrades. It looks like you will."

"And who will be our enemy, Comrade General?"

"The likelihood is that it will be China."

The class looks alarmed. "But Comrade General, we are 150 million people and they are about 1.5 billion. How can we possibly win?"

"Think about it. In modern war, it is not the quantity, but the quality that is the key. For example, in the Middle East, 5 million Jews fight against 50 million Arabs and the Jews have been the winners every time."

"But sir," asks the panicky officer. "Do we have enough Jews?"

A dentist was getting ready to clean an elderly lady's teeth. He noticed that she was a little nervous so he began to tell her a story as he was putting on his surgical gloves.

"Do you know how they make these rubber gloves?"

She said, "No."

"Well," he spoofed, "down in Mexico they have this big building set up with a large tank of latex and the workers are all picked according to hand size. Each individual walks up to the tank, dips their hands in, and then walks around for a bit while the latex sets up and dries right onto their hands. Then they peel off the gloves and throw them into the big 'Finished Goods' crate and start the process all over again."

And she didn't laugh a bit. But, five minutes later, he had to stop cleaning her teeth because she burst out laughing. She blushed and exclaimed, "I just suddenly thought about how they must make condoms."

A pirate walks into a bar with a steering wheel sticking out of his zipper.

The bartender says, "Hey, did you know you have a steering wheel attached to your willie?"

The pirate replies, "Aye, it's driving me nuts."

A drunken man staggers into a Catholic church and wanders over to the confessional box. He opens the door, sits down and says nothing.

The priest is quiet for a while, allowing the guy some time to collect his thoughts. Growing impatient, the priest coughs to attract his attention, but still the man says nothing. The priest then knocks on the wall three times in a final attempt to get the man to speak.

Finally, the drunk replies, "No use knockin' pal, there ain't no paper in this one either!"

The FDA officials today announced the release of the wonder drug Viagra in a new, easy to take liquid form.

It is sold under the name "Mydixadrill."

Now, when men come home from work in the evening, they can literally pour themselves a stiff one.

During the rush hour at Houston Airport, a flight was delayed due to a mechanical problem. Since they needed the gate for another flight, the aircraft was backed away from the gate while the maintenance crew worked on it. The passengers were then told the new gate number, which was some distance away. Everyone moved to the new gate, only to find a third gate had been designated for them.

After some further shuffling, everyone got on board and as they were settling in, the flight attendant made the standard announcement, "We apologize for the inconvenience of this last-minute gate change. This flight is going to Washington, D.C. If your destination in not Washington, D.C. you should deplane at this time."

A very confused looking and red-faced pilot emerged from the cockpit carrying his bags. "Sorry," he said. "Wrong plane."

In an American history discussion group, the professor was trying to explain how societies ideal of beauty changes with time. "For example," he said, "take the 1921 Miss America. She stood five feet, one inch tall, weighed 108 pounds and had measurements of 31-25-32. How do you think she'd do in today's version of the competition?"

The class fell silent for a moment. Then one student piped up, "Not very well."

"Why is that?" asked the professor.

"For one thing," the student pointed out, "She'd be about 100 years old."

A woman brought an old picture of her dead husband, wearing a hat, to a photographer. She wanted to know if the photographer could remove the hat from the picture. He convinced her he could easily do that and asked her what side of this head he parted his hair on.

"I forget," she said. "But you can see that for yourself when you take off his hat."

An elderly couple had been dating for some time and decided it was finally time to get married. Before the wedding, they had a long conversation regarding how their marriage might work. They discussed finances, living arrangement and so on. Finally the old man decided it was time to broach the subject of the physical relationship.

"How do you feel about sex?" he asked, rather hopefully.

"Well, I'd have to say I like it infrequently," she responded.

The old guy paused, then asked, "Was that one word or two?"

When the doctor called Mrs. Goldberg to tell her that her check came back, she replied, "So did my arthritis."

Two bored casino dealers are waiting at a craps table when a very attractive blonde comes in and wants to bet twenty thousand dollars on a single roll of the dice.

She says, "I hope you don't mind, but I feel much luckier when I am completely nude."

With that she strips naked and rolls the dice while yelling, "Momma needs new clothes!" Then she hollers, "YES! YES! I WON! I WON!" Then she begins jumping up and down and hugging each of the dealers.

With that she picks up her money and clothes and quickly leaves. The dealers just stare at each other dumbfounded. Finally, one of them asks, "What did she roll anyway?"

The other answers, "I thought YOU were watching!"

A guy goes into a restaurant with his shirt opened at the collar, but is stopped by a bouncer who tells him he must wear a necktie to get in. So the guy goes out to his car to look for a tie but discovers he doesn't have one. He sees a set of jumper cables in his trunk and in desperation ties them around his neck and goes back to the restaurant.

The bouncer looks him over and says, "Well, okay, I guess you can come in . . . . . just don't start anything."

A man, called to testify at the IRS, wondered what to wear. His accountant told him to wear his shabbiest clothing letting them think he is a pauper. His lawyer told him not to let them intimidate him and to wear his most elegant suit and tie. Confused, the man went to his rabbi, who said,

"Let me tell you a story. A woman, about to be married, asked her mother what to wear on her wedding night. Her mother told her to wear a long, flannel nightgown that goes right up to her neck. But when the woman asked her best friend, she told her to wear her sexiest negligee.

The man protested, "What does all this have to do with my problem with the IRS?"

"No matter what you wear, you are going to get screwed."

A father asks his 10-year-old son if he knows about the birds and the bees.

"I don't want to know!" the child says, bursting into tears. "Promise me you won't tell me!"

Flummoxed, the father asks what's wrong.

"Oh, dad," the boy sobs, "when I was six, I got the 'There's no Santa' speech. At seven, I got the 'There's no Easter Bunny' speech. When I was eight, you hit me with the 'There's no tooth fairy' speech. If you're going to tell me that grownups don't really fuck, I'll have nothing left to live for."

A beautiful woman loved growing tomatoes, but couldn't seem to get her tomatoes to turn red. One day while taking a stroll, she came upon a gentleman neighbor who had the most beautiful garden of huge red tomatoes.

She asked him, "What do you do to get your tomatoes so red?"

He responded, "Well, twice a day I stand in front of my tomato garden and expose myself, and my tomatoes turn red from blushing so much."

Well the woman was impressed, so she decided to try doing the same thing to her tomato garden to see if it would work for her. So twice a day for two weeks she exposed herself to her garden hoping for the best.

One day the gentleman was passing by and asked the woman, "By the way, how did you make out? Did your tomatoes turn red?"

"No," she replied, "but my cucumbers are enormous."

How can you tell when a man is well hung?
When you can just barely slip your finger in between his neck and the noose.

An older gentleman had an appointment to see a urologist who shared an office with several other doctors. The waiting room was filled with patients. He approached the receptionist desk. The receptionist was a large, imposing woman who looked like a wrestler. He gave her his name.

In a very loud voice the receptionist said, "Yes, I have your name here. You want to see the doctor about impotence, right?"

All the patients in the waiting room snapped their heads around to look at the very embarrassed man.

He recovered quickly though, and in an equally loud voice replied, "No, I've come to inquire about a sex change operation and I'd like the same doctor that did yours."

Jack was going to be married to Jill, so his father sat him down for a little chat. "Jack, let me tell you something. On my wedding night in our honeymoon suite, I took off my pants and handed them to your mother and said, 'Here, try these on.' So she did and said, 'These are too big; I can't wear them.' So I replied, 'Exactly. I wear the pants in this family and I always will.' Ever since that night we have never had any problems."

Jack thought that might be a good thing to try, so on his honeymoon he takes off his pants and says to Jill, "Here, try these on." So she does and says, "These are too large; they don't fit me."

So Jack says, "Exactly. I wear the pants in this family and I always will, and I don't want you to ever forget that."

Then Jill takes off her pants and hands them to Jack and says, "Here, you try on mine." So he does and says, "I can't get into your pants."

Jill says, "Exactly. And if you don't change your attitude, you never will."

Tell me the truth, doctor, how much longer do I have to live?"
"It's hard to predict," answered the doctor, "but let's just say that I wouldn't start watching any mini-series on TV if I were you, and for sure don't buy any green bananas."

An old Italian mafia don is dying and calls his grandson to his bed. "Grandson, I wanna you lisin to me. I wanna for you to take my chrome plated .38 revolver so you will always remember me."

"But, grandpa," said the grandson, "I really don't like guns, how about you leaving me your Rolex watch instead?"

"You lisina me, soma day you goina be runna da bussiness, you goina have a beautiful wife, lotsa money, a big home and maybe a coupla' bambino. Soma day you goina coma home and maybe finda you wife in bed with another man. Whadda' you do then? Point to you watch and say 'TIME'S UP?'"

Sister Marlena entered the Monastery of Silence and the Abbot said, "Sister, this is a silent monastery. You are welcome here as long as you like, but you may not speak until I direct you to do so."

Five years later the abbot said to the sister, "You may speak two words."

Sister Marlena said, "Hard bed."

"I'm sorry to hear that. We will get you a better bed."

Another five years pass and again the abbot tells Sister Marlena that she may say two words.

"Cold food," she said and the abbot assured her that the food would be better in the future.

On her 15th anniversary at the Monastery, the abbot calls Sister Marlena into his office and again tells her she may speak two words.

"I quit," said Sister Marlena.

'It's probably best," said the abbot. "You've done nothing but bitch since you've been here."

BARTENDER: I think you've had enough sir.
DRUNK: I just lost my wife, buddy.
BARTENDER: Well, it must be hard losing a wife . . . . .
DRUNK: It was almost impossible.

A businessman met a beautiful girl and asked her to spend the night with him for $500, and she did. Before he left in the morning, he told her that he did not have cash with him, but that he would have his secretary write a check and mail it to her, calling the payment "Rent for Apartment". On the way to the office, he regretted what he had done. Realizing that the whole event was not worth the price, he had his secretary send a check for $250 and enclose a note:

Dear Madam:

Enclosed, find a check in the amount of $250 for rent of your apartment. I am not sending the amount agreed upon because when I rented the apartment I was under that impression that:

it had never been occupied;
that there was plenty of heat; and
that it was small enough to make me feel cozy and at home.

Last night, however, I found out that it had been previously occupied, that there wasn't any heat and that it was entirely too large.

Upon receipt of the note, the girl immediately returned the check for $250 with the following note:
Dear Sir:

First of all, I cannot understand how you expect a beautiful apartment to remain unoccupied indefinitely. As for the heat, there is plenty of it if you know how to turn it on. Regarding the space, the apartment is indeed of regular size, but if you don't have enough furniture to fill it, please don't blame the landlord.

What does a dyslexic agnostic insomniac do? Stays awake all night wondering if there is a dog.

On our 25th wedding anniversary, my husband took me out to dinner. Our teenage daughters said they'd have dessert waiting for us when we returned. When we got home we saw that the dining room table was beautifully set with our fine china, crystal and candles. There was a note that read, "Your dessert is in the refrigerator. We are staying with friends, so go ahead and do something we wouldn't do!" My husband turned to me and said, "I suppose we could vacuum."

A man was sick and tired of going to work every day while his wife stayed home. He wanted her to see what he went through so he prayed, "Dear Lord, please create a trade in our bodies so my wife can see what I go through every day while she merely stays at home."

God, in his infinite wisdom, granted the man's wish. The next morning the man awoke as a woman. He cooked breakfast for his mate, awakened the kids, set out their school clothes, fed them breakfast, packed their lunches, drove them to school, came home to pick up the dry cleaning, took it to the cleaners and stopped at the bank to draw out some money, went grocery shopping and came home to put the groceries away.

He cleaned the cat's litter box and bathed the dog. Then it was already 1:00 and he hurried to make the beds, do the laundry, vacuum, dust and sweep and mop the kitchen floor. He picked the kids up at school, set out cookies and milk and got the kids organized to do their homework, then set up the ironing board and watched TV while he pressed the clothes.

At 4:30 he began peeling potatoes and washing greens for a salad, breaded the pork chops and snapped fresh beans for dinner. After dinner he cleaned up the kitchen, ran the dishwasher, folded the laundry, bathed the kids and put them to bed. At 9 p.m. he was exhausted, and although his chores weren't finished, he went to bed where he was expected to make love – which he managed to get through with complaint.

The next morning he awoke and immediately knelt by the bed and said, "Lord, I don't know what I was thinking. I was so wrong to envy my wife's being able to stay home all day. Please, oh please, let us trade back."

The Lord, in his infinite wisdom replied, "My son, I feel you have learned your lesson and I will be happy to change things back to the way they were. You'll have to wait 9 months, though. You got pregnant last night."

Light travels faster than sound. This is why some people appear bright until you hear them speak.

Reaching the end of a job interview, the human resources person asked a young engineer fresh out of MIT what kind of a salary we was looking for.

"In the neighborhood of $150,000 a year, depending on the benefits package."

"Well, what would you say to a package of 5 weeks vacation, 14 paid holidays, full medical and dental, company matching retirement fund to 50% of salary, and a company car, leased every 2 years, say a red Corvette?"

"Wow! Are you kidding?"

"Yeah, but you started it."

What is the difference between men and women?
A woman wants one man to satisfy her every need. A man wants every woman to satisfy his one need.

The sixth grade science teacher asked her class, "Which body part increases to 10 times its size when stimulated?"

No one answered for a long time until Mary stood up and said the teacher should not be asking sixth graders a question like that. She was going to tell her parents who would tell the principal who would fire the teacher.

The teacher ignored her and asked the question again, "Which body part increases to 10 times its size when stimulated?"

Finally, Billy stood up and said the answer is the pupil of the eye.

The teacher said, "Very good, Billy," and then turned to Mary and said, "As for you, young lady, I have three things to say to you: you have a very dirty mind, you didn't read your homework, and one day you will be very, very disappointed."

S ome days it's not even worth chewing through the restraints.

W hile on a golf tour in Ireland, Tiger Woods drives his huge BMW into a petrol station near Dublin. The attendant at the pump greets him in a typical Irish manner, unaware as to whom the golf pro is.

"Top of the morning to you sir," he says.

As Tiger Woods bends forward to pick up the pump, two tees fall out of his shirt pocket onto the ground.

"What are those, son? asks the attendant.

"They're called tees," replies Tiger.

"What they for?" inquires the Irishman.

"They're for putting my balls on while I'm driving," says Tiger.

"Hot damn, them boys at BMW think of everything!"

A sk any man, and he will tell you that any woman's ultimate fantasy is to have two men at once.

While this has been verified by a recent sociological study, it appears that most men do not realize that in this fantasy, one man is cooking and the other man is cleaning.

A man spoke frantically on the phone, clearly in a state of panic.

"My wife is pregnant and her contractions are only two minutes apart."

The doctor asked, "Is this her first child?"

"No, you idiot. This is her husband."

A middle-aged woman had a heart attack and was taken to the hospital. While on the operating table, she had a near death experience. Seeing God, she asked, "Is my time up?"

God said, "No, you have another 43 years, 2 months and 8 days to live."

Upon recovery, the woman decided to stay in the hospital and have a face-lift, brow lift, lip enhancement, boob job, liposuction and a tummy tuck. After her last operation, she was released from the hospital. While crossing the street on her way home she was hit and killed by an ambulance. Arriving in front of God, she demanded, "I thought you said I had another 40 years? Why didn't you pull me out of the path of the ambulance?"

God replied, "I'm sorry, I didn't recognize you."

Two campers were hiking in the forest when all of sudden a bear jumps out of a bush and starts chasing them. Both campers start running for their lives when one of them stops to put on his running shoes.

His partner says, "What are you doing? You can't outrun a bear."

His friend replies, "I don't have to outrun the bear. I only have to outrun you!"

A burglar broke into the house of a Quaker in the middle of the night and started to rob it. The Quaker heard the noise and went downstairs with his shotgun. When he found the burglar he pointed his gun at him and said gently,

"Friend, I mean thee no harm, but thou standest where I am about to shoot!"

He who laughs last, thinks slowest.

Walking can add years to your life. This enables you, at 85 years old, to spend an additional 2 years in a nursing home at $5,000 per month.

The Native Americans asked their Chief in autumn if the winter was going to be cold or not. Not really knowing the answer, the Chief replied that the winter was going to be cold and that the members of the village were to collect wood to be prepared.

Being a good leader, he then went to the next phone booth and called the National Weather Service and asked, "Is this winter going to be cold?"

The man on the phone responded, "This winter is going to be quite cold indeed."

So the Chief went back to speed up his people to collect even more wood to be prepared. A week later he call the National Weather Service again. "Is it going to be a cold winter?"

"Yes," replied the man, "it's going to be a very cold winter."

So the Chief goes back to his people and orders them to go and find every scrap of wood they can find. Two weeks later he calls the National Weather Service again, "Are you absolutely sure that the winter is going to be very cold?"

"Absolutely. The Native Americans are collecting wood like crazy!"

An old friend invited a guy to dinner. His buddy preceded every request to his wife with endearing terms, calling her Honey, My Love, Darling, Sweetheart, Pumpkin, etc.

He was impressed since the couple had been married almost 70 years and while the wife was off in the kitchen he said to his buddy, "I think it's wonderful that after all the years you've been married, you still call your wife all those pet names."

His buddy hung his head. "To tell you the truth, I forgot her name about ten years ago."

When you go into court, you are putting yourself in the hands of 12 people who weren't smart enough to get out of jury duty.

Two priests died at the same time and met Saint Peter at the Pearly Gates. St. Peter said, "I'd like to get you guys in now but our computer's down. You'll have to go back to Earth for about a week. What'll it be?"

The first priest says, "I've always wanted to be an eagle, soaring above the Rocky Mountains."

"So be it," says St. Peter and off flies the first priest.

The second priest mulls this over for a moment and asks, "Will any of this week 'count,' St Peter?"

"No, I told you the computer's down. There's no way we can keep track of what you're doing. The week's a freebie."

"In that case," says the second priest, "I've always wanted to be a stud."

"So be it," says St. Peter and the second priest disappears.

A week goes by, the computer is fixed, and the Lord tells St. Peter to recall the two priests. "Will you have any trouble locating them?" he asks.

"The first one should be easy. He's somewhere over the Rockies, flying with the eagles. But the second one could prove to be more difficult."

"Why's that?" asked the Lord.

St. Peter answered, "He's on a snow tire, somewhere in North Dakota."

An Irish priest is driving down to New York and gets stopped for speeding in Connecticut. The state trooper smells alcohol on the priest's breath and then sees an empty wine bottle on the floor of the car.

He says, "Sir, have you been drinking?"
"Just water," says the priest.
The trooper says, "Then why do I smell wine?"
The priest looks at the bottle and says, "Good Lord! He's done it again!"

Joined a health club last year. Spent about $400 bucks. Haven't lost a pound. Apparently you have to show up.

*A*d in a New York newspaper:

For sale by owner:
Compete set of Encyclopedia, 45 Volumes. Excellent condition.
$1000 or best offer. No longer needed.
I was married last week.
My wife knows everything.

A man had been drinking at a pub all night. The bartender finally said that the bar was closing so the man stood up to leave and fell flat on his face. He tried to stand one more time, same result. He figured he'd crawl outside and get some fresh air and maybe that will sober him up.

Once outside he stood up and fell flat on his face. So he decided to crawl the four blocks to his home. When he arrived at the door he stood up and again fell flat on his face. He crawled through the door and into his bedroom and when he reached his bed he tried one more time to stand up. This time he managed to pull himself upright and he quickly fell right into bed and was sound asleep as soon as his head hit the pillow.

He was awakened the next morning to his wife standing over him shouting, "So, you've been out drinking again!"

"What makes you say that?" he asked, putting on an innocent look.

"The pub called . . . . . you left your wheelchair there again."

A man receives a letter from his grandmother asking him to send her a current photo of himself in his new location. Too embarrassed to let her know that he lives in a nudist colony, he cuts a photo in half, but accidentally sends her the bottom half of the photo. He is really worried when he realizes that he sent the wrong half, but then remembers how bad his grandmother's eyesight is and hopes she won't notice.

A few weeks later he receives a letter from his grandmother saying, "Thank you for the picture. Change your hairstyle. It makes your nose look too short."

*C*hange is inevitable, except from a vending machine.

A man comes home from an exhausting day at work, plops down on the couch in front of the television, and tells his wife, "Get me a beer before it starts."

The wife sighs and gets him a beer.

Fifteen minutes later he says, "Get me another beer before it starts."

She looks cross, but fetches another beer and slams it down next to him.

He finishes that beer and a few minutes later says, "Quick, get me another beer, it's going to start any minute."

The wife is furious. She yells at him, "Is that all you're going to do tonight? Drink beer and sit in front of that TV? You're nothing but a lazy, drunken, fat slob and furthermore . . . ."

The man sighs and says, "It's started . . ."

A gynecologist had a burning desire to change careers and become a mechanic. So she found out from her local tech college what was involved, signed up for evening classes, attended diligently and learned all she could. When the time for the practical exam approached, she prepared carefully for weeks and completed the exam with tremendous skill.

When the results came back, she was surprised to find that she had obtained a mark of 150%. Fearing an error, she went to the instructor, saying, "I don't want to appear ungrateful for such an outstanding result, but I wondered if there had been an error which needed adjusting."

The instructor said, "During the exam, you took the engine apart perfectly, which was worth 50% of the total grade. You put the engine back together again perfectly, which was also worth 50%. I gave you an extra 50% because you did all of it through the MUFFLER."

The 50-50-90 rule: Anytime you have a 50-50 chance of getting something right, there's a 90% probability you'll get it wrong.

Bubba decided it was time to purchase a new saw to help clear his heavily timbered property. A salesman showed him the latest model chain saw and assured him that he could easily cut three or four cords of wood per day with it.

But the first day, Bubba barely cut one cord of wood. The second morning he arose an hour earlier and managed to cut a little over one cord. The third day he got up even earlier but only managed to achieve a total of 1½ cords of wood.

Bubba returned the saw to the store the next day and explained the situation.

"Well," said the salesman, "let's see what's the matter." He then pulled the cable and the chain saw sprang into action.

Leaping back, Bubba shouted, "What the heck is that noise?"

Father Murphy walks into a pub in Donegal, and says to the first man he meets, "Do you want to go to heaven?"

The man said, "I do, Father."

The priest said, "Then stand over there against the wall."

Then the priest asked the second man, "Do you want to go to heaven?"

"Certainly, Father," was the man's reply.

"Then stand over there against the wall," said the priest.

Then Father Murphy walked up to O'Toole and said, "Do you want to go to heaven?"

O'Toole said, "No, I don't Father."

The priest said, "I don't believe this. You mean to tell me that when you die you don't want to go to heaven?"

O'Toole said, "Oh, when I die, yes. I thought you were getting a group together to go right now."

Nothing is foolproof to a sufficiently talented fool.

Walking into the bar, Mike said to Charlie the bartender, "Pour me a stiff one - just had another fight with the little woman."

"Oh yeah?" said Charlie, "And how did this one end?"

"When it was over," Mike replied, "She came to me on her hands and knees."

"Really," said Charlie, "Now that's a switch! What did she say?"

She said, "Come out from under the bed, you little chicken."

Flynn staggered home very late after another evening with his drinking buddy, Paddy. He took off his shoes to avoid waking his wife, Mary. He tiptoed as quietly as he could toward the stairs leading to their upstairs bedroom, but misjudged the bottom step. As he caught himself by grabbing the banister, his body swung around and he landed heavily on his rump. A whiskey bottle in each back pocket broke and made the landing especially painful.

Managing not to yell, Flynn sprung up, pulled down his pants, and looked in the hall mirror to see that his butt cheeks were cut and bleeding. He managed to quietly find a full box of Band-Aids and began putting a Band-Aid as best he could on each place he saw blood.

He then hid the now almost empty Band-Aid box and shuffled and stumbled his way to bed. In the morning, Flynn woke up with searing pain in both his head and butt and Mary staring at him from across the room.

She said, "You were drunk again last night weren't you?"

Flynn said, "Why you say such a mean thing?"

"Well," Mary said, "it could be the open front door, it could be the broken glass at the bottom of the stairs, it could be the drops of blood trailing through the house, it could be your bloodshot eyes, but mostly it's all those Band-Aids stuck on the hall mirror.

Gallagher opened the morning newspaper and was dumbfounded to read in the obituary column that he had died. He quickly phoned his best friend, Finney.

"Did you see the paper?" asked Gallagher. "They say I died!!"

"Yes, I saw it!" replied Finney. "Where are ye callin' from?"

What's the difference between a new husband and a new dog? After a year, the dog is still excited to see you

A newlywed couple was spending their honeymoon in a remote log cabin resort far up in the mountains. They had registered on Saturday and they had not been seen for 5 days.

An elderly couple ran the resort and they were getting concerned about the welfare of these newlyweds. The old man decided to go and see if they were all right.

He knocked on the door of the cabin and a weak voice from inside answered. The old man asked if they were okay.

"Yes, we're fine. We're living on the fruits of love."

The old man replied, "I thought so . . . would you mind not throwing the peels out the window? They're choking my ducks."

Murphy was selling his house and put the matter in an agent's hands. The agent wrote up a sales blurb for the house that made wonderful reading.

After Murphy read it, he turned to the agent and asked, "Have I got all you say there?"

The agent said, "You certainly have. Why do you ask?"

Murphy replied, "Cancel the sale. It's too good to part with."

This redneck couple gets married. They go back to the motel after the ceremony and she changes into a sexy nightgown, lies on the bed and says, "Please be gentle with me. I'm a virgin."

At this, her new husband bursts into tears, pulls on his clothes, jumps into his pickup truck and drives home. He tells his father what happened.

"Son, you done right," says his pop. "If she weren't good enough for her own family, she ain't good enough for ours."

From a passenger ship, everyone can see a bearded man on a small island, shouting and desperately waving his hands.
"Who is it?" a passenger asks the captain.
"I've no idea. Every year when we pass, he goes nuts."

Linda & Kathy were comparing notes on the difficulties of running a small business.

"I started a new practice last year," Linda said. "I insist that each of my employees take at least a week off every three months."

"Why in the world would you do that?" Kathy asked.

"It's the best way I know of to learn which ones I can do without," Linda said.

An out-of-towner accidentally drove his car into a ditch in a desolate area. Luckily, a local farmer happened by with his horse, Buddy. He hitched Buddy up to the car and yelled, "Pull, Nellie, pull!"

Buddy didn't move. Once more the farmer hollered, "Pull, Buster, pull!" Buddy did not respond.

Then the farmer nonchalantly said, "Pull, Buddy, pull!" And the horse finally dragged the car out of the ditch.

The motorist was most appreciative and very curious. He asked the farmer why he kept calling his horse by the wrong name.

The farmer said, "Oh, Buddy is blind and if he thought he was the only one pulling, he wouldn't even try."

A woman arrived at the gates of Heaven. While she was waiting for Saint Peter to greet her, she peeked through the gates. She saw a beautiful banquet table. Sitting all around were her parents and all the other people she had loved and who had died before her. They saw her and began calling greetings to her: "Hello! How are you! We've been waiting for you! Good to see you."

When Saint Peter came by, the woman said to him, "This is such a wonderful place! How do I get in?"

"You have to spell a word," Saint Peter told her.

"Which word?" the woman asked.

"Love."

The woman correctly spelled "love" and Saint Peter welcomed her into Heaven.

About a year later, Saint Peter came to the woman and asked her to watch the gates of Heaven for him that day. While the woman was guarding the gates of Heaven, her husband arrived.

"I'm surprised to see you," the woman said. "How have you been?"

"Oh, I've been doing pretty well since you died," her husband told her. "I married the beautiful young nurse who took care of you while you were ill. And then I won the multi-state lottery. I sold the little house you and I lived in and bought a huge mansion. And my wife and I traveled all around the world. We were on vacation in Cancun and I went water skiing today. I fell and hit my head, and here I am. What a bummer! How do I get in?"

"You have to spell a word," the woman told him.

"Which word?" her husband asked.

"Czechoslovakia."

Sooooooo . . . . . you want to become my son-in-law," says the mother. "Not really," replies the suitor, "but I don't see any other way to marry your daughter."

What's the fastest way to a man's heart?
Through his chest with a sharp knife

Although he was a qualified meteorologist, Hopkins had a terrible record of forecasting for the TV news program. He became something of a local joke when a newspaper began keeping a record of his predictions and showed that he'd been wrong almost three hundred times in a single year. That kind of notoriety was enough to get him fired.

He moved to another part of the country and applied for a similar job. One blank on the job application called for the reason for leaving his previous position.

Hopkins wrote, "The climate didn't agree with me."

So this guy walks into a bar and orders a beer. As he sits there drinking it, he hears a voice say, "Nice tie!" He looks around and sees that he's the only person at the bar. He can't figure out who said it.

He keeps working on his beer and after a couple of minutes he hears another voice say, "Sharp shirt!" He's really puzzled this time because there's still nobody else in the bar.

He's about to finish his beer when he hears a third voice say, "Great haircut!" He's had enough at this point and he calls the bartender over.

"I keep hearing voices that say I've got a nice tie and a sharp shirt and a great haircut, but there's nobody around. What's going on?"

The bartender says, "Oh, that's the peanuts. They're complimentary."

If you lined up all the cars in the world end to end, someone would be stupid enough to try to pass them, five or six at a time, on a hill, in the fog.

A guy just died and he's at the pearly gates waiting to be admitted, while St. Peter is leafing through the big book to see if the guy is worthy.

St. Peter furrows his brow and says to the guy, "You know, I've gone through the book several times and I can't see that you ever did anything really bad in your life, but you never did anything really good either. If you can point to even one really good deed, you're in."

He thinks for a moment and says, "There was this one time when I was driving down the highway and saw a giant group of thugs assaulting this poor girl. I slowed down my car to see what was going on. Infuriated, I got out of my car, grabbed a tire iron out of my trunk and walked up to the leader of the gang, a huge guy with a studded leather jacket and a chain running from his nose to his ear. As I walked up to the leader, the thugs formed a circle around me. So I ripped the leader's chain off his face and smashed him over the head with the tire iron. Laid him out. Then I turned and yelled at the rest of them, "Leave this poor, innocent girl alone! You're all a bunch of sick, deranged animals! Go home before I teach you all a lesson in pain!"

St. Peter, impressed, says, "Really? When did this happen?"

"Oh, about two minutes ago."

Save the Earth...it's the only planet with chocolate.

It was a really hot day at the office due to a malfunction with the air conditioning system. There were about twenty people in close quarters and everyone was sweating, even with a fan on.
All of a sudden, people started to wrinkle their noses at an odor passing through the air. It was the most hideous smell anyone had ever smelled. One man, popping his head out of his cubicle said, "Oh, man! Someone's deodorant isn't working."
An overweight man in the corner replied, "Well, it can't be me. I'm not wearing any."

The shinbone is a device for finding furniture in a dark room.

A little boy comes down to breakfast. Since they live on a farm, his mother asks if he had done his chores. "Not yet," said the little boy. His mother tells him no breakfast till the chores are done. Well, he's a little pissed.

He goes to feed the chickens, and he kicks a chicken.
He goes to feed the cows, and he kicks a cow.
He goes to feed the pigs, and he kicks a pig.
He goes back in for breakfast, and his mother gives him a bowl of dry cereal.
"How come I don't get any eggs and bacon? Why don't I have any milk in my cereal?" he asks.
"Well," his mother says, "I saw you kick a chicken, so you don't get any eggs for a week. I saw you kick the pig, so you don't get any bacon for a week either. I also saw you kick the cow, so for a week you aren't getting any milk."
Just then, his father comes down for breakfast and kicks the cat halfway across the kitchen.
The little boy looks up at his mother and says: "Are you going to tell him, or should I?"

What are you watching, Dad?"
"Basketball game."
"What's the score?"
"117 to 114."
"Who's winning?"
"The team with 117."

A lawyer and a blonde are sitting next to each other on a long flight from LA to NY. The lawyer leans over to her and asks if she would like to play a fun game. The blonde just wants to take a nap so she politely declines and turns toward the window to catch a few winks.

The lawyer persists and explains that the game is really easy and lots of fun. "I ask you a question, and if you don't know the answer, you pay me $5, and visa-versa." Again she politely declines.

The lawyer tries again, "Okay, if you don't know the answer you pay me $5 and if I don't know the answer, I'll pay you $50," figuring that since she is a blond that he will easily win the match. This catches the blonde's attention and figuring that there will be no end to this torment unless she plays, agrees to the game.

The lawyer asks the first question. "What's the distance from the earth to the moon?" The blonde doesn't say a word, reaches into her purse, pulls out a five-dollar bill and hands it to the lawyer.

Now it's the blonde's turn. She asks the lawyer, "What goes up a hill with three legs and comes down with four?"

The lawyer looks at her with a puzzled look. He takes out his laptop and searches the Internet. After over an hour he wakes the blonde and hands her $50. The blonde takes the $50 and turns away to get back to sleep.

The lawyer taps her on the shoulder and asks, "Well, so what is the answer?"

Without a word, the blonde reaches into her purse, hands the lawyer $5 and goes back to sleep.

A Texan and his bride ask the hotel desk clerk for a room, telling him they just got married that morning.

"Congratulations!" says the clerk. Looking at the cowboy he asks, "Would you like the bridal then?"

"No thanks, I reckon I'll just hold her by the ears 'til she gets the hang of it."

A group of senior citizens were exchanging complaints about their ailments.
"My arm is so weak that I can hardly hold this coffee cup."
"Yes, I know. My cataracts are so bad that I can't see to pour my coffee."
"I can't turn my head because of the arthritis in my neck."
"My blood pressure pills make me dizzy."
"I guess that's the price we pay for getting old."
"Well, it's not all bad. We should be thankful that we can still drive."

The CIA had an opening for an assassin. After all the background checks, interviews and testing were done, there were three finalists, two men and a woman. For the final test, the CIA agents took one of the men to a large metal door and handed him a gun.

"We must know that you will follow our instructions, no matter what the circumstances. Inside of this room you will find your wife sitting in a chair. Kill her!"

The man said, "You can't be serious. I could never shoot my wife."

The agent said, "Then you're not the right man for this job."

The second man was given the same instructions. He took the gun and went into the room. All was quiet for about five minutes. Then the man came out with tears in his eyes, "I tried, but I can't kill my wife."

The agent said, "You don't have what it takes. Take your wife and go home."

Finally, it was the woman's turn. She was given the same instructions, to kill her husband. She took the gun and went into the room. Shots were heard, one shot after another. They heard screaming, crashing, banging on the walls. After a few minutes, all was quiet. The door opened slowly and there stood the woman. She wiped the sweat from her brow and said, "This gun was loaded with blanks. I had to beat him to death with the chair."

Flashlight: A case for holding dead batteries.

Doctor, doctor, what's the news?" asked Hal when his doctor called with his test results.

"I have some bad news and some really bad news," admitted the doctor. "The bad news is that you only have twenty-four hours to live."

"Oh my God," gasped Hal, sinking to his knees. "What could be worse than that?"

"I couldn't get a hold of you yesterday."

The blonde went into a shoe store to buy a pair of alligator shoes. After trying them on, she asked about the price. Learning that the shoes were very expensive, she decided she would go out into the bayou and get her own alligator shoes.

Later that afternoon, the shopkeeper was on his way home, going through the bayou, when he noticed the same blonde with a 12-gauge shotgun. She was dragging a 12-foot alligator onto the bank, where she stacked it near a large pile of alligators. As she turned the gator over, he heard her shout, "Damn it! This one isn't wearing shoes either."

In pharmacology, all medications have a generic name: Tylenol is acetaminophen, Advil is ibuprofen, Rogaine is minoxodil, and so on.

The FDA has been looking for a generic name for Viagra and today settled on the new name: mycoxafloppin.

An old man was walking in the forest when he heard a very weak voice by his feet. He bent down to look and saw that the voice came from a little frog that said to him, "I'm a beautiful, erotic and sensual princess, skilled in all the carnal pleasures of love. An evil queen, envious of my charms, turned me into a frog, but if you kiss me I will once again be a fair maiden and I will provide you with all the joys and delights you desire."

The old man picked up the little frog and put her into his pocket.

Bewildered, the frog looked out and asked, "What, you're not going to kiss me?"

"Nope," replied the old man. "At my age, I'd rather have a talking frog."

A 10 year old, under the tutelage of her grandmother, was becoming quite knowledgeable about the Bible.

Then one day she floored her grandmother by asking, "Which Virgin was the mother of Jesus? The Virgin Mary or the King James Virgin?"

A man walks out of a bar, stumbling back and forth with a key in his hand. A cop on the beat sees him and approaches.

"Can I help you sir?"

"Yesssh! Ssssshomebody ssshtole my car!"

The cop asks, "Where was the car the last time you saw it?"

"It wassss at the end of thisssh key!

About that time the officer looks down to see that the man's wiener is hanging out of his fly for the entire world to see. He asks the man, "Sir, are you aware that you are exposing yourself?"

Momentarily confused, the drunk looks down woefully at his crotch and, without missing a beat, blurts out, "SON-OF-A-BITCH . . . . . THEY GOT MY GIRLFRIEND TOO!"

A high school student came home one afternoon rather depressed.

"What's the matter, son?" asked his mother.

"It's my grades. They're all wet," said her son.

"What do you mean 'all wet?'"

"You know," he replied, " below C-level."

A couple of drinking buddies who are airplane mechanics are in a hangar at JFK in New York. It's fogged in and they have nothing to do.

"Man, have you got anything to drink?"

"Nah, but I hear you can drink jet fuel and it will kinda give you a buzz."

So they drink it, get smashed and have a great time, like only drinking buddies can. The following morning, one of the men wakes up and he just knows his head will explode if he gets up, but it doesn't. He gets up and feels good. In fact, he feels great! No hangover!"

The phone rings. It's his buddy. "Hey, how do you feel?"

"Great, just great!" he says.

"Yeah, I feel great too, and no hangover. That jet fuel stuff is great. We should do this more often."

"We could, but there's just one thing . . . . ."

"What's that?"

"Did you fart yet?"

"No . . . . ."

"Well, DON'T, 'cause I'm in Phoenix."

It's just a cold," the doctor said. "There is no cure, so you'll just have to live with it until it goes away."

"But Doctor, it's making me so miserable."

The doctor rolled his eyes toward the ceiling. The he said, "Look, go home and take a hot bath. Then put on a bathing suit and run around the block three or four times."

"What!?!" the patient exclaimed. "I'll get pneumonia!"

"We have a cure for pneumonia," the doctor said.

During a recent outing, Christy sneaked off to visit a fortune teller of some local repute. She found her in a dark and hazy room, the mystic peering into a crystal ball. The mystic delivered the grave news. "There's no easy way to say this, so I'll just be blunt. Prepare yourself to be a widow. Your husband will die a violent and horrible death this year."

Visibly shaken, Christy stared at the woman's lined face, then at the flickering candle, then down at her hands. She took a few deep breaths to compose herself. She simply had to know. She met the fortune teller's gaze, steadied her voice, and asked the question,

"Will I be acquitted?"

A young woman teacher with obvious liberal tendencies explains to her class of young children that she is an atheist. She asks her class if they are atheists too. Not really knowing what atheism is but wanting to be like their teacher, all their hands went up.

There was, however, one exception. A beautiful girl named Sarah has not gone along with the crowd. The teacher asks her why she had decided to be different.

"Because I'm not an atheist."

Then, asks the teacher, "What are you?"

"I'm Jewish."

The teacher is a little perturbed now and she asks Sarah why she is Jewish.

"Well, I was brought up knowing and loving God. My mom is Jewish and my dad is Jewish, so I am Jewish."

The teacher is now angry. "That's no reason," she says loudly. "What if your mom was a moron and your dad was a moron. What would you be then?"

"Then," says Sarah with a smile, "I'd be an atheist."

A store that sells husbands has just opened in New York City, where a woman may go to choose a husband. Among the instructions at the entrance is a description of how the store operates. You may visit the store ONLY ONCE! There are six floors and the attributes of the men increase as the shopper ascends the flights. There is, however, a catch. You may choose any man from a particular floor, or you may choose to go up a floor, but you cannot go back down except to exit the building!

So, a woman goes to the Husband Store to find a husband. On the first floor, the sign on the door reads:

Floor 1 - These men have jobs and love the Lord.

Floor 2 - These men have jobs, love the Lord, and love kids.

Floor 3 – These men have jobs, love the Lord, love kids and are extremely good looking.

"Wow," she thinks, but feels compelled to keep going.

She goes to the fourth floor and the sign reads:

Floor 4 - These men have jobs, love the Lord, love kids, are drop-dead gorgeous and help with the housework.

"Oh, mercy me!" she exclaims, "I can hardly stand it!" Still, she goes on!

The fifth floor sign reads:

Floor 5 - These men have jobs, love the Lord, love kids, are drop-dead gorgeous, help with the housework, and have a strong romantic streak.

She is so tempted to stay, but she goes to the sixth floor and the sign reads:

Floor 6 – You are visitor 4,637,012 to this floor. There are no men on this floor. This floor exists solely as proof that women are impossible to please.

Thank you for shopping at the Husband Store. Watch your step as you exit the building, and have a nice day!

Fred was applying for a job as a flagman/switch operator on the railroad. The chief engineer was conducting the interview.

"What would you do if the Northern Express was heading north on Track 1 and the Southern Central was heading south on Track 1?"

Fred quickly answered, "Well, I'd call my brother."

The chief engineer just sat there for a second. "Why would you call your brother?"

"He's never seen a train wreck before."

A regular walks into the bar and says, "Bartender, one round for everyone, on me!"

The bartender says, "Well, seems you're in a really good mood tonight."

"Oh, you can bet on it! I just got hired by the city to go around and remove all the money from parking meters. I start on Monday."

The bartender congratulates the man and proceeds to pour the round. A few days later, the same man walks into the bar.

"Bartender, TWO rounds for everyone, on me!"

The bartender says, "If you're so happy just having this new job, I can't imagine how happy you'll be when you get your paycheck!"

With a wondrous look on his face, the man pulls out a handful of quarters from his pocket and says, "You mean they PAY me too?"

A local charity office realized that it had never received a donation from the town's most successful lawyer. The person in charge of contributions called him to persuade him to contribute.

"Our research shows that out of a yearly income of at least $500,000, you give not a penny to charity. Wouldn't you like to give back to the community in some way?"

The lawyer mulled this over for a moment and replied, "First, did your research also show that my mother is dying after a long illness and has medical bills that are several times her annual income?"

Embarrassed, the rep mumbled, "Um . . . no."

"Or that my brother, a disabled veteran, is blind and confined to a wheelchair?"

The stricken rep began to stammer out an apology, but was interrupted,

"Or that my sister's husband died in a traffic accident leaving her penniless with three small children?" the lawyer's voice rising in indignation.

The humiliated rep, completely beaten, said simply, "I had no idea . . ."

On a roll, the lawyer cut him off once again: "and if I don't give them a penny, why should I give any to you?"

After three months of nagging, the old man finally goes to the doctor. "This is embarrassing, but I'd like to get a prescription for Viagra."

"Not a problem," said the doctor as he writes out the prescription.

The old man interrupts, "Doc, I forgot to tell you I need each pill cut into four pieces."

"I know the pills are expensive, but you have to take the entire pill for it to work properly," said the Doctor.

"You don't understand. I am almost 90 years old. I only want it to stick out far enough so I don't pee on my shoes."

I play golf in the low 80s," the little old man was telling one of the young boys at the club.

"Wow," said the young man. "That's pretty impressive."

"Not really," said the little old man, "any hotter and I'd probably have a stroke."

This woman was having an affair during the day while her husband was at work. One day she was in bed with her lover and she heard her husband's car pull into the driveway. She yelled at the boyfriend, "Hurry! Grab you clothes and jump out the window. My husband is home early."

The boyfriend looked out the window and said, "I can't jump out the window! It's raining like hell out there!"

She said, "If my husband catches up in here, he will kill us both."

So the boyfriend grabs his clothes and jumps out the window. When he landed outside he was in the middle of a marathon, so he started running along beside the others, only he was in the nude and carrying his clothes on his arm.

One of the runners asked him, "Do you always run in the nude?"

"Oh yes," he answered gasping for air. "It feels so free having the air blow over your skin while you are running."

The other runner then asked, "Do you always run carrying your clothes on your arm?"

"Oh yes, that way I can get dressed at the end of the run and get in my car and go home."

Then the other runner asked, "Do you always wear a condom when you run?"

"Only if it's raining," said the naked man.

A police officer in a small town stopped a motorist who was speeding down Main Street.

"But officer," the man said, "I can explain."

"Just be quiet!" snapped the officer, "or I'm going to let you cool off in jail until the chief gets back."

"But officer, all I wanted to say . . . . "

"You just don't listen, do you? Well, you're going to jail!"

A few hours later, the officer checks up on his prisoner and says, "Lucky for you that the chief's at his daughter's wedding. He'll be in a good mood when he gets back."

"Don't count on it," said the man in the cell. "I'm the groom."

Two engineering students were walking across campus when one said, "Where did you get such a great bike?"

The second engineer replied, "Well, I was walking along yesterday minding my own business when a beautiful woman rode up on this bike. She threw the bike to the ground, took off all her clothes and said, "Take what you want."

The first engineer nodded approvingly, "Good choice, the clothes probably wouldn't have fit."

Presenter to paleontologist: "So what would happen if you mated the woolly mammoth with, say, an elephant?"

Expert: "Well, in the same way that a horse and a donkey produce a mule, we'd get a sort of half-mammoth."

Presenter: "So it'd be like some sort of hairy gorilla?"

Expert: "Er, well yes, but elephant-shaped, and with tusks."

Sex Egg-ucation

Baby chick: "Am I a people?"
Mama Chick: "No, you're a chicken."
Baby chick: "Do chickens come from people?"
Mama Chick, "No, chickens come from eggs."
Baby Chick: "Are eggs born?"
Mama Chick: "No, eggs are laid."
Baby Chick: "Are people laid?"
Mama Chick: "Some are. Others are chicken."
Baby Chick, "????????"

A drunk stumbles along a baptismal service on a Sunday afternoon down by the river. He proceeds down to the water and stands next to the minister. The minister turns and notices the old drunk and says,

"Mister, are you ready to find Jesus?"

The drunk looks back and says, "Yes sir, I am."

The minister then dunks the fellow under the water and pulls him right back up. "Have you found Jesus?"

"No, I didn't!" said the drunk.

The minister then dunks him under again, this time for quite a bit longer, brings him up and says, "Now brother, have you found Jesus?"

"No. I did not!" the drunk said again.

Disgusted, the minister holds the man under the water for at least 30 seconds this time. He brings him back up and demands, "For the love of God, have you found Jesus yet?"

The old drunk wipes his eyes and pleads, "Are you sure this is where he fell in?"

The woman was more than a little upset when her car stalled in the middle of a busy street. As the light turned from red to green a second time and the car still wouldn't start, the honking fellow in the car behind her grew even more insistent.

Finally, the woman got out and walked over to his car.

"Excuse me, sir," she said politely, "if you'd like to help out by trying to get my car started yourself, I'll be glad to sit here and honk your horn for you."

Four men went golfing one day. Three of them headed to the first tee and the fourth went into the clubhouse to take care of the bill. The three men started talking and bragging about their sons.

The first man told the others, "My son is a home builder and he is so successful that he gave a friend a new home for free."

The second man said, "My son was a car salesman and now he owns a multi-line dealership. He's so successful that he gave a friend a new Mercedes, fully loaded."

The third man, not wanted to be outdone, bragged, my son is a stockbroker, and he is doing so well that he gave his friend an entire portfolio."

The fourth man joined them on the tee. The first man mentioned, "We were just talking about our sons. How's yours doing?"

The fourth man replied, "Well, my son is gay and dances in a gay bar."

The other three men grew silent as he continued.

"I'm not totally thrilled about the dancing job, but he must be doing good. His last three boyfriends gave him a house, a brand new Mercedes and a stock portfolio."

Three engineering students were gathered together discussing the possible designers of the human body.

One said, "It was a mechanical engineer. Just look at all the joints."

Another said, " No, it was an electrical engineer. The nervous system has many thousands of electrical connections."

The last said, "Actually it was a civil engineer. Who else would run a toxic waste pipeline through a recreational area?"

When the Jones family moved into their new house, a visiting relative asked the little five-year-old how he like the new place.

"It's terrific," he said. "I have my own room, Mike has his own room and Laura has her own room. But poor Mom is still in with Dad."

Two friends were playing golf when one pulled out a cigar. He didn't have a lighter so he asked his friend if he had one.

"I sure do," he replied while he reached into his golf bag and pulled out a 12 inch Bic lighter.

"Wow! Where did you get that monster lighter?"

"I got it from my genie."

"You have a genie?"

"Yes, right here in my golf bag."

"Could I see him?"

He opens his golf bag and out pops a genie. The friend asks the genie, "Since I am a good friend of your master, will you grant me one wish?"

"Yes, I will," the genie replies.

The friend asks the genie for a million bucks.

The genie hops back into the golf bag and leaves him standing there waiting for his million bucks. Suddenly, the sky begins to darken and the sound of a million ducks flying overhead is heard. The friend tells his golfing partner, "I asked for a million bucks, not a million ducks."

He answers, "I forgot to tell you that the genie is hard of hearing. Do you really think I asked him for a 12-inch Bic?"

The couple had not been getting along for years, so the husband thinks; "I'll buy my wife a cemetery plot for her birthday." Well, you can imagine her disappointment. The next year, her birthday rolls around again and he doesn't get her anything.

She says, "Why didn't you get me a birthday present?"

He says, "You didn't use what I got you last year!"

Over breakfast one morning, a woman said to her husband, "I'll bet you don't know what day this is."

"Of course I do," he answered as if he was offended and left for the office.

At 10:00 a.m., the doorbell rang and when she opened the door she was handed a box of a dozen long stemmed red roses. At 1:00 p.m., a foil-wrapped, 2-pound box of her favorite chocolates was delivered. Later, a boutique delivered a designer dress.

The woman couldn't wait for her husband to come home.

"First the flowers, then the chocolates and then the dress! I've never had a more wonderful Groundhog Day in my life."

People are more violently opposed to fur than they are to leather because it's safer to harrass rich women than motorcycle gangs.

A 60-year-old man went to a doctor for a checkup. The doctor told him, "You are in terrific shape. There's nothing wrong with you. Why, you might live forever – you have the body of a 35-year-old. By the way, how old was your father when he died?"

"Did I say he was dead?"

The doctor was surprised and asked, "How old is your father and is he very active?"

"Well, he's 82 years old and still goes skiing three times a season and surfing three times a week during the summer."

The doctor couldn't believe it. So he said, "How old was your grandfather when he died?"

"Did I say he was dead?"

The doctor was astonished. "You mean to tell me you are 60 years old and both your father and your grandfather are alive! Is your grandfather very active?"

"He goes skiing at least once every season and surfing once a week during the summer. Not only that, my grandfather is 106 years old and next week he is getting married."

"Heavens," the doctor said, "At 106 years, why on earth would your grandfather want to get married?"

"Did I say he wanted to?"

A judge asks the prisoner, "What are you charged with?

"Doing my Christmas shopping early," he replied.

"That's no offense. How early were you doing this shopping?"

"Before the store opened."

An American soldier, serving in World War II, had just returned from several weeks of intense action on the German front lines. He had finally been granted R&R and was on a train bound for London. The train was very crowded, so the soldier walked the length of the train looking for an empty seat. The only unoccupied seat was directly adjacent to a well-dressed middle-aged lady and was being used by her little dog.

The war-weary soldier asked, "Please ma'am, may I sit in that seat?"

The English woman looked down her nose at the soldier and said, "You Americans. You are such a rude class of people. Can't you see my little Fifi is using that seat?"

The soldier walked away determined to find a place to rest, but after another trip down to the end of the train, found himself again facing the woman with the dog.

Again he asked, "Please lady, may I please sit there? I'm very tired."

The English woman wrinkled her nose and snorted, "You Americans are not only rude, you are also arrogant. Imagine!"

The soldier didn't' say anything else. He leaned over, picked up the little dog, tossed it out the window of the train and sat down in the empty seat. The women shrieked and demanded that someone defend her and chastise the soldier.

An English gentleman sitting across the aisle spoke up. "You know sir, you Americans do seem to have a penchant for doing the wrong thing. You eat holding the fork in the wrong hand. You drive your autos on the wrong side of the road. And now sir, you've thrown the wrong bitch out of the window."

Suffering from a bad case of the flu, the outraged patient bellowed, "Three weeks? The doctor can't see me for three weeks? I could well be dead by then!"

Calmly, the voice at the other end of the line replied, "If so, would you have your wife call to cancel the appointment?"

An old man was sitting on a bench at the mall. A young man walked up to the bench and sat down. He had spiked hair all different colors – green, red, orange, blue and yellow. The old man stared.

The young man said, "What's the matter, old timer? Never done anything wild in your life?"

The old man replied, "Got drunk once and had sex with a parrot. I was just wondering if you were my son."

One afternoon a man came home from work to find total mayhem in his house. His three children were outside, still in their pajamas, playing in the mud. Empty food boxes and wrappers were scattered all around the front yard. The door of his wife's car was open as was the front door to the house.

Proceeding into the entry, he found an even bigger mess. A lamp had been knocked over and the throw rug was wadded up against one wall. In the front room the TV was loudly blaring a cartoon channel and the family room was strewn with toys and various items of clothing.

In the kitchen, dishes filled the sink, breakfast food was spilled on the counter, dog food was all over the floor, a broken glass lay under the table and a small pile of sand was spread by the back door. He quickly headed up the stairs, stepping over toys and more piles of clothes, looking for his wife.

He was worried she may be ill, or that something serious had happened. He found her lounging in the bedroom, still curled up in bed in her pajamas, reading a novel. She looked up at him and smiled and asked how his day went. He looked bewildered and asked, "What happened here today?"

She again smiled and answered, "You know every day when you come home from work and ask me what in the world did I do today?"

"Yes."

"Well, today I didn't do it."

A guy with a black eye boards his plane bound for Pittsburgh and sits down in his seat. He immediately notices that the guy next to him has a black eye, too. He says to him, "Hey, this is a coincidence, we both have black eyes. Mind if I ask how you got yours?"

The other guy says, "Well it just happened. It was a tongue twister accident. See, I was at the ticket counter and this gorgeous blonde with the most massive breasts in the world was there. So instead of saying 'I'd like two tickets to Pittsburgh,' I accidentally said 'I'd like two pickets to Tittsburgh,' and she socked me a good one."

The first guy replies, "Wow, this is unbelievable. Mine was a tongue twister, too! I was at the breakfast table and wanted to say to my wife 'Please pour me a bowl of Frosties, honey.' But I accidentally said, 'You ruined my life you evil, self-centered, fat-assed bitch.'"

A soldier was asked to report to headquarters for assignment. The sergeant said, "We have a critical shortage of typists. I'll give you a little test. Type this," he ordered, pointing to a desk that held a typewriter and an adding machine.

The man, quite reluctant to become a clerk typist, made a point of typing very slowly and made as many errors as possible.

The sergeant gave the typed copy only a brief glance and said, "That's fine. Report for work at 8 tomorrow."

"But aren't you going to check the test?" the prospective clerk asked.

The sergeant grinned, "You passed the test when you sat down at the typewriter instead of the adding machine."

It was many years ago since the embarrassing day when a young woman, with a baby in her arms, entered his butcher shop and confronted him with the news that the baby she was holding was his and asked what he was going to do about it.

Finally he offered to provide her with free meat until the boy was 16. She agreed.

He had been counting the years off on his calendar and one day the teenager, who had been collecting the meat each week, came into the shop and said, "I'll be 16 tomorrow."

"I know," said the butcher with a smile. "I've been counting too. Tell your mother that this is the last free meat she'll get, and watch the expression on her face."

When the boy arrived home he told his mother. The woman nodded and said, "Son, go back to the butcher and tell him I have also had free bread, free milk, and free groceries for the last 16 years and watch the expression on HIS face!"

Old Aunt Dora went to her doctor to see what could be done about her constipation.
"It's terrible," she said. "I haven't moved my bowels in a week."
"I see. Have you done anything about it?" asked the doctor.
"Yes. I sit in the bathroom for a half-hour in the morning and again at night."
"No," the doctor said. "I mean do you take anything?"
"Naturally," she answered. "I take a book."

A couple had only been married for two weeks and the husband, although very much in love, couldn't wait to go out on the town and party with his old buddies.

So, he said to his new wife, "Honey, I'll be right back."

"Where are you going, Coochy Coo?" asked the wife.

"I'm going to the bar, Pretty Face," he answered. "I'm going to have a beer."

The wife said, "You want a beer, my love?" She opened the door to the refrigerator and showed him 25 different kinds of beer, brands from 12 different countries: Germany, Holland, Japan, India, etc.

The husband didn't know what to do, and the only thing that he could think of saying was, "Yes, Lollipop...but at the bar...you know...they have frozen glasses..."

He didn't get to finish the sentence, because the wife interrupted him by saying, "You want a frozen glass, Puppy Face?" She took a huge beer mug out of the freezer, so frozen that she was getting chills just holding it.

The husband, looking a bit pale, said, "Yes, Tootsie Roll, but at the bar they have those hors d'oeuvres that are really delicious...I won't be long. I'll be right back. I promise. Okay?"

"You want hors d'oeuvres, Poochie Pooh?" She opened the oven and took out dishes of different hors d'oeuvres: chicken wings, pigs in blankets, mushroom caps, and little quiches.

"But my sweet honey . . . at the bar, you know, there's swearing, dirty words and all that."

"You want dirty words, Cutie Pie? LISTEN UP CHICKEN SHIT! SIT YOUR ASS DOWN, SHUT THE HELL UP, DRINK YOUR BEER IN YOUR FROZEN MUG AND EAT YOUR HORS D'OEUVRES BECAUSE YOUR MARRIED ASS ISN'T GOING TO A DAMNED BAR! THAT SHIT'S OVER, GOT IT, JACKASS?" and . . . they lived happily ever after.

One day, shortly after the birth of their first baby, the mother had to go out to run some errands. The proud papa stayed home to watch his new son. Soon after the mother left, the baby started to cry. The father did everything he could think of doing, but the baby wouldn't stop crying.

Finally, dad got so worried that he decided to take the infant to the doctor. After a brief examination the doctor undid the diaper and found that it was quite full. "Here's the problem," he said. "He needs to be changed."

The father said, "Impossible, the diaper package says it's good for up to 10 pounds!"

The children were now in the first grade and their teacher wanted them to be more grown up since they were no longer in kindergarten. She told them to use grown-up words instead of baby words. She then asked them to tell her what they did during their summer vacation.

The first little one said he went to see Nana. The teacher said, "No, you went to see your grandmother. Use the grown-up word."

The next child said she went for a trip on a choo-choo. The teacher said, "No, you went for a trip on a train. That's the grown-up word."

Then the teacher asked Johnny what he did during the summer. He proudly stated that he read a book. The teacher asked him what book he had read.

He puffed out his chest and in a very adult way replied, "Winnie the Shit."

A woman was driving down the highway about 75 miles per hour when she noticed a motorcycle policeman following her. Instead of slowing down, she picked up speed. When she looked again, there were two motorcycles following her. She shot up to 90 miles per hour. The next time she looked back, there were three cops following her.

Suddenly she spotted a gas station up ahead. She screeched to a stop and ran into the ladies room. Ten minutes later, she innocently walked out.

The three cops were standing there waiting for her. Without batting an eye, she said coyly, "I'll bet none of you thought I would make it."

Two men from Arkansas are walking along Sam Houston Street when they see a sign that reads, "Suits $5.00 each, Shirts $2.00 each, Trousers $2.50 per pair."

Bubba says to his pal, Billy Ray "LOOK! We could buy a whole lot of those, and when we get back home we could make a fortune. Now when we go into the shop, you be quiet, okay? Just let me do all the talking 'cause if they hear our accent, they might not serve us. I'll speak in my best Arkansas drawl."

They go in and Bubba orders 50 suits at $5.00 each, 100 shirts at $2.00 each and 50 pairs of trousers at $2.50 each.

"I'll back up my pickup and. . . ." The owner of the shop interrupts, "You're from Arkansas, aren't you?"

"Oh, yes," says a surprised Bubba. "How come you know that?"

The owner says, "This is a dry-cleaners."

One day at kindergarten, the teacher said to the class, "I'll give $2 to the child who can tell me who was the most famous man who ever lived."

An Irish boy put up his hand and said, "It was St. Patrick."

The teacher said, "Sorry, Sean, that's not correct."

Then a Scottish boy put up his hand and said, "It was St. Andrew."

The teacher replied, "I'm sorry Hamish, that's not right either."

Finally, a Jewish by raised his hand and said, "It was Jesus Christ."

The teacher said, "That's absolutely right, Marvin, come up here and I'll give you your $2."

As the teacher was giving Marvin his money, she said, "You know, Marvin, you being Jewish, I was very surprised you said Jesus Christ."

Marvin replied, "I know. In my heart I knew it was Moses, but business is business."

A man was walking on the beach and spied another man sunning himself. He was a well-built, muscular individual, obviously a body builder, but his body was much larger in proportion to his extremely tiny head. He opened his eyes and caught the walking man staring at him.

"I'm so sorry, I shouldn't stare, but I couldn't help noticing that your body and your head are not in proportion."

"That's an interesting story," the other man said sitting up on his towel. "Sit down here with me and have a beer and I'll tell you all about it."

"You see, I was on this very beach, walking along like you were, when I saw a mermaid out there by the rocks. I swam out and sneaked up on her and caught her. As you might know, mermaids will give you three wishes so that you will release them. Well, I'd always been a 97-pound weakling sort of guy and couldn't get girls, so the first wish I wished was to have the body of Arnold Schwarzenegger. And POOF! I was changed instantly into a strong, virile man – a magnificent specimen."

"Next, I thought to myself, I will need a place to take the girls I will be attracting, so I wished for a million dollar beach front mansion, and behind you is my magnificent home. So now I have the body and the place, all I need is the girl, right? So I turned to the mermaid and wished that I could make love to her. She explained to me that she was just a fish from the waist down and could not make love with a human."

"So I said to her, "Well, how's about a little head?""

Two tourists were driving through Wisconsin. As they were approaching Oconomowoc, they started arguing about the pronunciation of the town's name. They argued back and forth until they stopped for lunch.

As they stood at the counter, one tourist asked the blonde employee, "Before we order, could you please settle an argument for us? Would you please pronounce where we are . . . . . very slowly?"

The blonde girl leaned over the counter and said, "Burrrrrrr, gerrrrrrrr, Kiiiiiiing."

A woman rushed into the supermarket to pick up a few items. She headed for the express line where the clerk was talking on the phone with his back turned to her.

"Excuse me," she said, "I'm in a hurry. Could you check me out please?"

The clerk turned, looked her up and down, and smiled, "Not bad."

A linguistics professor was lecturing to his class. "In English, a double negative forms a positive. In some languages, though, such as Russian, a double negative is still a negative. However, there is no language wherein a double positive can form a negative.

A voice from the back of the room piped up, "Yeah, right."

When the newlywed couple got back from their honeymoon, the bride immediately called her mother.

"Oh mama, the honeymoon was wonderful, so romantic." Suddenly she burst out crying. "But mama, as soon as we returned, Sam started using the most horrible language – things I'd never heard before! I mean, all these awful 4-letter words. You've got to come get me and take me home. Please, mama!"

"Sarah, Sarah, calm down! Tell me, what could be so awful? What 4 letter words?"

"Please don't make me tell you mama. I'm so embarrassed. They're just too awful! Come and get me, please!"

"Darling, baby, you must tell me what had you so upset. Tell your mother these horrible 4-letter words."

Still sobbing, the bride said, "Oh, mama, words like DUST, WASH, IRON, COOK!"

A woman sued a man for defamation of character. She charged that he had called her a pig. The man was found guilty and fined. After the trial he asked the judge, "This means that I cannot call Mrs. Johnson a pig?"

The judge said that was true. "Does this mean I cannot call a pig 'Mrs. Johnson?'" the man asked.

The judge replied that he could indeed call a pig "Mrs. Johnson" with no fear of legal action.

The man looked directly at Mrs. Johnson and said. "Good afternoon, Mrs. Johnson."

After two years of marriage, Tom was still questioning his wife about her lurid past.

"C'mon, tell me," Tom asked for the umpteenth time. "How many men have you been with?"

"Baby," she protested, "if I told you, you'd throw a fit."

Tom promised he wouldn't get angry and convinced his wife to tell him.

"Okay," she said, then started to count on her fingers, "One, two, three, four, five, six, seven – then there's you – nine, ten, eleven, twelve, thirteen . . . . ."

John, looking as if he had lost his last friend, entered a restaurant one morning and sat down at a table. He said to the waitress, "Bring me two eggs fried hard, a slice of toast burned to a cinder and a cup of very weak coffee."

As she set the order in front of him, she asked, "Anything else, sir?"

"Yes," he answered, "now sit down and nag me. I'm homesick."

How do you get down from an elephant?
You don't get down from an elephant; you get down from a goose.

THINGS ONLY WOMEN UNDERSTAND:

Why you need to have five pairs of black shoes
The difference between cream, ivory and off-white
Crying can be fun
FAT CLOTHES
A salad, diet drink and a hot fudge sundae make a balanced lunch
Discovering a designer dress on the clearance rack can be considered a
peak life experience
The inaccuracy of every bathroom scale ever made
A good man might be hard to find, but a good hairdresser is next
to impossible
Why a phone call between two women never lasts under ten minutes
OTHER WOMEN

A young man at his first job as a waiter in a diner has a large trucker sit down at the counter and order, "Gimme three flat tires and a couple of headlights."

He goes to the kitchen and tells the cook, "I think this guy's in the wrong place. Look what he ordered."

The cook says, "He wants 3 pancakes and 2 eggs sunny-side-up."

"I get it," replies the waiter. So on his way back out to the counter he takes a bowl of beans to the trucker.

He looks at it and says, "I didn't order this!"

The young man tells him, "I figured while you were waiting for your parts, you might as well gas up!"

May I take your order?" the waiter asked.

"Yes, I'm just wondering, how do you prepare your chickens?"

"Nothing special sir," he replied. "We just tell them straight out that they're going to die."

A lady came to the hospital to visit a friend. She had not been in a hospital for several years and felt very ignorant about all the new technology. A man followed her into the elevator wheeling a large, intimidating looking machine with tubes and wires and dials.

"Boy, would I hate to be hooked up to that thing," she said.

"So would I," replied the technician. "It's a floor-cleaning machine."

A student was heading home for the holidays and when she got to the airline counter she presented her ticket to New York. As she gave the agent her luggage, she said, "I'd like you to send my green suitcase to Hawaii and my red suitcase to London."

The confused agent said, "I'm sorry, but we can't do that."

"Really? I am so relieved to hear you say that, because that's exactly what you did to my luggage last year!"

A little girl was asked what she wanted most for her birthday and she declared, "A baby brother."

"Daddy and I would like to give you a baby brother," said her mom, "but there isn't time before your birthday."

"Why don't you do like they do down at Daddy's factory when they want something in a hurry? Put more men on the job."

Most people hate to parallel park. The other day I saw this woman trying to get out of a tight parking space. She'd bump the car in front, then back up and hit the car behind her. This went on for two minutes.

I walked over to see if I could help somehow. My offer was declined and she said, "Why have bumpers if you're not going to use them once in a while?"

A couple, on their honeymoon, is about to consummate their marriage, when the new bride says to the husband, "I have a confession to make. I'm not a virgin. But I've only been with one guy."

"Oh yeah? Who was the guy?"

"Tiger Woods."

"Tiger Woods, the golfer?"

"Yeah."

"Well, he's rich, famous and handsome. I can see why you went to bed with him." The husband and wife then make passionate love. When they get done the husband rolls over and picks up the telephone.

"What are you doing?

"I'm hungry. I was going to call room service and get some food."

"Tiger wouldn't do that."

"Oh yeah? What would Tiger do?"

"He'd come back to bed and do it a second time."

The husband puts down the phone and makes love with his wife a second time. When they finish, he rolls over and picks up the phone.

"What are you doing?" she asks.

"I'm still hungry, so I was going to get room service to send up some food."

"Tiger wouldn't do that."

"Oh yeah? What would Tiger do?"

"He'd come back and do it one more time."

The guy slams down the phone and makes love to his wife one more time. When they finish he drags himself over to the phone and starts to dial. The wife asks, "Are you calling room service?"

"No! I'm calling Tiger Woods to find out what's par for this hole."

A lady was lost in her car during a bad snowstorm. She remembered what her dad had once told her. If you ever get stuck in a snowstorm, wait for a snowplow and follow it. Pretty soon a snowplow came by and she followed it for about 45 minutes. Finally, the driver of the truck got out and asked her what she was doing.

She explained that her dad had told her that if she ever got stuck in a snowstorm she should follow a plow.

The driver nodded and said, "Well I'm through with the Wal-Mart lot. You can follow me over to K-Mart if you'd like."

Little Johnny was practicing the violin in the living room while his father was trying to read in the den. The family dog was lying in the den, and as the screeching sounds of little Johnny's violin reached his ears, he began to howl loudly.

The father listened to the dog and the violin as long as he could. Then he jumped up, slammed the paper to the floor and yelled above the noise. "For Pete's sake, can't you play something the dog doesn't know?"

After being away on business, Tim thought it would be nice to bring his wife a little gift. "How about some perfume?" he asked the cosmetics clerk. She showed him a bottle costing $50.

"That's a bit much," said Tim, so she returned with a smaller bottle for $30. "That's still quite a bit," complained Tim.

Growing annoyed, the clerk brought out a tiny $15 bottle. "What I mean," said Tim, "is I'd like to see something really cheap."

The clerk handed him a mirror.

A termite walks into a bar room and asks, "Is the bar tender here?"

PREGNANCY QUESTIONS:

Q: I'm two months pregnant now. When will my baby move?
A: With any luck, right after he finishes college.

Q: How will I know if my vomiting is morning sickness or the flu?
A: If it's the flu, you'll get better.

Q: What is the most reliable method to determine a baby's sex?
A: Childbirth.

Q: My wife is five months pregnant and so moody that sometimes she is borderline irrational.
A: So what's your question?

Q: How long is the average woman in labor?
A: Whatever she says divided by two.

Q: My childbirth instructor says it's not pain I'll feel during labor, but pressure. Is she right?
A: Yes, in the same way that a tornado might be called an air current.

Q: When is the best time to get an epidural?
A: Right after you find out you're pregnant.

Q: Is there any reason I have to be in the delivery room while my wife is in labor?
A: Not unless the word "alimony" means anything to you.

Q: Is there anything I should avoid while recovering from childbirth?
A: Yes, pregnancy.

Q: Does pregnancy cause hemorrhoids?
A: Pregnancy causes anything you want to blame it for.

Q: Do I have to have a baby shower?
A: Not if you change the baby's diaper very quickly.

Q: Our baby was born last week. When will my wife begin to feel and act normal again?
A: When the kids are in college.

A little girl was diligently pounding away on her father's computer. She told him she was writing a story.

"What's it about?" he asked.

"I don't know," she replied. "I can't read."

Three friends – two straight guys and a gay guy and their significant others were on a cruise. A tidal wave came up and swamped the ship; they all perished, and the next thing you know, they're all standing before St. Peter.

First came one of the straight guys and his wife. St. Peter shook his head sadly. "I can't let you in. You loved money too much. You loved it so much, you even married a woman named Penny."

Then came the second straight guy. "Sorry, can't let you in either. You loved food too much. You loved to eat so much, you even married a woman named Candy!"

The gay guy turned to his boyfriend and whispered nervously, "This isn't looking good, Dick."

During his surgical residency, the doctor was called out of a sound sleep to the emergency room. Unshaven and with bed head, he showed up with an equally rumpled medical student. In the ER they encountered the on-call medical resident and his student, both neatly attired in clean white lab coats.

The resident said to his student, "You can always tell the surgeons by their absolute disregard for appearance."

Two evenings later, the resident was at a banquet when called to the ER for yet another emergency.

He was stitching away – wearing a tuxedo – when he encountered that same medical resident. He looked at him and then said to his student, "Sure is sensitive to criticism, isn't he?"

A man leaves a bar, gets into his car and drives away. A mile down the road, he's stopped by a police officer. The officer walks up to the driver's side window holding a Breathalyzer and says, "Good evening sir. We're testing for drunk driving. Would you please blow into this machine?"

The man replies, "I'm sorry, I can't do that. I have asthma. If I blow in that machine, I will have an attack."

"In that case, I'm going to have to ask you to come back to the station for a blood test."

The man says, "I can't do that. I have anemia and if you stick a needle in me I will bleed to death."

The officer says, "Then you'll have to get out and walk five yards along this white line."

"Can't do that either," said the man.

The officer was getting irritated. "And why not?"

"Because I'm dead drunk."

At a banquet, a woman found herself seated next to a gentleman about her age, in his seventies. She stared at him until she had his attention.

Finally she said, "Please forgive me for staring at you like this, but I can't help it. You see, you look exactly like my third husband."

"Oh," he responded. "How many times have you been married?"

With a warm smile and a twinkle in her eye, she patted his hand and answered, "Twice."

What happens if you get a gigabyte?
It megahertz!

A small boy is sent to bed by his father. Five minutes later:
"Da-addy!"

"What?"

"I'm thirsty, Can you bring me a drink of water?"

"No, you had your chance. Lights out." Five minutes later . . . . .

"Da-addy!"

"WHAT?"

"I'm THIRSTY . . . . . Can I have a drink of water?"

"I told you NO! If you ask again I'll have to come up there and spank you." Five minutes later . . .

"Daaaaa-aaaaaady!"

"WHAT?"

"When you come in to spank me, can you bring me a drink of water?"

Girl: "When we get married, I want to share all your worries and troubles and lighten your burden."

Boy: "It's very kind of you, darling. But I don't have any worries or troubles."

Girl: "Well that's because we aren't married yet."

A traveling salesman knocked on a farmer's door and requested a place to sleep for the night.

"We're a little tight on space, so I'm going to have to put you in with my three sons."

"Oh, pardon me," said the salesman, "I must be in the wrong joke."

Taxiing down the tarmac, the jetliner abruptly stopped and returned to the gate. After an hour-long wait, it finally took off. A concerned passenger asked the flight attendant what the problem was.

"The pilot was bothered by a noise he heard in the engine. It took us a while to find a new pilot."

One night a grasshopper hops into a bar and the bartender turns to him and says, "Hi little fella, did you know that we serve a drink here that's named after you?"

The grasshopper looks at him with surprise and says, "You mean to say you have a drink named Irving?"

A state government employee sits in his office and out of boredom, decides to see what's in his old filing cabinet. He pokes through the contents and comes across an old brass lamp.

"This will look great on my mantelpiece," he decides and takes it home with him. While polishing the lamp, a genie appears and grants him three wishes.

"I wish for an ice cold beer right now!"

POOF! He gets his beer and drinks it. Now that he can think more clearly, he states his second wish.

"I wish to be on an island where beautiful nymphomaniacs reside."

POOF! Suddenly he is on an island with gorgeous women eyeing him lustfully. He tells the genie this third and last wish:

"I wish I'd never have to work again."

POOF! He's back in his government office.

One day a five-year-old girl excitedly approached her mother and announced that she had learned how you get a baby.

The mother was amused and said, "Oh really sweetie? Why don't you tell me all about it?"

The little girl explained, "Well, the mommy and daddy take off all their clothes and the daddy's wiener stands way up high and the mommy kneels on the floor and puts the daddy's wiener in her mouth and then the daddy's wiener sort of explodes and makes a sticky juice into the mommy's mouth and then the mommy swallows the sticky juice and that's how you get a baby."

The mother looked lovingly at her daughter, leaned over to meet her eye to eye and said, "Oh honey, that's sweet, but that's not how you get a baby. That's how you get jewelry."

Fifteen minutes into a flight, the pilot announced, "Ladies and gentlemen, one of our engines has failed. There is nothing to worry about. Out flight will take an hour longer than scheduled, but we still have three engines left."

Thirty minutes later the pilot announced, "One more engine has failed and the flight will take an additional 2 hours. But don't worry; we can fly just fine on two engines.

An hour later the pilot announced, "One more engine has failed and our arrival will be delayed another three hours. But don't worry, we still have one engine left."

The blonde in seat 17A turned to the man next to her and said, "If we lose one more engine, we'll be up here all day!"

A blind guy on a bar stool shouts to the bartender, "Wanna hear a blond joke?"

In a hushed voice, the guy sitting next to him says, "Before you tell that joke, you should know something. Our bartender is blond and the bouncer is blond. I'm a 6' tall, 200 pounds black belt. The guy sitting next to me is 6'2", weighs 225 and he's a rugby player. The fella to your right is 6'5", pushing 300 lbs. and he's a wrestler. Each one of us is blond. Think about it, mister. You still wanna tell that joke?"

The blind guy says, "No. Not if I'm gonna have to explain it five times."

A pregnant woman gets into a car accident and falls into a deep coma. Asleep for nearly six months, she wakes up and sees that she is no longer pregnant.

Frantically, she asks the doctor about her baby.

The doctor replies, "Ma'am, you had twins - a boy and a girl. The babies are fine. Your brother came in and named them."

The woman thinks to herself, "Oh no, not my brother – he's an idiot!" Expecting the worst, she asks the doctor, "Well, what's the girl's name?"

"Denise," the doctor says.

The new mother thinks, "Wow, that's not a bad name. Guess I was wrong about my brother. I like Denise." Then she asks the doctor, "What's the boy's name?

"Denephew."

T wo bowling teams, one of all blondes and one of all brunettes, charter a double-decker bus for a weekend gambling trip to Louisiana. The brunette team rode on the bottom of the bus, and the blonde team rode on the top level.

The brunette team down below really whooped it up, having a great time, when one of them realized she hadn't heard anything from the blondes upstairs. She decided to go up and investigate. When the brunette reached the top, she found all the blondes in fear, staring straight ahead at the road, clutching the seats in front of them with white knuckles.

The brunette asked, "What the heck's going on up here? We're having a great time downstairs!"

One of the blondes looked at her, swallowed hard and whispered, "Yeah, but you've got a driver!"

S am was driving down the road and gets pulled over by a policeman. Walking up to Sam's car, the policeman says, "Your wife fell out of the car 5 miles back."

"Thank God for that . . . I'd thought I'd gone deaf."

A husband and wife are lying in bed watching "Who wants to be a Millionaire." The husband turns to his wife and says, "Honey, do you wanna have sex?"

The wife replies, "Not tonight, I have a headache."

Husband: "Is that your final answer?"

Wife: "Final answer!"

Husband: "Can I phone a friend?"

Wife: "See the palm of your hand?"

Husband: "Yes."

Wife: "You use the phone, you'll lose THAT life line."

The Queen of England was visiting one of Canada's top hospitals and during her tour of the floors, she passed a room where a male patient was masturbating.

"Oh my God!" said the Queen, "That's disgraceful, what's the meaning of this?"

The doctor leading tour explains, "I'm sorry your ladyship, this man has very serious condition where his testicles rapidly fill with semen. If he doesn't do that five times a day, they would explode and he would most likely die instantly."

"Oh, I'm sorry," said the Queen.

On the next floor, they passed a room where a young nurse was giving a patient a blow job.

"Oh my God, what's happening in there?"

"Same problem, better health plan."

A highway patrolman pulled alongside a speeding car on the freeway. Glancing at the driver, he was astounded to see a blonde behind the wheel, knitting. Realizing that she was oblivious to his flashing lights and siren, the trooper cranked down his window, turned on his bullhorn and yelled:

"PULL OVER!"

"NO," the blonde yelled back. "IT'S A SCARF!"

There were these two old sisters, both virgins. It's Saturday night and Sadie looks at Molly and says, "I will not die a virgin. I'm going out and I'm not coming home until I've been laid."

Molly says, "Well make sure you're home by 10 so I don't worry about you." Ten o'clock rolls around and there is no sign of Sadie.

11 o'clock . . . . . 12 o'clock . . . . . and finally at 1:15, the front door flies open. In comes Sadie and she heads straight for the bathroom.

Molly knocks on the door. No answer so she opens the door and there sits Sadie with her panties around her ankles, legs wide apart and her head down between her legs looking at her privates.

"What's the matter, Sadie? What's wrong?"

"Molly, it was 10 inches long when it went in and 5 inches when it came out. When I find the other half, you're gonna have the time of your life."

In here we will speak proper English. There are two words I don't allow in my class," said the professor, "One is gross and the other is cool."

From the back of the room a voice called out, "So what are the words?"

Aging Aunt Mildred was 93 years old and was particularly despondent over the recent death of her husband. She decided she would just kill herself and join him in death. Thinking that it would be best to get it over with quickly, she took out his old Army pistol and made the decision to shoot herself in the heart since it was so badly broken in the first place.

Not wanting to miss the vital organ and become a vegetable and a burden to someone, she called her doctor's office to inquire as to just exactly where the heart would be.

"On a woman," the doctor said, "your heart would be just below your left breast."

Later that night, Mildred was admitted to the hospital with a gunshot wound to her left knee.

A very flat-chested woman entered an upscale department store and approached the saleslady in lingerie. "Do you have a size 28AA bra?"

The clerk said that she didn't, so the woman left the store and went to another department store where she met with the same results. She was becoming quite frustrated and finally decided to try K-Mart.

Marching up to the sales clerk, she unbuttoned and threw open her blouse and yelled, "Do you have anything for this?"

The clerk looked closely at her and replied, "Have you tried Clearasil?"

The orthopedic surgeon was moving to a new office and his staff was helping transport many of the items. One of his staff put the display skeleton in the front seat of her car with his bony arm across the back of the seat without realizing the impact to other drivers. At one traffic light the stares of the people in the cars next to her became obvious and she looked across and explained, "I'm delivering him to my doctor's office."

The other driver leaned out of his window. "I hate to tell you lady, but I think it's too late."

Two keys hang in a undertaker's office – one for the organ in the chapel; the other for one of the cars in the garage; two small signs above the keys read, "HYMN" and "HEARSE".

Sarah was reading a newspaper while her husband was engrossed in a magazine. Suddenly she burst out laughing.

"Listen to this," she said. "There's a classified ad here where a guy is offering to swap his wife for a season ticket to the stadium."

"Hmmmm," her husband said, not looking up from his reading.

Teasing him, Sarah said, "Would you swap me for a season ticket?"

"Absolutely not," he said.

"How sweet! Tell me why not."

"Season's more than half over," he said.

How come you're late today?" asked the bartender as the blonde waitress walked into the bar.

"It was awful," she explained. "I was walking down Elm Street and there was a terrible accident. A man was thrown from his car and he was lying in the middle of the street. His leg was broken, his skull was fractured, and there was blood everywhere. Thank God I took that first-aid course."

"Oh my God, what did you do?"

"I sat down and put my head between my knees to keep from fainting!"

A woman was in a casino for the first time. At the roulette wheel she says, "I have no idea what number to play."

A young, good-looking man nearby suggests she play her age. Smiling at the man, she puts her money down on number 32.

The wheel is spun, and the number 41 comes up.

The smile drifted from the woman's face and she fainted.

Toward the end of the senior year in high school, the students were required to take a CPR course. The classes used the well-known mannequin victim, Rescue Anne, to practice. The group's model was legless to allow for storage in a carrying case.

The class went off in groups to practice. As instructed, one the of classmates gently shook the doll and asked, "Are you all right?" He then put his ear over the mannequin's mouth to listen for breathing.

Suddenly, he turned to the instructor and exclaimed, "She said she can't feel her legs."

One day the sheriff sees Billy Bob walking down the street with nothing on except his boots. The sheriff says, "Billy Bob, what the hell are you doing walking around town dressed like that?"

Billy Bob replies, "Well, sheriff, me and Mary Lou was down on the farm and we started a-cuddlin.' Mary Lou said we should go in the barn, and we did. In the barn we started a-kissin' and a-cuddlin' and things got pretty hot and heavy. Well, then Mary Lou took off all her clothes and said that I should do the same. Well, I took off all my clothes except my boots. Then Mary Lou laid herself on the hay and said, 'Okay, Billy Bob, let's go to town!'"

"I guess I'm the first one here."

A Polish couple was delighted when their long wait to adopt a baby came to an end. The adoption agency called and told them that they had a wonderful Russian baby boy and the couple took him without hesitation.

On the way home from the adoption agency, they stopped by the local college to enroll in night courses. After they filled out the forms, the registration clerk inquired, "Whatever possessed you to study Russian?"

The couple proudly said, "We just adopted a Russian baby and in a year or so he'll start to talk. We just want to be able to understand him."

A bear walks into a bar in Billings, Montana and sits down. He bangs on the bar with his paw and demands a beer. The bartender approaches and says, "We don't serve beer to bears in bars in Billings."

The bear, becoming angry, demands again that he be served a beer. The bartender tells him again, more forcefully,

"We don't serve beer to belligerent bears in bars in Billings."

The bear, very angry now, says, "If you don't serve me a beer, I'm going to eat that lady sitting at the end of the bar."

"Sorry, we don't serve beer to belligerent, bully bears in bars in Billings."

The bear goes to the end of the bar, and as promised, eats the woman. He comes back to his seat and again demands a beer. The bartender states,

"Sorry, we don't serve beer to belligerent, bully bears in bars in Billings who are on drugs."

The bear says, "I'm not on drugs."

The bartender says, "You are now. That was a barbitchyouate."

A clever elderly woman decided to have her portrait painted. So she told the artist, "Paint me with diamond earrings, a diamond necklace, an emerald bracelet and a gold Rolex."

"But you're not wearing any of those things," the artist pointed out.

"I know," she said. "It's in case I die before my husband. If he remarries right away, I want his new wife to go crazy looking for the jewelry."

A 65-year-old man goes to his doctor and says, "Doc, I have a problem. My girlfriend is sleeping over on Friday, my ex-wife is sleeping over on Saturday and my wife is coming home on Sunday. I need 3 Viagra pills to satisfy them all."

The doctor says, "You know, 3 Viagra pills 3 nights in a row is pretty dangerous for a man of your age. I will give them to you on the condition that you return to my office on Monday so that I can check you out."

The man agrees and on Monday he returns to the doctor's office with his arm in a sling.

"What happened?" asked the doctor.

"Nobody showed up!"

A little old lady was going up and down the halls in the nursing home, flipping up the hem of her nightgown and saying, "Supersex! Supersex! She walked up to an elderly man in a wheelchair, flipped her gown at him and said, "Supersex!"

He sat silently for a moment or two looking up at her and finally said,

"I'll take the soup."

Two old women were sitting on a bench waiting for their bus. The buses were running late and a lot of time had passed.

Finally, one woman turned to the other and said, "You know, I've been sitting here so long, my butt fell asleep!"

The other woman turned to her and said, "I know! I heard it snoring!"

A retired gentleman went to the Social Security office to apply for benefits. The woman behind the counter asked him for his driver's license to verify his age. He looked in his pockets and realized he had left his wallet at home. He told the woman that he was very sorry and asked if he would have to come back another day.

The woman says, "Unbutton your shirt." He opens his shirt revealing lots of curly silver hair.

She says, "That silver hair on your chest is proof enough for me," and she goes ahead and processes his Social Security application.

When he gets home, the man tells his wife about what happened.

She said, "You should have dropped your pants. You might have qualified for disability too."

Heck is a place for people who don't believe in Gosh.

There was this Midwestern phone company that was going to hire one team of telephone pole installers and the boss had to choose between a team of blonds and a team of brown-haired guys.

So the boss said to both teams, "Here's what we'll do. Each team will be installing poles out on the new road. The team that installs the most poles gets the job."

Both teams headed right out. At the end of the shift, the brown-haired guys had installed 12 poles. When the blond team returned 45 minutes later, they were exhausted. But they had only installed three poles.

The boss gasped, "Three? The other team installed 12."

"Yeah," said the blond leader. "But you should see how much they left sticking out."

Two men go on a fishing trip. They rent all the equipment: the rods and reels, wading suits, rowboat, their car and even a cabin in the woods.

The first day they go fishing they don't catch anything. The same thing happens on the second day and everyday until finally on the last day of their vacation, one of the men catches a fish.

As they are driving home they are feeling really depressed. One guy turns to the other and says, "Do you realize that this one lousy fish we caught cost us fifteen hundred bucks?"

The other guy says, "Wow! Then it's a good thing we didn't catch any more."

NEW DRUGS FOR WOMEN

DAMNITOL – Take two and the rest of the world can go to hell for up to 8 full hours.

EMPTYNESTROGEN – Suppository that eliminates melancholy and loneliness by reminding you of how awful they were as teenagers and how you couldn't wait till they moved out.

ST. MOMMA'S WORT – Plant extract that treats mom's depression by rendering preschoolers unconscious for up to two days.

PEPTOBIMBO – Liquid silicone drink for single women. Two full cups swallowed before an evening out increases breast size, decreases intelligence, and prevents conception.

DUMBEROL – When taken with Pepto-bimbo, can cause dangerously low IQ, resulting in enjoyment of country music and pickup trucks.

FLIPITOR – Increases life expectancy of commuters by controlling road rage and the urge to flip off other drivers.

MENICILLIN – Potent anti-boy-otic for older women. Increases resistance to such lethal lines as, "You make me want to be a better person."

BUYAGRA – Injectable stimulant taken prior to shopping. Increases potency, duration, and credit limit of spending spree.

JACKASSPIRIN – Relieves headache caused by a man who can't remember your birthday, anniversary, phone number, or to lift the toilet seat.

ANTI-TALKSIDENT – A spray carried in a purse or wallet to be used on anyone too eager to share their life stories with total strangers in elevators.

NAGAMENT – When administered to a boyfriend or husband provides the same irritation level as nagging him.

During class, the chemistry professor was demonstrating the properties of various acids. "Now I'm dropping this silver coin into this glass of acid. Will it dissolve?"

"No, sir," a student called out.

"No?" queried the professor. "Perhaps you can explain why the silver coin won't dissolve."

"Because if it would, you wouldn't have dropped it in."

Vernon, where's your homework?" Miss Martin asked sternly.

"My dog ate it," was his solemn response.

"Vernon, I've been a teacher for eighteen years. Do you really expect me to believe that story?"

"It's true, Miss Martin, I swear," insisted the boy. "I had to force him, but he ate it."

Two elderly women were out driving in a large car, both barely able to see over the dashboard. As they were cruising along they came to an intersection. The stoplight was red but they just went on through. The woman in the passenger seat thought to herself, "I must be losing it. I could have sworn we just went through a red light."

She was getting nervous and decided to pay very close attention to the road and the next intersection to see what was going on.

Sure enough, at the next intersection the light was definitely red and they went right through it again. She turned to the other woman and said, "Mildred! Did you know we just ran through two red lights in a row? You could have killed us!"

Mildred turned to her and said, "Oh, am I driving?"

Ed arrives home some six hours late from his usual Saturday golf foursome. Edna, his wife, immediately lit into him, "You have some nerve leaving me home alone all day. I had to cancel dinner with our friends and send the babysitter home. You better have a good explanation."

Ed told Edna that their game was interrupted by the untimely death of Stan, one of their playing partners.

"Edna, honey, Stan died of a massive heart attack just as we were about to tee off on the second hole. If there's a silver lining, it's that he died doing what he loved best."

Saddened, Edna comforted her husband, "I'm so sorry. But tell me something," Edna asked with a note of anger returning to her voice. "If he died on the second tee, what took you so long?"

"Well," said Ed, "for the next 17 holes it was the same thing: Hit the ball and drag Stan, hit the ball and drag Stan."

A man walks into a drug store with his eight-year-old son. As they walk by a condom display, the boy asks, "What are these, Dad?" To which the man, matter-of-factly replies, "Those are called condoms, son. Men use them to have safe sex."

The young boy looks over the display and picks up a package of 3 condoms and asks, "Why are there 3 in this package?"

The dad replies, "Those are for high-school boys. One for Friday, one for Saturday and one for Sunday.'

"Cool!" says the boy. Then he notices a 6-pack and asks, "Then who are these for?"

"Those are for college men. Two for Friday, two for Saturday and two for Sunday."

"WOW!" exclaims the boy. "Then who uses THESE?" he asks, picking up a 12-pack.

With a sigh, the dad replies, "Those are for married men. One for January, one for February, one for . . . . . ."

Before going to Europe on business, a man drove his Rolls Royce to a downtown New York City bank and went in to ask for an immediate loan of $5,000. The loan officer requested collateral. So the man gave him the keys to his Rolls Royce. The loan officer had the car driven into the bank's underground garage for safekeeping and gave the man his money.

Two weeks later, the man walked back into the bank and asked to settle up his loan and get his car back. "That will be $5,000 in principal and $15.40 in interest." The man wrote a check and started to walk away.

"Wait, sir. While you were gone, I found out that your are a millionaire. Why in the world would you need to borrow $5,000?"

"Where else in Manhattan could I park my Rolls Royce for two weeks and pay only $15.40?"

An elderly married couple scheduled their annual medical examinations on the same day. Afterwards, the doctor said to the man, "You appear to be in good health. Do you have any medical concerns that you would like to discuss with me?"

"In fact I do. After I have sex with my wife for the first time, I am usually hot and sweaty. And then, after having sex with her the second time, I'm usually cold and chilly."

"This is very interesting," replied the doctor. "Let me do some research and get back to you."

After examining the elderly lady, the doctor said, "Everything appears to be fine. Do you have any medical concerns that you would like to discuss with me?"

The lady replied that she had none. Then the doctor asked, "Your husband had an unusual concern. He claims that he is usually hot and sweaty after having sex the first time with you and then cold and chilly after the second time. Do you know why?"

"Oh, that old buzzard! That's because the first time is usually in July and the second time is usually in December."

A woman walks into a drugstore and asks the pharmacist if he sells extra large condoms.

He replies, "Yes we do. Would you like to buy some?"

"No sir, but do you mind if I wait around here until someone does?"

As a man was driving down the freeway, his car phone rang. Answering, he heard his wife's voice urgently warning him, "Herman, I just heard on the news that there's a car going the wrong way on Interstate 480. Please be careful."

"Geez," said Herman. "It's not just one car. It's hundreds of them."

A man returns from the Middle East feeling very ill. He goes to see his doctor who immediately rushes the man to the hospital to undergo tests. After the tests are completed, the man wakes up to the ringing of the telephone in his private room at the hospital. On the other end of the line, the doctor explains,

"We've received the results back from your tests and found that you have an extremely nasty STD called G.A.S.H., which is a combination of gonorrhea, AIDS, syphilis and herpes."

"Oh my God," cries the man. "Doc, what am I going to do?"

"Well, we're going to put you an a diet of pizza, pancakes and pita bread."

"Will that cure me?"

"Well no, but it's the only food we can get under the door."

An elderly woman entered a large furniture store and was greeted by a salesman. "Is there something in particular I can show you?" he asked.

"Yes, I want to buy a sexual sofa."
"You mean a sectional sofa?"
"No! All I want is an occasional piece in the living room."

A man was sitting in his seat on an airplane waiting for take-off. Imagine his surprise when the Pope sat down in the seat next to him. Still, the man was too shy to speak to the Pope. Shortly after take-off the Pope began a crossword puzzle.

"This is fantastic," thought the man. "I'm really good at crosswords. Perhaps, if the Pope gets stuck, he'll ask me for assistance."

Almost immediately, the Pope turned to him and said, "Excuse me, but do you know a four letter word that ends in 'unt' and refers to a woman?

Only one word leapt to the man's mind – a vulgar one. "I can't tell the Pope that," he thought. There must be another." Then it hit him.

He turned to the Pope and said. "I think you're looking for the word 'aunt.'"

"Of course!" exclaimed the Pope. "I don't suppose you happen to have an eraser?"

A farmer got pulled over by a state trooper for speeding, and the trooper started to lecture the farmer about his speed and in general began to throw his weight around to try and make the farmer uncomfortable. Finally, the trooper got around to writing out the ticket but kept having to swat at some flies that were buzzing around his head.

The farmer said, "Having some problems with circle flies there, are ya?"

The trooper stopped writing the ticket and said, "Well, yeah, if that's what they are. I've never heard of circle flies."

So the farmer says, "Well, circle flies are common on farms. See, they're called circle flies because they're almost always found circling around the back end of a horse."

The trooper says, "Oh," then he stops and says, "Hey, wait a minute, are you trying to call me a horse's ass?"

The farmer says, "Oh no, officer. I have too much respect for the law and police officers to even think about calling you a horse's ass."

The trooper says, "Well, that's a good thing," and goes back to writing the ticket.

After a long pause, the farmer says, "Hard to fool them flies, though."

A nd on the sixth day, God created the platypus.
And God said, "Let's see the evolutionists try and figure this one out."

S am and Bessie are senior citizens and Sam always wanted an expensive pair of alligator cowboy boots. Seeing some on sale, he buys a pair and wears them home, and asks Bessie if she notices anything different about him.

"What's different? It's the same shirt you wore yesterday and the same pants. What's different?"

Frustrated, Sam goes into the bathroom, undresses and comes out completely naked, wearing only his new boots. Again he asks Bessie if she notices anything different.

"What's different, Sam? It's hanging down today; it was hanging down yesterday and it will be hanging down tomorrow."

Angrily, Sam yells, "Do you know why it's hanging down? 'Cause it's looking at my new boots!!!"

Bessie replies, "You shoulda bought a hat!"

I t was an elegant dinner party and the hostess had left nothing to chance, except that a little water had splashed on the marble floor. When the waiter came into the dining room carrying the beautiful roast suckling pig, he slipped and fell flat, sending the roast flying.

"Don't worry, Charles," said the hostess calmly. "Just take the roast back to the kitchen and bring out the other one."

HOW TO INSTALL A HOME SECURITY SYSTEM

1. Go to a second-hand store and buy a pair of men's used size 14-16 work boots.

2. Place them on your front porch, along with several empty beer cans, a copy of Guns & Ammo magazine and several NRA magazines.

3. Put a few giant dog dishes next to the boots and magazines.

4. Leave a note on your door that reads:

Hey Bubba, Big Jim, Duke and Slim, I went to the gun shop for more ammunition. Back in an hour. Don't mess with the pit bulls -- they attacked the mailman this morning and messed him up real bad. I don't think Killer took part in it, but it was hard to tell from all the blood.

PS - I locked all four of 'em in the house. Better wait outside.

An Irishman, an Italian and a Polish guy are in a bar. They are having a good time and all agree that the bar is a nice place.

Then the Irishman says, "Aye, this is a nice bar, but where I come from, back in Dublin, there's a better one. At MacDougal's, you buy a drink, you buy another drink, and MacDougal himself will buy your third drink."

Then the Italian says, "Yeah, that's a nice bar, but where I come from there's an even better one. Over in Brooklyn, there's this place, Vinny's. You buy a drink, Vinny buys you a drink. You buy anudda drink, Vinny buys you anudda drink."

Then the Polish guy says, "You think that's great? Where I come from, there's this place called Warshowski's. At Warshowski's, they buy you your first drink, they buy you your second drink, they buy you your third drink and then they take you in the back and get you laid."

"Wow!" says the other two. "That's fantastic! Did that actually happen to you?"

"No," replies the Polish guy, "but it happened to my sister."

A seaman meets a pirate in a bar. The pirate has a peg leg, a hook and an eye patch. "How'd you end up with a peg leg?" asks the sailor.

"I was swept overboard in a storm. A shark bit off me whole leg."

"Wow! said the seaman, "What about the hook?"

"We were boarding an enemy ship, battling the other sailors with swords. One of them cut me hand clean off."

"Incredible!" remarked the seaman. "And the eye patch?"

"A seagull dropping fell in me eye."

"You lost your eye to a seagull dropping?"

"It was me first day with me hook."

A young girl was about to go out on her first date and she was talking to her grandmother about it.

The grandmother says, "Sit here and let me tell you about those young boys. He is going to try to kiss you; you are going to like it, but don't let him do that."

"He is going to try to feel your breast, you are going to like it, but don't let him do that."

"He is going to try to put his hand between your legs, you are going to like it, but don't let him do that."

"But most important, he is going to try to get on top of you and have his way with you. You are going to like it, but don't let him do that. It will disgrace the family."

With that bit of advice, the granddaughter went on her date and could not wait to tell her grandmother about it. The next day she told her grandmother that her date went just like she said.

"But," she said, "Grandmother, I didn't let him disgrace the family. When he tried, I turned over, got on top of him and disgraced his family."

A blonde and a brunette are walking down the street and the brunette spots her boyfriend in a flower shop. She sighs and says, "Oh shit, my boyfriend is buying me flowers again . . . for no reason."

The blonde looks quizzically at her and says, "What's the big deal? Don't you like getting flowers?"

The brunette says, "Oh sure . . . but he always has expectations after getting me flowers and I just don't feel like spending the next three days on my back with my legs in the air."

The blonde says, "Don't you have a vase?"

A 54-year-old accountant leaves a letter for his wife on Friday that reads:

Dear Wife (that's what he called her):

I am 54, and by the time you receive this letter I will be at the Grand Hotel with my beautiful and sexy 18-year-old secretary.

When he arrived at the hotel there was a letter waiting for him that read as follows:

Dear Husband:

I too am 54, and by the time you receive this letter I will be at the Breakwater Hotel with my handsome and virile 18-year-old boy toy. You being an accountant will therefore appreciate the fact that 18 goes into 54 many more times than 54 goes into 18.

I watched my wife's routine at breakfast. She made lots of trips to the refrigerator, stove, table and cabinets, often carrying just a single item at a time. I suggested carrying several things at once in order to save time."

"Did it save time?"

"Actually, yes. It used to take her twenty minutes to get breakfast ready. Now I do it in seven."

B ill and Marla had a small apartment in the city and they decided that the only way to pull off a Saturday afternoon quickie with their 10-year-old son home was to send him out onto the balcony and order him to report on all the neighborhood activities. To a young boy, spying would be a lot of fun and would distract him for an hour or so.

The boy began his commentary as his parents put their plan into operation.

"There's a car being towed from the parking lot," he said. "An ambulance just drove by." A few moments passed. "Looks like the Andersons have company. Matt's riding a new bike and the Coopers are having sex."

Mom and Dad sat up in bed. "How do you know that?" the startled father asked.

"Their kid is standing out on the balcony too."

A panda bear walks into a bar, sits on a stool and starts munching on some peanuts. He finishes the bowl and pulls out a gun. He shoots the guy sitting beside him and starts to make for the door.

"Why'd you do that?" the bartender asks, stunned.

"Look 'Panda' up in the encyclopedia," the bear answers as he walks out the door and starts down the street.

Puzzled, the bartender shakes his head and goes back to work. Later that night when the he gets home, he looks in his encyclopedia and is startled by what he sees:

PANDA: A wild animal that eats shoots and leaves."

A doctor who specialized in circumcisions was retiring after 30 years. The nurses had been saving the foreskins from the last 50 circumcisions and had a wallet made out of them. This was presented to the doctor at his retirement party. He said, "Is this all I get after 30 years of service?"

The head nurse replied, "Stroke it – it will turn into a suitcase!"

Sitting on the side of the highway waiting to catch speeding drivers, a state trooper sees a car puttering along at 22 mph. He thinks to himself, "This driver is just as dangerous as a speeder." So he turns on his lights and pulls the driver over.

Approaching the car, he notices that there are five old ladies – two in the front seat and three in the back, wide-eyed and white as ghosts. The driver, obviously confused, says to him, "Officer, I don't understand. I was doing exactly the speed limit. What seems to be the problem?"

"Ma'am, you weren't speeding, but you should know that driving slower than the speed limit can also be a danger to other drivers."

"Slower than the speed limit? No Sir, I was doing the speed limit - exactly 22 miles per hour."

The state trooper, trying to contain a chuckle, explained to her that 22 was the route number, not the speed limit.

A bit embarrassed, the woman grinned and thanked the officer for pointing out her error.

"But before I let you go, ma'am, I have to ask, is everyone in this car OK? These women seem awfully shaken and they haven't muttered a single peep this whole time."

"Oh, they'll be all right in a minute, officer. We just got off Route 119."

A pipe burst in the lawyer's house, so he called a plumber. The plumber arrived, unpacked his tools, did mysterious plumber type things for a while, and handed the lawyer a bill for $600.

The lawyer exclaimed, "This is ridiculous! I don't even make that much and I'm a lawyer!"

The plumber quietly replied, "Neither did I, when I was a lawyer."

It is pouring rain in the Mississippi Valley and the rising river begins to threaten all manner of private homes, including that of the local priest. With the water coming into the ground floor, a rowboat with police comes by and the officer shouts, "Father, let us evacuate you! The water level is getting dangerous." The priest replies, "No thank you. I am a righteous man, who trusts in the Almighty, and I am confident He will deliver me."

Three hours go by and the rains intensify, at which point the priest is forced up to the second floor. A second police rowboat comes by and tries to convince the priest to evacuate. Again the Priest refuses saying that he is a righteous man, who trusts in the Almighty and is confident that he will be saved.

The rain does not stop and the priest is forced onto the roof of his house. A helicopter flies over and the officer shouts down, "Father, grab onto the rope and we'll pull you up! You're in terrible danger!"

The priest replies, "No thank you, I am a righteous man, who trusts in the Almighty, and I am confident He will deliver me."

The deluge continues and the priest is swept off the roof, is carried away by the current and drowns. He goes up to heaven and at the Pearly Gates he is admitted and comes before the Divine Presence.

The priest says, "Dear Lord, I don't understand. I've been a righteous observant person my whole life and depended on you to save me in my hour of need. Where were you?"

The Lord answered, "I sent two boats and a helicopter. What more do you want?"

Two buddies were in a bar, drinking and discussing their wives. "Do you and your wife ever do it doggie style?"

"Well, not exactly. She's more into the trick dog aspect of it."

"Oh? What do you mean?"

"I sit up and beg and she rolls over and plays dead."

A husband and wife, both in their eighties, were sitting on the couch watching the Playboy channel on TV. He looked at her and asked, "Do you think we can still do that?"

"Well, we can sure try!" she answered.

So they shuffled off to the bedroom. He went into the bathroom to get ready and she took off all her clothes in the bedroom. When he came out of the bathroom, he saw her standing on her head in the middle of the bedroom floor.

"What are you doing, sweetheart?" he asked.

"Well, I thought if you couldn't get it up, maybe you could just drop it in!"

A mother was walking past her daughter's bedroom when she heard a humming sound. When she opened the door she found her daughter naked on the bed with a vibrator.

"What are you doing?"

"I'm 35 and still living at home with my parents, and this is the closest I'll ever get to a husband."

Later that week the father was in the kitchen and heard a humming sound coming from the basement. When he went downstairs he found his daughter naked on the sofa with her vibrator.

"What are you doing?

"I'm 35 and still living at home with my parents, and this is the closest I'll ever get to a husband."

A couple of days later the mother heard the humming sound again, this time coming from the living room. Upon entering the room she found her husband watching television with the vibrator buzzing away beside him.

"What are you doing?" she asked.

"Watching the game with my son-in-law," he said.

An Irishman, a Mexican and a redneck were doing construction on scaffolding on the 20th floor of a building. They were eating lunch and the Irishman said, "Corned beef and cabbage. If I get corned beef and cabbage one more time for lunch, I'm going to jump off this building."

The Mexican opened his lunch box and exclaimed, "Burritos again! If I get burritos one more time, I'm going to jump off too."

The redneck opened his lunch and said, "Bologna again! If I get a bologna sandwich one more time, I'm jumping too."

Next day the Irishman opens his lunch box, sees corned beef and cabbage and jumps to his death. The Mexican opens his lunch box, sees a burrito and jumps, too. The redneck opens his lunch, sees a bologna sandwich and jumps to his death, too.

At the funeral, the Irishman's wife is weeping. She said, "If I'd known how really tired he was of corned beef and cabbage, I never would have given it to him again."

The Mexican's wife also weeps and says, "I could have given him tacos or enchiladas. I didn't realize he hated burritos so much."

Everyone turned and stared at the redneck's wife.

"Hey, don't look at me! That dumb-ass made his own lunch!"

A businessman boarded a plane to find, sitting next to him, an elegant woman wearing the largest, most stunning diamond ring he had ever seen.

He asked her about it.

"This is the Klopman diamond," she said. "It is beautiful, but there is a terrible curse that goes with it."

"What's the curse?" the man asks.

"Mr. Klopman."

John invited his mother over for dinner. During the meal, his mother couldn't help noticing how beautiful John's roommate, Julie, was. She had long been suspicious of a relationship between them and this only made her more curious.

Over the course of the evening, while watching the two interact, she started to wonder if there was more between John and Julie than met the eye. Reading this mom's thoughts, John volunteered, "I know what you must be thinking, but I assure you, Julie and I are just roommates."

About a week later, Julie came to John and said, ""Ever since your mother came to dinner, I can't find the beautiful silver gravy ladle. You don't suppose she took it, do you?"

John said, "Well, I doubt it, but I'll write her a letter just to be sure."

So he sat down and wrote, "Dear Mother, I'm not saying you 'did' take a gravy ladle from my house, and I'm not saying you 'did not' take a gravy ladle. But the fact remains that one has been missing ever since you were here for dinner. Love, John"

Several days later, John received a letter from his mother that read,

"Dear Son, I'm not saying that you 'do' sleep with Julie, and I'm not saying that you 'do not' sleep with Julie. But the fact remains that if she was sleeping in her own bed, she would have found the gravy ladle by now. Love, Mom"

A man walks into a bar. "Gimme a double before the shit hits the fan." A few minutes later, the same thing. "Gimme a beer before the shit hits the fan." This goes on for an hour or so.

Finally, the bartender goes up to him and says, "Listen buddy, maybe you should settle up before you get another drink."

"Oops, the shit just hit the fan."

A man stumbles up to the only other patron in a bar and asks if he could buy him a drink.

"Why of course," comes the reply. "Where you from?"

"I'm from Ireland," replies the second man.

The first man responds: "You don't say. I'm from Ireland, too. Let's have another round to Ireland."

Curious, the first man then asks, "Where in Ireland are you from?"

"Dublin."

"I can't believe it! I'm from Dublin too! Let's have another drink to Dublin."

Curiosity again strikes and the first man asks, "What school did you go to?"

"Saint Mary's. I graduated in '62."

"This is unbelievable! I went to Saint Mary's and graduated in '62 too!"

About that time, in comes one of the regulars and sits down at the bar.

"What's been going on?" he asks the bartender.

"Nothing much. The O'Malley twins are drunk again."

As an inspirational measure, the Boss had placed a sign in the restroom directly above the sink. It had a single word on it – "THINK!"

The next day when he went into the restroom, he looked at the sign and noticed that right below it, above the soap dispenser, someone had carefully lettered another sign, which read, "THOAP!"

Chemistry teacher: "What is the formula for water?"
Little Johnny: "H-I-J-K-L-M-N-O."
Chemistry teacher: "Why would you give a silly answer like that?"
Little Johnny: "You said it was H to O!"

An 80-year-old man is having his annual check-up. The doctor asks him how he's feeling.

"I've never been better! I've got an eighteen-year-old bride who's pregnant with my child. What do you think about that?"

The doctor considers this for a moment and says, "Well, let me tell you a story. I know a guy who's an avid hunter. He never misses a season. But one day he's in a hurry and accidentally grabs his umbrella instead of his gun. He's out walking in the woods near a creek and suddenly spots a beaver in some brush in front of him. He raises his umbrella, points it at the beaver and squeezes the handle. BAM! The beaver drops dead in front of him."

"That's impossible!" said the old man in disbelief, "Someone else must have shot that beaver."

"Exactly my point," said the doctor.

Tired of asking for Coke and being told all they have is Pepsi, and visa versa, a man thinks of a way to make life easier.

So one day at a snack bar he asked for a dark, carbonated beverage.

The young man behind the counter chuckled and asked the man, "Would you like a cylindrical plastic sucking device with that?"

What's the usual tip?" a man growled when the college boy delivered his pizza.

"Well," the student said, "this is my first delivery, but the other guys said that if I got a quarter out of you, I'd be doing great."

"That so?" grunted the man. "In that case, here's five dollars."

"Thanks, I'll put this in my college fund."

"By the way, what are you studying?"

"Applied psychology."

A man takes his wife to the stock show. They start heading down the alley that has the bulls. They come up to the first bull and his sign states: "This bull mated 50 times last year." The wife turns to her husband and says, "He mated 50 times in a year. You could learn from him."

They proceed to the next bull and his sign states, "This bull mated 65 times last year." The wife says to her husband, "That's over 5 times a month. You can learn from this one, too."

When they reach the last bull, his sign says: "This bull mated 365 times last year." The wife's mouth drops open and she says, "WOW! That's ONCE A DAY!!! You could really learn from this one!"

The man, finally fed up with the nagging, turns to his wife and says, "Go up and ask if it was 365 times with the same cow?"

A keen country lad applied for a salesman's job at a city department store. In fact, it was the biggest store in the world – you could get anything there.

The boss asked him, "Have you ever been a salesman before?"

"Yes, I was a salesman in the country," said the lad.

The boss liked the cut of him and said, "You can start tomorrow and I'll come and see you when we close up." The day was long and arduous for the young man, but finally 5:00 came around. The boss showed up as promised and asked, "How many sales did you make today?"

"One," said the young salesman.

"Only one?" blurted the boss. "Most of my staff makes 20 or 30 sales a day. How much was the sale worth?"

"Three hundred thousand, four hundred and sixty four dollars," said the young man.

"How did you manage that?" asked the flabbergasted boss.

"Well, this man came in and I sold him a small fish hook, then a medium hook and finally a really large hook. Then I sold him a small fishing line, a medium one and then a huge one. I asked him where he was going fishing and he said down the coast. I said he would probably need a boat, so I took him down to the boat department and sold him that twenty-foot schooner with the twin engines. Then he said his Volkswagen probably wouldn't be able to pull it, so I took him to the car department and sold him a new Deluxe Cruiser.

The boss took two steps back and asked in astonishment, "You sold all that to a guy who came in for a fish hook?"

"No . . . . . he came in to buy a box of tampons for his wife and I said to him, 'Your weekend's shot, you may as well go fishing.'"

A blind man is walking down the street with his seeing-eye dog. They come to a busy intersection and the dog, ignoring the high volume of traffic zooming by on the street, leads the blind man right out into the thick of traffic. This is followed by the screech of tires and the blaring of horns as panicked drivers try desperately not to run the pair down.

The blind man and the dog finally reach the safety of the other side of the street and he pulls a cookie out of his coat and offers it to his dog. A passerby, having observed this whole incident, can't control his amazement and says to the blind man, "Why on earth are you rewarding your dog with a cookie? He nearly got you killed!"

The blind man turns in his direction and replies, "To find out where his head is, so I can kick his ass!"

The manager of a large office noticed a new man one day and told him to come into his office. "What's your name?"

"John," the new guy replied.

The manager scowled, "Look, I don't know what kind of an office you worked at before, but I don't call anyone by their first name. It breeds familiarity and that leads to a breakdown in authority. I refer to my employees by their last names only: Smith, Jones, Baker. I am to be referred to only as Mr. Robertson. Now that we got that straight, what is your last name?"

"Darling. My name is John Darling."

"OK, John, the next thing I want to tell you is . . . . ."

Paddy was driving down the street in a sweat because he had an important meeting and couldn't find a parking place. Looking up to heaven he said, "Lord, take pity on me. If you find me a parking place I will go to Mass every Sunday for the rest of me life and give up me Irish whiskey!"

Miraculously, a parking place appeared. Paddy looked up again and said, "Never mind, I found one."

Nine-year-old Joey was asked by his mother what he had learned in Sunday school:

"Well, Mom, our teacher told us how God sent Moses behind enemy lines on a rescue mission to lead the Israelites out of Egypt. When he got to the Red Sea, he had his engineers build a pontoon bridge, and all the people walked across safely. He used his walkie-talkie to radio headquarters and call in an air strike. They sent in bombers to blow up the bridge and all the Israelites were saved."

"Now, Joey, is that REALLY what your teacher taught you?"

"Well, no, but if I told it the way the teacher did, you'd never believe it."

A guy hears a knocking on his door. He opens it up and no one is there. He looks all around and finally sees a little snail sitting on his doormat. He picks it up and throws it into a field across the street.

Ten years go by and one day he hears a knocking on his door. He opens it up and no one is there. He looks all around and finally sees a little snail sitting on the doormat.

The snail says, "What was that all about?"

John was a clerk in a small drug store but he was not much of a salesman. He could never find the item the customer wanted. Bob, the owner, had about enough and warned John that the next sale he missed would be his last. Just then a man came in coughing and asked John for their best cough syrup. Try as he might, John couldn't find the cough syrup. Remembering Bob's warning, he sold the man a box of Ex-Lax and told him to take it all at once.

The customer did as John said and then walked outside and leaned against a lamp post. Bob had seen the whole thing and come over to ask John what had transpired.

"He wanted something for his cough but I couldn't find cough syrup. I substituted Ex-Lax and told him to take it all at once," John explained.

"Ex-Lax won't cure a cough," Bob shouted angrily.

"Sure it will," John said and pointed at the man leaning against the lamp post. "Look at him. He's afraid to cough."

So tell me," asked the interviewer, "have you any other skills?"

"Actually, yes," said the applicant. "Last year I had two short stories published in national magazines and I finished my novel."

"Very impressive, but I was thinking of skills you could apply during office hours."

The applicant explained brightly, "Oh, that was during office hours."

A film crew was on location deep in the desert. One day an old Indian went up to the director and said, "Tomorrow rain." The next day it rained.

A week later, the Indian went up to the director and said, "Tomorrow storm." The next day there was a hailstorm.

"This Indian is incredible," said the director. The told his secretary to hire the Indian to predict the weather for the remainder of the shoot. However, after several successful predictions, the old Indian didn't show up for two weeks.

Finally the director sent for him. "I have to shoot a big scene tomorrow and I'm depending on you. What will the weather be like?"

The Indian shrugged his shoulders and said, "Don't know. My radio is broken."

Some great things about getting older . . . . .
- You get to eat dinner at 4:00
- Your investment in health insurance is finally beginning to pay off
- Kidnappers are not very interested in you
- It's harder and harder for sexual harassment charges to stick
- People no longer view you as a hypochondriac
- Your secrets are safe with friends because they can't remember them
- Your supply of brain cells is finally down to a manageable size
- Your eyes won't get much worse
- Adult diapers are actually kind of convenient
- Things you buy now won't wear out
- No one expects you to run into a burning building
- There's nothing left to learn the hard way
- Your joints are more accurate than the National Weather Service
- In a hostage situation you are likely to be released first
- If you've never smoked, you can start now and it won't have time to hurt you

Finding little Andy making faces at others on the playground, Ms. Smith stopped to gently reprove the child.

Smiling sweetly the teacher said, "When I was a child, I was told if I made ugly faces I would stay like that."

Andy looked up and replied, "Well, you can't say you weren't warned."

At age 4, success is not peeing in your pants.
At age 12, success is having friends.
At age 20, success is getting laid.
At age 35, success is making money.
At age 60, success is getting laid.
At age 70, success is having friends.
At age 80, success is not peeing in your pants.

Johnny went to visit the priest to give a confession. "Bless me, Father, for I have sinned. I have been with a loose girl."

"Is that you, little Johnny Parisi?" the priest asked.
"Yes, Father, it is," Johnny replied.
"And who was the girl you were with?" the priest asked.
"I can't tell you, Father. I don't want to ruin her reputation."

"Well, Johnny, I'm sure to find out her name sooner or later, so you may as well tell me now. Was it Tina Minetti?"
"I cannot say."
"Was it Teresa Volpe?"
"I'll never tell."
"Was it Nina Capelli?"
"I'm sorry, but I cannot name her."
"Was it Cathy Piriano?"
"My lips are sealed."
"Was it Rosa DiAngelo then?"
"Please, Father, I cannot tell you."

The priest sighed in frustration. "You're very tight lipped, Johnny Parisi, and I admire that. But you've sinned and have to atone. You cannot be an altar boy for four months. Now you go and behave yourself."

Johnny walked back to the pew. His friend Nino leaned over and whispered, "What'd you get?"

Johnny turned to him and whispered back, "Four months of vacation and five good leads."

Doctor, I have an earache."

2000 B.C.   "Here, eat this root."
1000 B.C.   "That root is heathen, say this prayer."
1850 A.D.   "That prayer is superstition, drink this potion."
1940 A.D.   "That potion is snake oil, swallow this pill."
1985 A.D.   "That pill is ineffective, take this antibiotic."
2000 A.D.   "That antibiotic is artificial. Here, eat this root."

This poor man had a mother-in-law from hell. Whenever she saw him she would hiss at him, "If you don't treat my daughter right, when I die I'll dig up from my grave and haunt you."

Well, the old lady finally died and a friend asked him, "Aren't you worried about her ominous threat?"

"Hell no! I had her buried face down. Let her dig!!!"

After submitting to X-rays, electrocardiograms and blood tests, the anxious patient waited for his doctor's opinion.

"Howard," the physician began, "I have good news and bad news."

"What's the good news?"

"My son has been accepted to the Harvard School of Medicine."

"And the bad news?"

"You're going to pay for it."

One day while jogging, a man noticed two tennis balls lying on the grass next to the sidewalk. He picked them up, put them in his pocket and proceeded on his way.

While waiting at the cross walk for the light to change, there was a beautiful blonde standing next to him.

"What are those big bulges in your running shorts?" she asked.

"Tennis balls."

"Wow," said the blonde looking upset. "That must hurt. I once had tennis elbow and the pain was unbearable."

Two Kansas farmers, Jim and Bob, are sitting at their favorite bar, drinking beer. Jim turns to Bob and says, "You know, I'm tired of going through life without an education. Tomorrow I think I'll go to the community college and sign up for some classes."

Bob thinks it's a good idea, and the two leave. The next day, Jim goes down to the college and meets the dean of admissions, who signs him up for the four basic classes: Math, English, History, and Logic.

"Logic?" Jim says. "What's that?"

The dean says, "I'll give you an example. Do you own a weed eater?"

"Yeah."

"Then logically speaking, because you own a weed eater, I think that you would have a yard."

"That's true, I do have a yard."

"I'm not done," the dean says. "Because you have a yard, I think logically that you would have a house."

"Yes, I do have a house."

"And because you have a house, I think that you might logically have a family."

"Yes, I have a family."

"I'm not done yet. Because you have a family, then logically you must have a wife. And because you have a wife, then logic tells me you must be a heterosexual."

"I am a heterosexual. That's amazing; you were able to find out all of that because I have a weed eater."

Excited to take the class now, Jim shakes the Dean's hand and leaves to go meet Bob at the bar. He tells Bob about his classes, how he is signed up for Math, English, History, and Logic.

"Logic?" Bob says, "What's that?"

Jim says, "I'll give you an example. Do you have a weed eater?"

"No."

"Then you're a queer."

Three women, two younger and one senior citizen, were sitting naked in a sauna. Suddenly there was a beeping sound. The young woman pressed her forearm and the beep stopped.

The others looked at her. "That was my pager," she said. "I have a microchip under the skin of my arm."

A few minutes later a phone rang. The second young woman lifted her palm to her ear. When she finished, she explained, "That was my mobile phone. I have a microchip in my hand."

The older woman felt very low-tech, and not to be outdone, she decided she had to do something just as impressive. She stepped out of the sauna and went to the bathroom.

She returned with a piece of toilet paper hanging from her rear end. The others raised their eyebrows and stared at her.

The older woman finally said, "Well, will you look at that . . . I'M GETTING A FAX!"

At a pharmacy, a blonde asked to use the infant scale to weigh the baby she held in her arms.

The clerk explained that the device was out for repairs, but said that she would figure the infant's weight by weighing the woman and baby together on the adult scale, then weighing the mother alone and subtracting the second amount from the first.

"That won't work," countered the blonde. "I'm not the mother, I'm the aunt."

Father Flanagan was visiting the nunnery to deliver some mail to the head nun, when he saw sister Margaret, whose stomach was a little bit bigger than usual.

"Is there something wrong with your stomach?" he asked.

"No," she replied, "it's just a little stomach gas."

A few weeks later, he visited again, and her stomach was even bigger. "Are you sure it's only gas?" he asked.

"Yes," she replied, "I'll get over it soon."

A few months later, Father Flanagan visited the nunnery, and saw Sister Margaret pushing a baby carriage.

Leaning over it, he said, "Cute little fart."

Alice and Frank are bungee jumping one day. Alice says to Frank, "You know, we could make a lot of money running our own bungee-jumping business in Mexico."

Frank thinks this is a great idea, so they pool their money and buy everything they need: a tower, an elastic cord, insurance, etc. They travel to Mexico and begin to set up on the square. As they are constructing the tower, a crowd begins to assemble. Slowly, more and more people gather to watch them at work. When they had finished, there was such a crowd they thought it would be a good idea to give a demonstration.

So, Alice jumps. She bounces at the end of the cord, but when she comes back up, Frank notices that she has a few cuts and scratches. Unfortunately, Frank isn't able to catch her and she falls again, bounces, and comes back up again. This time, she is bruised and bleeding. Again, Frank misses her. Alice falls again and bounces back up. This time, she comes back pretty messed up -- she's got a couple of broken bones and is almost unconscious. Luckily, Frank finally catches her this time and asks, "What happened? Was the cord too long?"

Barely able to speak, Alice gasps, "No, the bungee cord was fine. It was the crowd. What the hell is a piñata?!"

*A*n Amish woman and her daughter were riding in an old buggy one cold, blustery wintry day. The daughter said to her mother, "My hands are freezing cold."

The mother replied, "Put your hands between your legs. The body heat will warm them up." So the daughter did and her hands warmed up.

The next day the daughter was riding with her boyfriend, and he said, "My hands are freezing cold."

The girl replied, "Put them between my legs. They'll warm up."

Later that week the boyfriend was again driving the buggy with the daughter. He said, "My nose is freezing cold."

"Put it between my legs and it will warm up," she told him. He did, and his nose warmed up.

The next day while driving the buggy with the daughter, the boyfriend said, "My penis is frozen solid."

Later that same day, the daughter is driving the buggy with her mother when she says, "Mother, have you ever heard of a penis?"

The slightly concerned mother says, "Sure, why do you ask?"

The daughter says, "Well, they make one hell of a mess when they defrost."

*T*wo daughters had been given parts in the Christmas pageant at their church and they got into an argument as to who had the most important role. Finally the 10 year old said to her younger sister. "Well, you just ask Mom. She'll tell you that it's much harder to be a virgin than it is to be an angel."

A wife and her husband were having a dinner party for some very important guests. The wife was very excited and wanted everything to be perfect. At the very last minute she realized that she didn't have any snails to serve, so she asked her husband to run down to the beach with the bucket to gather some snails.

Very grudgingly he agreed, took the bucket, walked out the door, down the steps and out to the beach. As he was collecting the snails he noticed a beautiful woman strolling along side the water. He thought to himself, "Wouldn't it be great if she came over and talked to me?" and went back to collecting snails. When he looked up the woman was standing right over him. They started talking and she invited him back to her place. They ended up spending the night together.

At seven o'clock the next morning, he woke up and exclaimed, "Oh no! My wife's dinner party!" He got dressed, grabbed his bucket and ran out the door. He ran down the beach all the way to his apartment. He ran up the stairs of his apartment. He was in such a hurry that when he got to the top of the stairs, he dropped the bucket of snails all down the stairway.

Just then the door opened and a very angry wife was standing in the doorway wondering where he's been all this time. He looked at the snails on the steps, then looked at her, then back at the snails and said,

"Come on guys, we're almost there!"

A man went into a Santa Monica restaurant and was seated. All the waitresses were gorgeous. A particularly beautiful waitress with legs that wouldn't quit came to his table and asked if he was ready to order.

"What would you like sir?" the waitress in the short dress asked.

He looked at the menu and then scanned her beautiful frame from top to bottom. "A quickie," he replied.

The waitress turned and walked away in disgust. After she regained her composure, she returned to his table and asked again, "What would you like sir?"

The man thoroughly checked her out again and answered, "A quickie."

This time her anger took over. She reached across the table and slapped him with a resounding SMACK and stormed away.

Another man, sitting at the next table, leaned over and whispered, "Um, I think it's pronounced 'quiche.'"

A man phones home from his office and says to his wife, "I have the chance to go fishing for a week. It's the opportunity of a lifetime. I have to leave right away. Please pack my clothes, my fishing equipment and my blue silk pajamas. I'll be home in an hour to pick them up."

The man rushes home to grab everything, hugs his wife, apologizes for the short notice and hurries off. A week later the man returns home and his wife asks, "Did you have a good trip, dear?"

The husband replies, "Yep, the fishing was great . . . but you forgot to pack my blue silk pajamas."

His wife smiles, "Oh no I didn't . . . I put them in your tackle box."

A priest, a doctor and an engineer were playing golf behind a particularly slow foursome.

Engineer: "What's with these guys? We've been waiting for 15 minutes."

Doctor: "I don't know but I've never seen such ineptitude!"

Priest: "Here comes the greens keeper. Let's have a word with him."

Priest: "Hey George, what's with that group ahead of us? They're rather slow, aren't they?"

George: "Oh yes. That's the group of blind firefighters. They lost their sight while saving our club house last year so we let them play here anytime free of charge."

Priest: "That's so sad. I will say a special prayer for them tonight."

Doctor: "Good idea. And I'm going to contact my ophthalmologist buddy and see if there's anything he can do to help them."

Engineer: "Why can't these guys play at night?"

The graduate with a science degree asks, "Why does it work?"
The graduate with an engineering degree asks, "How does it work?"
The graduate with an accounting degree asks, "How much will it cost?"
The graduate with a liberal arts degree asks, "Do you want fries with that?"

One night at an economy motel a man ordered a 6 a.m. wakeup call. The next morning, he awoke at 6 a.m. but the phone didn't ring until 6:30. "Good morning," a young man said sheepishly. "This is your wakeup call."

Annoyed, he let the young man have it. "You were supposed to call me at 6 a.m. What if I had a million dollar deal to close this morning and your oversight made me miss out on it?"

"Well sir," the desk clerk quickly replied, "If you had a million dollar deal to close, you probably wouldn't be staying in this motel."

A couple from Minneapolis decided to go to Florida to thaw out during one particularly icy winter. They planned to stay at the very same hotel where they spent their honeymoon 20 years earlier. Because of hectic schedules, it was difficult to coordinate their travel schedules. So, the husband left Minnesota and flew to Florida on Thursday, with his wife flying down the following day.

The husband checked into the hotel. There was a computer in his room, so he decided to send an email to his wife. However, he accidentally left out one letter in her email address, and without realizing his error, he sent the e-mail.

Meanwhile, somewhere in Fairbanks, Alaska, a widow had just returned home from her husband's funeral. He was a minister of many years who was called home to glory following a sudden heart attack. The widow decided to check her e-mail expecting messages of condolence from relatives and friends.

After reading the first message, she fainted. The widow's son rushed into the room, found his mother on the floor, and saw the computer screen which read:

To: My Loving Wife
Subject: I've Arrived
Date: 20 January 2005

I know you're surprised to hear from me. They have computers here now and you are allowed to send e-mails to your loved ones. I've just arrived and have been checked in. I see that everything has been prepared for your arrival tomorrow. Looking forward to seeing you then!

Hope your journey is as uneventful as mine was.
P. S. Sure is hot down here.

An old hillbilly farmer had a wife that nagged him unmercifully from morning until night, and sometimes later. She was always complaining about something and the only time he got any relief was when he was out in the field plowing. He plowed a lot.

One day while he was out plowing his wife brought his lunch. He drove the old mule into the shade and sat down on a stump and began to eat. Immediately his wife started nagging and complaining. All of a sudden the old mule lashed out with both feet catching her smack in the back of the head killing her dead on the spot.

At the funeral the minister noticed something rather odd. When a woman mourner approached the farmer, he would listen for a moment and then nod his head in agreement. But when a man approached him, he would listen for a minute and then shake his head in disagreement. This was so consistent that the minister decided to ask the old farmer about it.

So after the funeral the minister asked the farmer why he nodded his head and agreed with the women, but always shook his head and disagreed with the men.

The old farmer said, "Well, the women would come up to me and say something about how nice my wife looked or how pretty her dress was, so I'd nod my head in agreement."

"And what about the men?" asked the minister.

"They all wanted to know if the mule was for sale."

A shipwrecked mariner had spent several years on a deserted island when one day he was thrilled to see a ship offshore and a smaller vessel pulling out toward him.

When the boat grounded on the beach, the officer in charge handed the marooned sailor a bundle of newspapers and told him, "With the Captain's compliments. He said to read through these and let us know if you still want to be rescued."

Three contractors were visiting a tourist attraction; one was from New York, another from Texas and the third was from Florida. At the end of the tour, the guard asked them what they did for a living. When they all replied that they were contractors, the guard said, "Hey, we need one of the rear fences rebuilt. Why don't you guys take a look at it and give me a bid?" So they all went out to the back fence to check it out.

The Florida contractor stepped up first, took out his tape measure and did some calculations and said, "Well, I figure the job will run about $900. $400 for materials, $400 for my crew and $100 profit for me."

The Texas contractor measured and did some quick figuring and said, "Looks like I can do this job for $700. $300 for materials, $300 for my crew and $100 profit for me."

Without so much as moving, the New York contractor said, "$2,700."

The guard looked at him and said, "You didn't even measure like the other guys. How did you come up with such a high figure?"

"Easy," he said. "$1,000 for me, $1,000 for you and we hire the guy from Texas."

A blonde was having a lot of trouble trying to sell her old car because it had almost 230,000 miles on it. As she was telling her problem to her girlfriend, the friend told her, "There is a possibility to make the car easier to sell but it's not legal.

"That doesn't matter," replied the blonde, "as long as I can sell the car."

"Okay," said her friend, "Here is the address of a friend of mine. He owns a car repair shop. Tell him I sent you and he will 'fix it.' Then you shouldn't have a problem anymore trying to sell your car."

The following weekend the blonde made the trip to the mechanic. Later that month she ran into her girlfriend. "Did you sell your car?"

"No," replied the blonde. "Why should I? It only has 50,000 miles on it."

It was a cold winter day. An old man walked out onto the frozen lake, cut a hole in the ice and dropped in his fishing line. He was there for almost an hour without even a nibble when a young boy walked out onto the ice and cut a hole not far from him. Minutes later the boy hooked a largemouth bass.

The old man couldn't believe his eyes, and chalked it up to plain luck, but shortly thereafter, the young boy pulled in another large catch. And he kept catching fish after fish.

The old man could take it no longer and asked, "Son, I've been here for over an hour without even a nibble. You've been here only a few minutes and have caught a half dozen fish. How do you do it?"

The boy responded, "Roo raf roo reep ra rums rarm."

"What was that?" the old man asked.

Again the boy responded, "Roo raf roo reep ra rums rarm."

"Look," said the old man, "I can't understand a word you're saying."

The boy spit the bait into his had and said, "You have to keep the worms warm!"

Dan married an identical twin. Less than a year later he was in court filing for divorce.

"Tell the court why you want a divorce," the judge said.

"Well, Your Honor, every once in a while my sister-in-law would come for a visit and because she and my wife are so identical, sometimes I'd end up making love to her by mistake."

"Now surely there must be some difference between the two women."

"Exactly, Your Honor. That's why I want the divorce."

A couple was celebrating their golden wedding anniversary. Their domestic tranquility had long been the talk of the town. A local newspaper reporter was inquiring as to the secret of their long and happy marriage.

"Well, it dates back to our honeymoon," explained the man. "We visited the Grand Canyon and took a trip down to the bottom of the canyon by pack mule. We hadn't gone too far when my wife's mule stumbled.

My wife quietly said, 'That's once.'

We proceeded a little further and the mule stumbled again. Then my wife quietly said, 'That's twice.'

We hadn't gone a half-mile when the mule stumbled a third time. My wife quietly removed a revolver from her pocket and shot the mule dead.

I started to protest over her treatment of the mule when she looked at me and quietly said, 'That's once.'"

Three guys go through an exit interview at a mental hospital. The doctor says he can release them if they can answer the simple mathematical problem: "What is 8 times 5?"

The first patient says, "139."

The second one says, "Wednesday."

The third says, "What a stupid question. It's obvious: The answer is 40."

The doctor is delighted. He gives the third guy his release. As the man is leaving, the doctor asks how he came up with the correct answer so quickly.

"It was easy, Doc. I just divided Wednesday into 139."

One day two old men at a retirement home were sitting on the front porch. One man says to the other, "Ya know, Bill, if you think about it, we are not that old. I mean, my memory is still very good."

As the man said this, he knocked on the wood chair he was sitting in. "Actually, sharp as ever."

After a couple of minutes of silence, he said, "So is anyone going to get the door or do I have to do it?"

It was a bitterly contested divorce hearing and after three weeks of testimony, the judge was ready to hand down his decision.

"Mr. Johnson, after hearing both sides of the case, we find that you are at fault and therefore the court will give your wife alimony at six hundred dollars a month."

Johnson replied, "Thanks, your Honor. And to show I'm not such a bad guy, I'll throw in a hundred myself."

A first grade teacher had a small number of children gathered around a table for a reading group. After she read them a story, she gave the children a work sheet to do. While they were working, she heard one little girl say very softly, "Damn!"

The teacher went over to the little girl, leaned over and said quietly, "We don't say that in school."

The little girl looked up at the teacher, her eyes got very big and wide and she asked, "Not even when things are all fucked up?"

A man is driving down a deserted highway and notices a sign that reads, SISTERS OF MERCY HOUSE OF PROSTITUTION, 12 MILES. He thinks it was a figment of his imagination, but soon he sees another sign that says, SISTERS OF MERCY HOUSE OF PROSTITUTION, 6 MILES.

Realizing that these signs are for real, he drives on and sure enough there is a sign, SISTERS OF MERCY HOUSE OF PROSTITUTION, NEXT RIGHT. Curiosity gets the best of him and he pulls off the highway into the driveway and sees an old stone building with a sign on the door that reads, SISTERS OF MERCY HOUSE OF PROSTITUTION.

He climbs the steps, rings the bell and the door is answered by a nun in a long black habit who asks, "What may we do for you my son?"

"I saw your signs along the highway and was interested in possibly doing some business."

"Very well, my son, please follow me." He is led through many winding hallways when the nun stops at a closed door and tells the man, "Please knock on this door," and she leaves. The man does as he is told and this door is opened by another nun in a long black habit, holding a tin cup. This nun instructs, "Please place $50 in the cup, then go through the large wooden door at the end of this hallway."

He places the money in the nun's cup and trots eagerly down the hall and slips through the door, pulling it shut behind him. As the door locks, he finds himself back in the parking lot, facing another sign . . . . .

GO IN PEACE. YOU HAVE JUST BEEN SCREWED BY THE SISTERS OF MERCY.

Here is a little known story of how God came to give us the Ten Commandments:

God first went to the Egyptians and asked them if they would like a commandment.

"What's a commandment?" they asked.

"Well, it's like, THOU SHALT NOT COMMIT ADULTERY," replied God.

The Egyptians thought about it and said, "No way, that would ruin our weekends."

So then God went to the Assyrians and asked them if they would like a commandment. They also wanted to know what a commandment was.

"Well, it's like THOU SHALT NOT STEAL."

The Assyrians immediately replied, "No way. That would ruin our economy."

So finally God went to the Jews and asked them if they wanted a commandment.

They asked, "How much?"

God said, "They're free."

The Jews said, "Great! We'll take TEN!"

A 92-year-old man went to the doctor to get a physical. A few days later, the doctor saw the man walking down the street with a gorgeous young lady on his arm.

At his follow up visit, the doctor talked to the man and said, "You're really doing great, aren't you?"

The man replied, "Just doing what you said Doc: 'Get a hot mamma and be cheerful.' "

The doctor said, "I didn't say that. I said you got a heart murmur. Be careful."

While in China, a man is very sexually promiscuous and does not use a condom all the time. A week after arriving back home in the States, he wakes one morning to find his penis covered with bright green and purple spots. Horrified, he immediately goes to see a doctor. The doctor, never having seen anything like this before, orders some tests and tells the man to return in two days for the results.

The man returns a couple of days later and the doctor says: "I've got bad news for you --- you've contracted Mongolian VD. It's very rare and almost unheard of here. We know very little about it."

The man looks a little perplexed and says: "Well, give me a shot or something and fix me up, Doc."

The doctor answers: "I'm sorry, there's no known cure. We're going to have to amputate your penis."

The man screams in horror, "Absolutely not! I want a second opinion."

The doctor replies: "Well, it's your choice. Go ahead if you want but surgery is your only choice."

The next day, the man seeks out a Chinese doctor, figuring that he'll know more about the disease. The Chinese doctor examines his penis and proclaims: "Ah, yes, Mongolian VD. Vely lare disease."

The guy says to the doctor: "Yeah, yeah, I already know that, but what can we do? My American doctor wants to operate and amputate my penis!"

The Chinese doctor shakes his head and laughs: "Stupid Amelican docta, always want to opelate. Make more money that way. No need to opelate!"

Oh, Thank God!" the man replies.

"Yes," says the Chinese doctor, "You no worry! Wait two weeks. Fawoff by itself!"

Three dogs are sitting in the waiting room of their veterinarian's office: a poodle, a schnauzer and a Great Dane. The poodle asks the schnauzer, "Why are you here?"

The schnauzer responds, "I'm 17 years old and I don't see or hear very well any longer. I've been having accidents in the house. My owner says I'm too old and sick so he brought me here to be put to sleep."

The schnauzer asks the poodle, "Why are you here?"

The poodle responds, "I've not been myself lately. I've been especially high-strung and I've been barking all the time. I've been snapping at people and I even bit one of the neighbor's kids. Nobody knows why this has been happening, and my owner says he can't risk me biting somebody else, so he brought me here to be put to sleep."

The poodle and the schnauzer ask the Great Dane why he is here and he responds, "My owner is this beautiful runway model. Yesterday she was walking around the house naked when she suddenly bent down to pick up something she dropped. While she was bent over nature took over and the next thing I know I'm on top of her doing the doggie thing. I couldn't help myself."

The poodle asks, "So your owner brought you here to have you put to sleep?"

"No. I'm just here to get my nails trimmed."

Two nuns, Sister Catherine and Sister Helen, are traveling through Europe in their car. They get to Transylvania and are stopped at a traffic light. Suddenly, out of nowhere, a tiny little Dracula jumps onto the hood of the car and hisses through the windshield.

"Quick, quick!" shouts Sister Catherine. "What shall we do?"
"Turn the windshield wipers on. That will get rid of the abomination," says Sister Helen.

Sister Catherine switches them on, knocking Dracula about, but he clings on and continues hissing at the nuns.

"What shall I do now?" she shouts.
"Switch on the windshield washer. I filled it up with Holy Water at the Vatican," says Sister Helen.

Sister Catherine turns on the windshield washer. Dracula screams as the water burns his skin, but he clings on and continues hissing at the nuns.

"Now what?" shouts Sister Catherine.
"Show him your cross," says Sister Helen.
"Now you're talking," says Sister Catherine.
She opens the window and shouts, "Get the fuck off the car"

An attorney arrived home late, after a very tough day trying to get a stay of execution for a client who was due to be hanged for murder at midnight. His last minute plea for clemency to the governor had failed and he was feeling worn out and de-pressed.

As soon as he walked through the door at home, his wife started on him about, 'What time of night to be getting home is this? Where have you been?' 'Dinner is cold and I'm not reheating it'. And on and on and on.

Too shattered to play his usual role in this familiar ritual, he poured himself a shot of whiskey and headed off for a long hot soak in the bathtub, pursued by the predictable sarcastic remarks as he dragged himself up the stairs. While he was in the bath, the phone rang. The wife answered and was told that her husband's client, John Wright, had been granted a stay of execution after all. Wright would not be hanged tonight.

Finally realizing what a terrible day he must have had, she decided to go upstairs and give him the good news. As she opened the bathroom door, she was greeted by the sight of her husband, bent over naked, drying his legs and feet.

'They're not hanging Wright tonight,' she said to which he whirled around and screamed,

'FOR THE LOVE OF GOD WOMAN, DON'T YOU EVER STOP?'

The Dentist tells the Cowboy, "That tooth has to come out. I'm going to give you a shot of Novocain."
"No way! I hate needles. I'm not having any shot!"
"Okay, we'll have to go with gas."
"Absolutely not! It makes me sick for days. I'm not having gas."
So the Dentist steps out of the room and returns with a glass of water and a pill.
The Cowboy asks, "What is that?"
"Viagra."
"Will that kill the pain?" he asked with surprise.
"No, but it will give you something to hang on to while I pull your tooth."

You don't stop laughing because you grow old. You grow old because you stop laughing.

— Michael Pritchard